Lara Temple was three years old when she begged her mother to take the dictation of her first adventure story. Since then she has led a double life—by day she is a high-tech investment professional, who has lived and worked on three continents, but when darkness falls she loses herself in history and romance...at least on the page. Luckily her husband and two beautiful and very energetic children help her weave it all together.

THE RAKE'S ENTICING PROPOSAL

Lara Temple

MILLS & BOON

First Published in Great Britain 2019
by Mills & Boon, an imprint of HarperCollins*Publishers*
1 London Bridge Street, London, SE1 9GF

© 2019 Ilana Treston

ISBN: 978-0-263-26919-2

MIX
Paper from
responsible sources
FSC® C007454

This book is produced from independently certified FSC™ paper
to ensure responsible forest management.
For more information visit www.harpercollins.co.uk/green.

Printed and bound in Spain
by CPI, Barcelona

This one is for my soul sisters.

Armed with tea or wine or cake—
they sweep in and rescue me from my worst selves
and let me do the same for them.

Wherever we are around the globe—
the sisterhood holds firm.

Chapter One

'*I have one last, but very important, quest for you, Chase...*'

Chase drew Brutus to a halt at the foot of Huxley's Folly.

The last time he'd seen his cousin, he'd stood precisely there in the arched doorway of the stone tower, his wispy grey hair weaving in the breeze like an underwater plant.

The last time he'd seen him and the first and last time Huxley had ever expressed any sentiment regarding Chase's chosen occupation.

'I do hope what you do for Oswald doesn't place you in too much peril, Chase. Tessa would be very upset if you joined her too soon.'

Huxley always referred to Chase's mother as if her death was merely a temporary absence. It was one of the reasons Chase found visiting Huxley a strain, but that was no excuse for neglecting him these past couple of years, no matter how busy Oswald kept him.

'It's my fault, Brutus.' He stroked the horse's thick black neck. 'I should have visited more often. Too late now.'

Brutus huffed, twin bursts of steam foaming into the chilly air.

Chase sighed and swung out of the saddle. Coming to Huxley Manor always stretched his patience, but without Huxley himself his stay would be purgatorial. Nothing wrong with postponing it a little longer with a visit to the ramshackle Folly tower. Every time he came it looked a little more stunted, but as children he and Lucas and Sam fantasised that it was populated with ogres, magical beasts and escaped princesses.

He approached the wall where Huxley kept a key behind a loose brick, when he noticed the door was slightly open. He frowned and slipped inside, a decade of working as emissary for his uncle at the Foreign Office coming into play even though he knew there was probably no need. Being sent to smooth out some of the less mentionable kinks in relations with Britain's allies meant one collected as many enemies as friends. Wariness had the advantage of increasing longevity, but it also flared up at inappropriate moments, and this was probably just such a case.

No doubt whoever was in the tower was merely

his cousin, Henry, the new Baron Huxley, or Huxley's trusted secretary, Mallory, Chase told himself as he climbed the stairs silently.

It was neither.

For a moment as he stood in the doorway of the first floor of the tower he wondered if he'd conjured one of their old tales into being—the Princess locked away and pining for her Prince.

His mouth quirked in amusement at his descent into fancy as he took in the details of her attire. Definitely not a princess.

She was seated at Huxley's desk, which was positioned to provide a view from the arched window, so she was facing away and all he could see was the curve of her cheek and tawny-brown hair gathered into a tightly coiled bun exposing the fragile line of her nape and a very drab-coloured pelisse with no visible ornamentation.

She was leaning over some papers on the desk with evident concentration and the opening words in Huxley's cryptic letter forced their way back into his mind.

There is something I have but recently uncovered that I must discuss with you. I think it will be best you not share this revelation with anyone, except perhaps with Lucas, as it can do more harm than good to those I care about most...

Huxley's letter, dated almost a month ago, awaited him on his return from St Petersburg two days ago, as well as a message from his man of business with news of Huxley's demise and his last will and testament.

Chase hadn't the slightest idea what Huxley was referring to, but he had every intention of finding out. Through the centuries the Sinclair name became synonymous with scandal, but now Lucas was married and Sam widowed Chase had every intention of keeping his family name out of the muck and mire it so loved wallowing in. If Huxley had uncovered something damaging and had it here at the Manor, Chase intended to destroy it as swiftly and quietly as possible.

Therefore, the sight of a strange woman seated at Huxley's desk and looking through his papers was not the most welcome vision at the moment.

As if sensing his tension, she straightened, like a rabbit pricking its ears, then turned and rose in one motion, sending the chair scraping backwards. For the briefest moment her eyes reflected fear, but then she did something quite different from most women he knew. Like a storm moving backwards she gathered all expression inwards and went utterly flat. It was like watching liquid drain out of a crack in a clay vessel, leaving it empty and dull.

They inspected each other in silence. With all trace of emotion gone from her face she was as unremarkable as her clothes—her height was perhaps a little on the tall side of middling, but what figure he could distinguish beneath her shapeless pelisse was too slim to fit society's vision of proper proportions and the pelisse's hue, a worn dun colour that hovered between grey and brown and was an offence to both, gave a sallow cast to her pale skin. Only her eyes were in any way remarkable—large and a deep honey-brown. Even devoid of expression they held a jewel-like glitter which made him think of a tigress watching its prey from the shadows.

'Who are you? What are you doing here?' she demanded, her voice surprisingly deep and husky for someone so slight. That, too, was unusual. Similar demands were fired at him by friend and foe since he'd joined the army and not nearly as imperiously. Predictably he felt his hackles rise along with his suspicions.

'I could ask the same question. Are you another of Lady Ermintrude's nieces? I thought I had met the lot.'

She moved along the desk as he approached, putting it between them, but he concentrated on what lay on top. Piled high with papers and books, it was much more chaotic than he remembered and he wondered if his cousin or the young woman were the cause.

He glanced at the slip of paper she'd inspected with such concentration. It was a caricature of a camel inspecting a pot of tea through a quizzing glass, grey hair swept back in an impressive cockade over a patrician brow. The resemblance to his cousin's antiquarian friend Phillip 'Poppy' Carmichael was impressive and a fraction of Chase's tension eased, but only a fraction. This particular scrap of paper might have nothing to do with Huxley's message, but any of the other papers here might hold the key to understanding it.

He returned his attention to the woman. She was younger than his first impression of her—perhaps in her mid-twenties. Her hand rested on a stack of books at the edge of the desk and she looked like a countrified statue of learning, or a schoolmistress waiting for her class to settle. She did have rather the look of a schoolmistress—proper, erect, a little impatient, as if he was not merely a slow pupil, but purposely recalcitrant. With her chin raised, her eyes had a faintly exotic slant, something an artist would attempt if he wanted to depict a goddess to be wary of.

And he was. If there was one thing he'd learned was that appearances could be and often were deceptive. So he leaned his hip on the desk, crossed his arms and gave her his best smile.

'It is impolite to read another person's correspondence. Even if he is dead.'

'I didn't mean…' The blank façade cracked a little, but the flash of contrition was gone as quickly as it appeared and she raised her chin, her mouth flattening into a stubborn line that compressed the appealing fullness of her lower lip. 'As I am betrothed to Lord Huxley I have every right to be here. Can you say the same?'

'Unfortunately not. He wouldn't have me.'

She gave a little gasp of laughter and it transformed her face as much as that brief flash of contrition—her eyes slanting further, her cheeks rounding and her mouth relaxing from its prim horizontal line. Then something else followed her amusement—recognition.

'I should have guessed immediately. You must be one of the Sinclairs, yes? Henry said one of you would likely come to Huxley Manor because of Lord Huxley's will.'

'One of us. You make us sound like a travelling troupe of theatrical performers.'

'Much more entertaining according to Miss Fenella.'

'My cousin Fen was always prone to gossip. You can stop edging towards the door; I have no intention of pouncing on Henry's freshly minted betrothed, whatever the requirements of my reputation. I am surprised, though. I had not heard he was engaged.'

'We…we are keeping it secret at the moment because of the bereavement. Only Lady Ermintrude and the Misses Ames know. I should not have told you, either, but I assume Henry will have to tell you if you are staying at the Manor.

Please do not mention it to anyone, though. It would be improper...while he is in mourning...'

Unlike her previous decisive tones, her voice faded into a breathy ramble and the defiance in her honey-warm eyes into bruised confusion. Perhaps she was hurt by Henry's refusal to acknowledge her position?

'Of course the proprieties must be observed,' he soothed. 'But that still does not explain why you are here alone at the Folly, reading Cousin Huxley's papers. Shouldn't you be at the Manor flirting with Henry or paying court to Lady Ermintrude along with everyone else?'

'Henry is fully occupied with his land steward and Lady Ermintrude and Miss Ames and Miss Fenella are busy with preparations for the annual meeting of the Women's Society, which apparently trumps all mourning proprieties. Since my embroidery skills are on the wrong side of atrocious, I am *persona non grata* and had to find some other way of passing the time.'

'I imagine your embroidery skills are the least cause of your lack of popularity among the womenfolk of the manor. However, that, too, doesn't explain why you are here.'

'Henry showed me the hidden key when we explored yesterday. I merely wanted some place quiet to read.'

'To read other people's letters,' he said softly. She flushed, but didn't answer, and he felt a twinge of contrition himself. He was becoming too much like Oswald—ready to suspect everyone of everything. She was no doubt bored of being slighted and indulging in a sulk—in which case he was being unfairly harsh.

'Is Lady Ermintrude making your life difficult? I am not surprised. She always intended that my cousin would marry one of her nieces.'

'Yes, she made that only too clear. I thought Henry was exaggerating, but…' She stopped and cleared her throat, throwing him a suspicious look, as if realising she was being far too frank with a stranger. He smiled and tried another tack.

'You still should not come to the Folly unaccompanied. The tower itself is solid enough, but all these boxes and stacks could prove hazardous. It always looked as though a whirlwind has passed through, but it appears to have reached new levels of chaos since I was last here. Is his study in the east wing as bad?'

'Henry did not take me there. He said the will specified all the contents of the east wing went to you and your siblings so he did not wish to meddle. He only showed me the Folly because it is such a peculiarity and I was curious to see inside. Perhaps I should not have insisted.'

Chase wondered at his growing sense of discomfort. There was something about this young woman that was…off. It put him at a disadvantage, which was precisely where he did not like being put.

'He was always a biddable fellow.'

'Henry is polite and considerate. That is very different from being biddable.'

'You are quite right, it is. I apologise for maligning him.'

She snorted, her opinion of his apology all too clear. The hesitation and vulnerability were gone once more and the watchful glitter was back. She looked too soft to be so hard, another discordant note. Chase considered moving so she could access the stairway, but remained where he was.

'Excuse me, Mr Sinclair.' She looked up and he saw the schoolmistress again—in the light from the window the honey in her eyes was sparked with tiny shards of green just around the iris, like jade slivers dipped in gold.

'For what?' he asked, not budging.

'I was not begging your pardon,' she replied, spacing out the words as if to someone hard of hearing. 'I was asking you to stand aside so I may pass.'

'In a moment. Congratulations on your betrothal, by the way. Where did you meet Henry?'

She eyed the space between him and the doorway, clearly calculating her odds of slipping by.

'We are neighbours in Nettleton.'

'How charming. I didn't know Nettleton har-

boured such hidden gems. How are you enjoying Huxley?'

'We only arrived two days ago.'

'A diplomatic but revealing answer. Not at all,
then.'

She laughed and the tiny lines at the corners
of her eyes hinted she smiled easily, which surprised him.

'Judging by Lady Ermintrude's comments
about the Sinclairs, my welcome may be warmer
than yours.'

'You shouldn't say that with such relish.'

'True. It is very uncharitable of me. I hope
Lady Ermintrude welcomes you with open arms,
Mr Sinclair.'

'That sounds a far worse prospect. May I ask
how you would benefit from that unlikely sce-
nario?'

'Anything that puts a smile on her face would
be welcome.'

'Having never seen her smile, I cannot judge if it
would be an improvement, but when that unlikely
event occurs I doubt I will have been its cause.'

'Was she always like that? Or is her stony
façade a concession to mourning her brother-
in-law?'

'*Façade* implies something hidden, but after
years of observation I can safely say her interior
is completely consistent with her exterior. There
is no inner sanctum, complete with crackling fire-

place and a good book, so do not waste your time searching for it. Ermy is as devoid of emotion as she is of humour.'

'That is what Henry says, but one cannot help wondering... Everyone has redeeming features. She appears devoted to her nieces.'

'Yes, poor Dru and Fen. They would have fared better without it. Though devotion isn't quite the word.'

'What is, then?'

He opened his mouth to answer and paused, surprised by his willingness to satisfy her curiosity. He was not usually so revealing to a complete stranger.

'You do know that in Aunt Ermy's small universe, Henry marrying one of her nieces was as obvious as the sun rising in the east or two plus two equals four.'

'My brother would point out that while the latter is indeed a given, there is nothing to say the sun must always rise in the east.'

'Good God, I hope you didn't make that Humean point to Aunt Ermy. Is that why you have banished yourself to the Folly?'

Her smile flashed again and was tucked away.

'I had best return now. Good day, sir.'

She took a step forward, but stopped once more as he did not move out of the way. It was childish to be toying with her, but he was curious about Henry's bride-to-be. His memories of his awkward but good-natured cousin did not tally well with this intelligent and curious specimen of femininity.

'I must return to the Manor, sir.'

'In a moment. Since there is no one here to help us follow convention, shall we break with it and introduce ourselves? I am Charles Sinclair, though my friends and quite a few of my enemies call me Chase. May I know the name of my cousin-to-be?'

'Then will you stand aside and allow me to leave?'

He bowed. 'My word on it.'

She huffed a little, as if considering a snort of disdain.

'Miss Walsh.'

'Walsh. Walsh of Nettleton.' He shouldn't have spoken aloud. Her eyes widened at his tone and their coolness turned to frost.

She didn't look anything like the Fergus Walsh he'd once met in London. That man had been a red-haired Celt with charm and a temperament to match. He'd also been a charming wastrel and inveterate gambler who'd frequented all the clubs and gaming hells until bad debts drove him to ever more dissolute establishments. He'd brought his family to the brink of ruin and then compounded his shame by drowning in a ditch outside a gambling hell off the Fleet while inebriated.

Chase had also heard of him from Huxley who'd been bemused by his younger brother's friendship with the man. Arthur Whelford, father to new Lord Huxley, was a vicar and possessed all the virtues of his calling. But despite these differences the Whelfords and Walshes had been the best of friends. And now the wastrel's daughter was engaged to the vicar's son and new Lord Huxley.

'I shan't keep you from your betrothed any longer, Miss Walsh. You may run along.'

'How kind of you, Mr Sinclair.' Resentment seethed in her deep voice, but as she moved towards the doorway something else caught his attention—a folded slip of paper held in her hand. The world shifted, both his pity and the last remnant of his enjoyment of the absurd little scene draining away in an instant, and he tweaked the letter from her hand.

'I believe my cousin's will stipulated that the contents of the Folly are mine and my siblings', so I suggest you leave this here.'

'How *dare* you! Return that to me this instant!'

She reached for the letter and in his surprise he raised it above his head, just as he would when he and Sam squabbled over something as children. And just like Sam, Fergus Walsh's daughter lunged for it. Her move was so unexpected she almost made it, but just as her fingers grazed the letter he raised it further and she grabbed the lapel of his coat, staggering against him and shoving him back on to the stack of boxes that stood by the stairway.

He should have steadied himself on the wall, but instead he found his other arm around her waist as he toppled backwards. The top boxes tumbled down the stairway in a series of deafening crashes and he abandoned the letter to brace himself against the doorjamb before he followed them into the void. He saw the moment the anger in her eyes transformed to shock and fear as they sank towards the stairs, her hand fisting hard in his coat as if she could still prevent him from falling. The impact against the tumbled boxes and the top step was painful, but nowhere near as painful as their precipitous descent down them might have been.

'My God, I am so sorry. Are you hurt?' She was still on him, one hand fisted on his greatcoat, the other splayed against his chest. Her eyes were wide with concern and he could see all the shades of gold and amber and jade that meshed together around the dilated pupils and he had the peculiar sensation he was still sinking, as if the fall hadn't stopped, just slowed.

'Are you hurt?' she demanded again, giving his coat a little tug. Out of the peculiar numbness he noticed her elbow was digging painfully into his abdomen and he forced himself to shake his head. At last the strange sensation ebbed, but now his body woke and instead of reconnoitring and reporting back on the damage, it focused on something completely different. She was sprawled on top of him, astride his thigh, her legs spread and her own thigh tucked so snugly between his if he shifted the slightest bit he…

'You *are* hurt,' she stated, her fist tightening further in his coat, her gaze running over him as if trying to locate his wounds and, though he hadn't felt a blow, he wondered if perhaps he had after all struck his head on the wall and that accounted for this strange floating feeling.

'Not hurt. Just winded,' he croaked and managed a smile and thankfully her brows drew together into a frown.

'Serves you right! That is *my* letter. Not Lord Huxley's.'

She struggled to rise, her thigh dragging against his groin with startling effectiveness and his normally obedient body shocked him by leaping into readiness. Instinctively his arm tightened around her and with a cry she slipped and fell back against him, leaving him doubly winded, her hair a silky cushion under his chin. Perhaps if he had not been so surprised and not a little embarrassed by his body's perfidy, he might have kept quiet. But instead of helping her as a gentleman should, he kept his arm where it was and succumbed to the urge to turn his head to test the softness of her hair with his lips.

'Don't go yet…we've just got comfortable,' he

murmured against her hair, absorbing the scent of lilies and something else, sweet and tempting… Vanilla? Her elbow sank even more painfully into the soft flesh under his ribs, but he felt the pain less than he noticed the rest of her anatomy as she wriggled off him and shoved to her feet.

'Henry is utterly right about you!'

He levered himself into a sitting position and watched as she picked up the letter with a gesture that was a perfect reflection of her scold. She didn't even glance at him as she stepped over him and stalked down the stairs.

'And you may tidy up that mess you made.' Her scold echoed up the stairwell the moment before the slamming of the wooden door sent a whoosh of cold air up towards him. He heard Brutus's shrill whinny and hauled himself to his feet with a spurt of fear only to hear her voice, faint but all too clear as she admonished his sixteen-hand fiend of a horse.

'Out of my way, you great lug. You're as ill mannered as your master!'

Chase inspected the tear in the seat of his buckskins where the shattered box had ripped through the sturdy material. It stung and throbbed and he began laughing.

His brother Lucas would love that he found himself flat on his backside with his head handed to him within minutes of arriving. What a fitting beginning to what was likely to prove a dismal week.

Chapter Two

'Ellie, wait.'

Ellie stopped halfway up the stairs, indulging in a string of mental curses. She didn't wish to speak to anyone in her present state, not even Henry.

'I've escaped the steward and was just about to set off in search of you, Ellie. There is tea in… Good Lord, what happened to you? Have you fallen down a coal chute?' Henry's eyes widened as they took in the state of her skirts and the uncharacteristic anger on her face.

'I must change, Henry.'

'First come into the parlour and tell me what's about before the three witches find us. Come, tea and lemon seed cake are just what you need…' Henry coaxed.

The smile and the concern in his sky-blue eyes were a balm after the look of distaste that had doused the laughter in Mr Sinclair's grey eyes the moment he realised who her father was.

Though how someone with his reputation had the gall to look down upon a fellow reprobate…

She shouldn't be surprised—it was the way of the world that even rakes and rascals felt superior to those of their breed foolish enough to sink into debt and disgrace. Apparently the notion of *there but for the grace of God go I* didn't occur to the likes of Charles Sinclair. Chase, Indeed! She would like to chase him off with a croquet mallet!

'You're looking fierce, Ellie. Is this Lady Ermintrude's fault?'

'No. I had an encounter with your cousin,' she said and he grinned, looking even more angelically boyish.

'Dru or Fen did this? Over me? Good lord, I wouldn't have thought they had the pluck!'

'Not them, you vain popinjay. Your cousin The Right Honourable Charles Sinclair. Though I saw nothing very honourable about him.'

His grin vanished.

'Oh, lord, is Chase here already? And what the devil do you mean you had an encounter? I've heard he's a devil with the ladies, but…'

'Henry Giles Whelford!'

'Sorry, Eleanor. I was funning… Never mind. I thought you were at the Folly escaping Aunt Ermintrude.'

'I was. He appeared there while I was trying

to read Susan's letter. And he is a hundred times worse than you said.'

'Is he? I mean…what on earth did he do?'

'He accused me of stealing! And then he took my letter and when I tried to take it back we almost fell down the stairs.'

'No! Ellie, are you hurt? Do let me see.'

Her anger fizzled at the concern in her friend's voice.

'I'm not hurt, but I never should have allowed you to convince me to masquerade as your betrothed. I knew everything would go wrong.'

'Hush!' Henry flapped his hands, glancing at the closed door. 'You never know when that sneaky Pruitt might be hovering about listening at keyholes. If I am to protect your reputation, the engagement must remain just between us, Lady Ermintrude and her nieces.'

'I know, but I've already blurted it out to Mr Sinclair.'

'*What?* Why on earth…?'

'I don't know. He looked at me so suspiciously and the words were out before I could think. I warned you I am dreadful at subterfuge. If I had not been so desperate…'

'We are both desperate, remember?'

'My problems are slightly more serious than yours,' she replied sharply. 'If I cannot find the funds to prevent the banks from foreclosing on Whitworth, Edmund and Susan and Anne and

Hugh will lose their home at best and end up in debtors' prison at worst. I think that is a little more fateful than whether you can withstand Lady Ermintrude's pressure to wed one of her nieces. I did try to recover my mistake by telling him it was to remain a secret while you were in mourning.'

'Well, that should be enough—Chase was never one to spill. Matters are a little more complicated here than I thought, but once I untangle the accounts I am certain to find a way to raise the funds to prevent the banks foreclosing on Whitworth. And then in a few weeks you may jilt me and I will mope around, declaring myself inconsolable and determined never to wed and that will put an end to Aunt Ermintrude's plans to force me into marrying Dru or Fen. By the time she overcomes her scruples I will hopefully have the Manor sufficiently on its feet so I can dispense with her funds.'

'I still think this is madness, Henry. I don't know if I shall uphold this masquerade for days, let alone weeks. Besides, the children never had to manage without me...'

'Well, high time they did. Susan and Edmund wouldn't thank you for calling them children. Why, Susan is almost on the shelf herself.'

'Thank you kindly, Henry. I'm well aware of my advancing years.'

'You're still a year younger than I so listen to

a wise old man—it will come right in the end.
I promise. All you must do is be precisely who
you are—the indomitable Miss Eleanor Walsh. If
you could keep Whitworth afloat for the past five
years, beating back bankers and creditors from
the doorstep, you can take on one ill-tempered
spinster. Well, three of them. You've already
made grand progress last night, admiring Aunt
Ermintrude's brooch. Now she is convinced you
are a scheming golddigger.'

'I was trying to make polite conversation!'

'Well, some more of that politeness and she'll
be mighty pleased with me when you jilt me. It's
deuced uncomfortable that Uncle Huxley allowed
the estate to become dependent on her funds, but
I suspect that was her doing, trying to make herself indispensable. No doubt she wished it was her
and not her sister Hattie my poor uncle married.'

'I feel rather sorry for her…'

'Well, don't be. There isn't a shred of kindness in her.'

'It was kind of her to take Drusilla and Fenella
in when their parents died.'

'That isn't kindness. She brought them here
like two dolls and treated them just the same. If
they weren't so annoying, I would feel sorry for
them. Why, Dru is twenty-three and has never
had a true Season even though she is an heiress
in her own right. It's shameful.'

'There, that is something for you to do. Really, you led me to believe they were much worse than they are. Once I break your heart, I suggest you take your cousins to town and find them husbands.'

'Fen might enjoy it, but Dru prefers the country. You should have seen her today when she came with me and the steward out to the pastures, the two of them rattling on about sheep and wool and lambing until I was ready to cry. I can't see her enjoying the brouhaha of London any more than I would.'

'I think it a good sign Dru made such a gesture of goodwill. You should encourage her to come out with you more often, knowing she will enjoy it more than embroidering with her aunt.'

'It feels more like a cross between a lecture and a scold than a gesture of goodwill.'

'Well, she is rather shy…'

'Shy? *Dru?* The girl tore strips out of me that time I put frogs in her bed. Had me carry them all the way back to the pond in the dark.'

'Well, you *were* a horrid little boy and I would have done the same.'

Henry laughed, his freckled cheeks a little pink, and not for the first time since her arrival at Huxley, Ellie wondered if he was being quite honest with himself. His tales of Huxley Manor over the years led her to expect a household of scheming harpies, but it was clear only Lady Ermintrude merited that title.

She decided to toss one more stone into the well.

'Once the period of strict mourning is over, you should hold a ball here at the Manor and bring all the landed gentry so she can find a nice country squire. Then settling Fen would be her and her husband's task.'

'I don't fancy playing matchmaker, if you don't mind. But perhaps I should ask Dru to help with the da—the darling sheep. I might as well derive some benefit from her superior airs. But even if Dru isn't…well, you know…that doesn't mean my aunt wouldn't try to force my hand with her. I told you about that time three years ago when Aunt Ermintrude arranged matters so that we were left stranded in a carriage on the way back from an assembly. If the Philbys had not come along we'd have been long married, believe me. I left the next day before the old witch could try something else. You're my only defence, Ellie.'

Ellie sighed. She might think Dru rather suited Henry, but she could not argue against his aversion to being coerced into marriage. She knew enough about being coerced into situations not of one's choosing.

'It's only a few weeks, Ellie. In fact, it's dashed good news Chase has come. My aunt always resented Huxley's strong ties to the Sinclairs. After his wife passed, he spent much more time with them and their widowed mother in Egypt than he ever spent here and when they did come to visit they always managed to rub her the wrong way. Perhaps you could flirt with him and then...'

'No!'

'Oh, very well. It was only a thought.'

'A typically noddy-headed one, Henry! Though if I were at all sensible I should encourage anything that will hasten your plan. I couldn't bear it if Edmund lost everything because I failed. I had it all planned, you know. All we needed were a few more years of decent harvests and for nothing terrible to go wrong with the livestock or the tenants, then poor Mr Phillips fell ill so of course we could not press for rents and then there was the drought last year and...'

Her voice cracked as she recalled the last summons to meet with Mr Soames at the bank. He'd been regretful, but very clear. They'd shown far too much leniency already. Problems of their own... Pressure from the board... Fiscal duty... Three months...

Three months...

Her head and stomach had reeled and halfway back on that endless walk from town she'd hurried into the bushes and been viciously ill. She'd only told Henry because he'd been waiting at Whitworth to tell her of Huxley's passing and somehow the truth tumbled out of her. So when he said it was fate and proposed this mad plan she'd agreed. For once, just for once, she wanted someone to swoop in and save her, like a sorcerer in a story.

She'd forgotten that most swooping-in sorcerers tended to exact a hefty price for their services.

But three months…

She felt another wave of weariness and fear beat at her embattlements. It was even stronger now that she was away from Whitworth where she didn't have the constant reminders of her duty. Even coming here felt like a betrayal despite the fact that this was her only hope of saving her family's home. She didn't know what to think any longer.

Just that she was so very, very tired. And scared.

'Oh, God, Henry, I'm so frightened,' she whispered and the tears began to burn. She would not cry. She hadn't cried since her mother and baby sister died that horrible day five years ago and she would not begin now.

'Dash it all, Ellie, don't come apart at the seams now,' Henry said, his eyes widening in alarm, but he put his arm around her shoulders, drawing her to him. 'You're the indomitable Eleanor Walsh, remember? Nothing is too difficult for you. So buck up, everything will come right in the end. Word of honour. I…'

'Henry Giles Whelford! I will have none of that in my household!'

They both jerked apart at the command. For such an ancient house, the door hinges were well oiled—neither had noticed the door open. Lady Ermintrude stood flanked by Drusilla and Fenella Ames, their cheeks flaming, and behind them, as out of place as a panther in a litter of kittens, stood the dark and impassive Mr Sinclair.

Ellie's face flamed in embarrassment and lingering misery, her pulse tumbling forward as it had when he appeared behind her in the Folly. It was not quite fear, more like the sensation of waking in the middle of a vivid dream, her mind struggling to separate fact from fiction. She had an utterly outrageous thought that he was not really there, just a figment of her imagination—that if she blinked he would disappear and all she would see were the three disapproving women.

'I didn't…we weren't…' Henry stammered, but Lady Ermintrude waved a hand, cutting him off as she turned.

'Supper is in an hour. Do not be late.' She sailed away and the cousins trailed in her wake, but Mr Sinclair remained, leaning on the doorjamb. As the silence stretched the absurdly fanciful sensation that he was not quite corporeal faded, but he still looked utterly out of place. He must only have entered because he was still wearing his greatcoat and Ellie noticed his buckskins were as streaked with dust and grime from their fall as her skirts.

Peculiarly, this mundane observation reassured her a little, but when she looked up he smiled and her well-developed inner alarms began pealing once more. Instinctively she donned the supercilious look she reserved for visits from creditors and bank officials, but his smile merely deepened and he turned to Henry.

'Hello, Henry. You really must train Aunt Ermy to call you by your title now. Hard to establish your authority when she's calling you Henry Giles.'

Henry stood and tugged at his waistcoat, his face flushed.

'I don't need to establish my authority. I'm Lord Huxley now. Why didn't you send word you were arriving today? Will you be staying here or in town?'

'Well, that puts me in my place.'

Henry's stiff look crumbled.

'Oh, deuce take you, Chase. I hope you are staying here because we need to even the odds.'

'I hadn't realised I was being enlisted into battle again. Aren't you planning to introduce me to the other troops, by the way?'

The mocking edge was gone from his smile and Ellie felt her own lips curve in answer. She wasn't surprised Henry found it hard to be annoyed at his cousin—no doubt this man was accustomed to deploying his easy humour to smooth his path. It was probably not genuine, but it was very effective.

'Eleanor said the two of you already did that,' Henry replied. 'So, how long shall you be staying?'

'I have to see what awaits me in the East Wing. If it is anything like the chaos of the Folly, it will take more than a couple of days, I'm afraid.'

'Oh, Good. Supper last night was dreadfully dull, but hopefully now you are here you will liven things up. I'm dashed glad you're here, Chase.'

Chase Sinclair's gaze flickered past Henry to assess Ellie's less-welcoming expression.

'Well, that makes one of us, Henry.'

Chapter Three

Ellie paused halfway down the stairs, wondering how she had sunk so low that her stomach was contracting just as nervously at going down to supper as it did when facing Mr Soames at the bank. Henry called her indomitable, but she could not seem to find her balance now she was away from Whitworth.

Now she would not only have to face the combined hostility of Lady Ermintrude and the two Misses Ames, but also the mocking and perceptive Chase Sinclair. It would be a wonder if the masquerade didn't unravel that very evening.

She didn't even have any finery to hide behind. Her one good dress was pathetically dowdy compared to the cousins' ostentatious mourning dresses and the under-chambermaid assigned to assist her had no experience being a lady's maid, so Ellie had simply twisted her hair into a bun at her nape as she always did. At Whitworth none of this mattered, but here...

Perhaps she should plead a headache?

She sighed, gathering her courage as Pruitt opened the door to the yellow salon just as the clock finished chiming the hour.

'You are late, Miss Walsh. I said five o'clock.' Lady Ermintrude announced before her foot even crossed the threshold.

'But...'

Henry raised his hands behind his aunt's back and Ellie swallowed her words.

'My apologies, Lady Ermintrude.' She curtsied, something she had not done in years, wobbling a little on the way up. Henry stood by the window next to Mr Sinclair and the setting sun encased the two men in a red-gold halo, making Henry look more angelic than ever, in stark contrast to Mr Sinclair's sharply hewn face, deep-set grey eyes, and black hair. Together they could have modelled for a painting of Gabriel and Lucifer.

Though perhaps not—one wouldn't want to have Lucifer dominating that painting and Mr Sinclair certainly took up more than his fair share of space. He had changed out of his riding clothes and was dressed in a style she would have found hard to describe, but next to Henry's tightly nipped waist and high shirt points he looked both less fashionable and much more elegant. Perhaps it was his sheer size. He appeared even taller in the civilised pale-yellow and walnut-wood colours that dominated the drawing room than he had in the shambolic room in the Folly. Without his greatcoat she could see the impressive breadth of his shoulders had nothing to do with its many capes.

It was strange that after the first disorienting moments of his appearance at the Folly and earlier in the parlour she hadn't felt any real apprehension, but now in the safety of the yellow salon he suddenly looked dangerous.

He raised his glass as he met her eyes, his mouth quirking slightly at one corner. Lady Ermintrude's eyes narrowed and Henry stepped forward hurriedly.

'Eleanor, may I introduce my cousin, Mr Charles Sinclair. Chase, this is Miss Walsh.'

Mr Sinclair put down his glass and Ellie straightened her shoulders and waited for the man to add to her destruction in Lady Ermintrude's estimation.

'Miss Walsh.' He bowed slightly, his voice cool and polite and nothing like the familiar tones he had employed in the Folly or with Henry. But just as her shoulders dropped a little he turned to Henry.

'I didn't know you had it in you, Cousin.'

Henry floundered at the ambiguous comment

and there was a moment's awkward silence, but Chase Sinclair merely went to stand by the fireplace, watching them as if waiting for the next act to commence.

There was a sudden stifled giggle from Fenella and both Lady Ermintrude and Drusilla directed a dampening look at her.

'The betrothal is not yet a public fact, Charles,' Lady Ermintrude said in her most damping tones. 'It is hardly appropriate to be contemplating such matters while still in mourning. We would all appreciate if you refrain from referring to it in public or in front of the servants. Indeed, in any setting.'

Mr Sinclair arched one dark brow, but he gave a slight, mocking bow. Ellie indulged in some very satisfying silent rejoinders to Lady Ermintrude, but went to sit meekly on the sofa. Henry approached the sofa as well, but at a lift of Lady Ermintrude's veined hand he chose a spindly chair instead.

For a moment there was no sound but the rustle and snap of the fire and Ellie battled against the absurd urge to succumb to giggles like Fenella even as she struggled to think of something, anything to say that wouldn't make matters more uncomfortable. She caught sight of a book on the low table between the open fashion plates of

La Belle Assemblée. She knew nothing of fashion, but surely Ovid was unexceptionable?

'That is my favourite translation of the *Metamorphoses.*' The words tumbled out of her and into a silence more awful than before.

'I beg your pardon?' Lady Ermintrude demanded. 'You have been permitted to read such salacious blasphemy?'

'I don't think it is quite fair to call Ovid's *Metamorphoses* blasphemy, Aunt Ermy,' Mr Sinclair interjected. 'His *Ars Amatoria*, on the other hand, can be safely called salacious, but I sincerely doubt Miss Walsh has read that. Or have you, Miss Walsh? If not, I recommend the third volume in particular.'

Ellie met her tormentor's gaze, not at all certain she should be grateful to him for drawing Lady Ermintrude's fire.

'I won't have you discussing such topics in front of my dear Drusilla and Fenella, Charles Sinclair! And you may take that book and put it with the rest of Huxley's belongings. I do not know why it is here at all.'

'Yes, Lady Ermintrude.'

Mr Sinclair obediently took the book and went to sit on a chair across from Fenella. Fenella giggled again, but subsided under her aunt's glare.

'How long do you believe it will take you to sort through the East Wing, Charles?'

'I will try to be as quick as possible and not

allow myself to be distracted by any salacious antiquities, Aunt Ermy,' he replied and her ladyship snorted.

'I sincerely doubt Huxley had anything salacious there aside from those horrid books. You will need help. I suggest that since Henry is engaged in estate matters and since Miss Walsh appears to be proficient in Latin and all that heathenish nonsense, she may be of some use in helping you sort through Huxley's belongings. I do not believe in sitting idle.'

Ellie stared at her and Henry roused himself.

'But Aunt, surely…' His voice dwindled under her gaze.

'Surely what, Henry? Speak up! I detest mumbling. Drusilla and Fenella are hard at work helping me with the embroidering for the parish's Poor Widows and Orphans Society and do not have time to entertain your…betrothed. And since she so charmingly admitted she cannot set a stitch she will hardly be of use to us in our duties.'

'Surely I could help with the housekeeping; I am…'

'*I* oversee the housekeeping,' Lady Ermintrude snapped. 'You are not yet wed and until that day I see no reason to upheave Mrs Slocum's routine. Meanwhile you may either be of use assisting the clearing of the East Wing or entertain yourself while Henry is engaged elsewhere. Now it is time for supper.'

'Sorry, Eleanor,' Henry whispered as they stood to follow Lady Ermintrude into supper. He looked so miserable she smiled and patted his arm.

'Never mind, Henry. We shall laugh about it later.'

'You might. This is my destiny.' He sighed.

'Coming, Henry?' Lady Ermintrude barked and Henry took Ellie's arms and propelled her after his cousins.

Inside the supper room Ellie realised Lady Ermintrude had taken another step in her battle to separate her from Henry. Leaves had been added to the already impressive table, lengthening it by several yards. Now Henry sat at one end, flanked by Dru and Lady Ermintrude, while she was seated at the other end with Charles Sinclair and Fenella. At least that meant she was far from Lady Ermintrude's sharp comments and Drusilla's brooding silences, but she felt sorry for Henry. If he'd hoped Mr Sinclair would swell the ranks of his supporters, he'd underestimated the superior tactical skills of his enemy. Though Ellie was a little surprised Lady Ermintrude felt Fen was safe in her sinful cousin's presence, especially given Fen's rather mischievous streak. This was immediately in evidence as Fen demanded 'Cousin Chase' regale her with London gossip, though she kept her gaze demurely on her plate, hiding her giggles behind her napkin.

* * *

In the end supper was not as horrid as Ellie had expected. She listened idly to the fashionable nonsense Mr Sinclair offered his cousin, rather in the manner of a man tossing a stick to a puppy. She herself had no interest in gossip about fashionable fribbles, but at least he was amusing and neither of them appeared to want her to contribute which suited her, leaving her to stew in her own concerns.

When these became too depressing, Ellie turned her attention to the dining room. It was very grand, but from experience she recognised the signs of economy in the draughts whistling faintly past the warped window frames, in the threadbare carpet and in the creaking of the uncomfortable chairs. Lady Ermintrude might be a wealthy woman, but it was evident she kept the household on a short string. Ellie's hopes that Henry might be able to save Whitworth, already sinking since her arrival, sank further—what were the chances of Lady Ermintrude giving Henry funds merely for the asking?

She was deep in her morose calculations, but her ears perked up when Fen leaned towards Mr Sinclair and asked in a whisper, 'What was that book you mentioned, Cousin Chase? Is it very wicked?'

Ellie glanced at Mr Sinclair. Surely he wouldn't? He met her gaze with a slow, speculative smile that drew her into full alertness. Just as in the Folly she was suddenly utterly present, her senses absorbing everything—the sound of cutlery on china, the whisper of the draught just touching her nape, the flicker of the fire piercing the ruby-rich liquid in his wine glass.

'Is it, Miss Walsh? Wicked?'

The single word twisted out of its mould and became an entity in itself. She had read several Greek and Latin tomes from her father's library that might be considered fast for a proper young woman, but she had never thought they deserved the label wicked. Now, under the force of that smile, she was no longer certain. Of anything.

'No! Have you read it, Miss Walsh? Is it one of *those* books?' For the first time there was a glimmer of respect in Fenella's eyes as she turned to Ellie.

'I don't think your aunt will approve you discussing such matters, Miss Fenella; certainly not with Mr Sinclair.'

'You *have* read it. Do you think there is an English copy in the library?'

'If I remember correctly there is one in Latin, Fen,' Sinclair answered. 'It would do you good to apply yourself to something other than embroidery and gossip.'

Fen wrinkled her nose.

'Aunt never allowed us to study Latin. Only a

little Italian so we can sing. She says German rots the mind and French enlarges the heart.'

'Good Lord. I had no idea Ermy was a student of medieval medicine. I'm afraid to ask what she thinks about Greek. Something unmentionable in polite society, no doubt.'

Lady Ermintrude swivelled in their direction, causing Fen to stifle her giggle and apply herself to her syllabub. Chase motioned to Pruitt to refill his glass, then turned to Ellie.

'I was wondering what it would take for you to smile again,' he murmured. 'Don't let Ermy see you do that too often. Her hopes to scuttle your plans will only intensify if she sees that smile.'

'Thank you for your concern on my behalf, Mr Sinclair.'

'Being called Mr Sinclair always reminds me of my uncle. Not a nice man. Call me Chase, or, if you must, Cousin Chase like Fen does.'

'It would hardly be proper for me to call you Chase and we are not cousins.'

'We will be soon and since we are apparently to work together over the next few days, I suggest you try. I don't answer to Mr Sinclair.'

'Oh, good. That means our time together is likely to be very quiet and I much prefer working without interruptions.'

He laughed.

'I see your weapon of choice is the sharp rebuke of silence. I cannot remember if that is among Ovid's suggestions to women in his *Art of Love*. Did you really read it or is that merely bravado?'

'Did *you* really read it or is that merely braggadocio?'

'My God, Henry has no idea what he is in for. And you are quite right—I only read the interesting parts and skimmed the rest. I particularly liked the segment where he suggests women take a variety of lovers of all types and ages…'

'Cousin Chase!' Fen gasped, her spoon halfway to her mouth and her eyes as wide as saucers, darting from him in the direction of her aunt.

'You are quite right, Fen, this is not a suitable topic to be discussed at the supper table, certainly not while such horrible pap is being served. Miss Walsh and I will discuss it later.'

'Miss Walsh would as soon spend her day practising cross-stitches, Mr Sinclair.' Ellie replied.

'Is that a euphemism?'

Ellie did her best not to smile. The more he talked, the more her discomfort faded. He might be the irreverent rogue Henry said, but to regard him as a threat was ludicrous. In fact, she could see the wisdom of Henry's hopes that at least with him in the house Lady Ermintrude's fire would not be directed solely at her. And helping him in the East Wing would be an improvement to further demolishing her fingers with embroidery.

'All that energy you expend trying not to smile

could be better spent, you know?' he said and be-hind the humour she saw the same speculation as in the Folly. It was a strange combination. Discor-dant. As if he were two wholly different people, like the two-faced god Janus—half-rogue, half-jester. And something else as well...

'What then could be said about all the energy you expend in maintaining your rogue's mask?' she asked, curious which aspect would respond to her thrust. He didn't answer immediately, watch-ing her as he raised his glass.

'A mask implies something to conceal. I am not so complex a fellow. Just like Lady Ermin-trude I possess no hidden depths, I'm afraid. Fen could tell you as much. She has known me for dogs' years, right, Fen?'

He flashed his cousin a smile and she shook her head.

'He is hopeless. Aunt says it is only a matter of time before he and Lord Sinclair end in gaol or debtors' prison or worse.'

'With a hopeful emphasis on *worse*,' Chase added.

'I thought Henry said your brother was recently married.' Ellie said and his smile shifted for a mo-ment, went inwards, and contrarily Ellie felt her shoulders tense.

'Lucas was always the serious one in our fam-ily. As befits the eldest sibling.'

'Besides, she is an heiress,' Fen said, leaning forward conspiratorially. 'Aunt Ermintrude says…'

'Do tell us what Aunt Ermy says about my sister-in-law.' His voice did not change, but the table fell silent. Even Pruitt stopped in mid-motion, Henry's plate of uneaten syllabub hovering. The power of Chase Sinclair's stillness was as shocking as a full outburst of fury might have been and Ellie's curiosity sharpened.

'N-nothing,' Fen replied, her shoulders hunched, and Ellie threw herself into the breach.

'Henry told me she employs a man of business to manage her extensive financial concerns. I am very envious.'

His smile returned, a little wry.

'You like the idea of ordering men about, Miss Walsh?'

'I can see its merits.'

'You may always practise on me, if you wish. When you aren't smoothing over troubled waters.'

'Ah, the mask is back in place. And just in time for Lady Ermintrude to call a halt to our evening's entertainment.'

They stood as Lady Ermintrude rose and announced the women would retire.

'Goodnight, Miss Walsh. Cousin Fenella.' Chase Sinclair bowed properly, but ruined the polite gesture by murmuring in Latin as she passed, *'Spero autem frigus cor calida fovere somnia.'*

She could not prevent the flush that rose to her

cheeks at the suggestive quote from Ovid, but she answered as coolly as his assessment of her heart.

'I shall leave that office to my betrothed, thank you, Mr Sinclair.'

'What did he say?' Fen whispered as they left the supper room. 'Something about sparrows in autumn and insomnia?'

'Precisely. His Latin is quite atrocious,' she lied, grateful that the darkened corridors masked her blush. The thought of hot dreams warming cool hearts did not sound quite as innocently romantic as when she and her sister Susan read that particular section of the *Ars Amatoria*. 'He was merely trying to be clever and failing.'

'Well, I am glad he is here. He is so wickedly amusing.'

'Fenella!' Drusilla admonished and Fen sighed and hurried after her aunt and sister. Ellie trailed behind them, looking forward to reading a book in bed.

Her siblings were rarely amenable to retiring before dusk and she could not remember the last time she had the luxury of reading herself to sleep. Bedtime at Whitworth was always a hectic time, rather like trying to herd stampeding bulls. By the time she herself reached her room she was too exhausted to do more than fall into bed and even then her mind was a whirl of worries about debts and mortgages that leaked into her dreams.

But instead of sinking into this all-too-temporary respite from her world, she sat staring at the walls well into the night, her mind full of fear of the future and the peculiar nature of the Huxleys. And Sinclairs.

'Thank God!'

Henry collapsed into an armchair as Pruitt closed the door after the women's departure. 'I don't know how much more of that I can bear.'

'You shall have to develop an immunity, I'm afraid.' Chase handed him a glass of port. 'At least until after your wedding. Then I suggest you allow your bluestocking betrothed to deliver Aunt Ermy her marching papers. Having the two of them in one house is likely to prove disastrous. How the devil did you convince that unflappable piece of work to marry you, Henry? She is hardly your type.'

'She is more my type than yours,' Henry snapped.

'I don't have a type. It limits me.'

'Well, I do. Ellie is the best woman I know.'

'That still doesn't explain why you are marrying her and certainly not why she is marrying you.'

'You leave her alone, Chase.'

Chase laughed. Having observed Miss Walsh throughout that interminable meal, he realised his initial concerns about her were probably completely unfounded. Whatever sins her father had committed and whatever hidden currents existed in her own character, that core of schoolmistress's rectitude was not assumed. But there was still something that did not quite ring true and it pricked his curiosity.

'Don't worry, Henry. I don't poach and certainly not on virgin territory. I'm merely curious. Besides, you ought to have more faith in your beloved's constancy than your concern implies.'

'I'm not worried she will fancy someone like you; she is far too sensible. But I don't want you bothering her with your teasing. This is hard enough for her as it is.'

'Very gallant of you. I am doing you a service, though.'

Henry's brows lowered, creating a sandy bar over his blue eyes, and Chase continued.

'The more your beloved disapproves of me, the more Ermy is likely to approve of her.'

'Blast you, Chase, you always make having your own way sound so reasonable.' A grin replaced his frown and he sighed. 'I hadn't realised how awful matters are until we arrived this week. Have you had a look at the East Wing? Is it bad?'

'Bad enough that I'm afraid I might go missing in that bog never to be found again, but it must be done. I am certain that if I left Huxley's belongings to the care of Aunt Ermy she will have the lot of it thrown on to a bonfire and I cannot allow that; I do have some scruples.'

'Why not let someone else see if there is anything worth salvaging so you can run back to London and your ladies?'

'I am between ladies at the moment. Besides, I would rather see if there is anything of more than cultural value before I hand over the remains to the dry sticks at the Museum.'

'What, have you run aground? Even with a new heiress in the family?'

Chase gathered in his temper once more and counted to ten. Henry's freckles dimmed as he flushed.

'Sorry. That was uncalled for. I only… Oh, blast. I'm in over my head. I never wanted to be Lord Huxley or a landowner. I was content working with the solicitors in Nettleton and I don't know a dashed thing about sheep or land management or…or anything.'

'That's comprehensive. Chin up, Henry, it will become easier with time.'

'No, it won't. At least not until we can revive the estate to turn a profit. Uncle might have been a brilliant scholar, but he was a terrible landlord and it's only Ermy's money that keeps this place afloat. He spent every penny he had on travel and curios. It really isn't fair he left them to you.'

'Ah, I see the point of sensitivity about heiresses. I presume Miss Walsh is not bringing funds to this union?'

Henry's expression was an answer in itself.

Clearly Fergus Walsh's estate had not recovered with his demise.

'You should have proposed to Dru or Fen, Henry. Two plump heiresses ripe for the plucking and emblazoned with Ermy's approval. They suit you better than Miss Walsh, anyway.'

'How the devil do you know what suits me?'

Chase didn't answer. His encounters thus far with his prim cousin-to-be were not conclusive and he had nothing to support his conviction Henry was making a very serious mistake. In fact, he could not quite make sense of Henry's engagement. The title was modest but respectable and, without Huxley draining the accounts to pay for his travels and artefacts, in a few years the estate could be dragged into profitability.

If Henry chose, he could do better than an impoverished neighbour from a scandal-stricken family, past her first blush of youth and with nothing but passable good looks and a sharp tongue to recommend her. Strangely, though, Chase didn't think she had done the running. Or perhaps it was merely his unexpected reaction to her accidental proximity in the Folly that was colouring his judgement. And his inability to pin her down. She was… He was not quite certain what she was. In her plain dress and her hair sternly disciplined into a depressingly practical bun, she looked every inch the spinster schoolmistress. She even ate like one—as if measuring each bite for its utility and dismissing the syllabub as pure frivolity.

But though her cool haughtiness did not appear assumed, it did not accord with that burst of temper in the Folly or her sudden and unsettling flashes of humour. Under the ice he sensed there were volatile forces at work and he wondered if she suffered from any of her father's instability of character. For Henry's sake he hoped not.

Henry sighed and put down his glass, dragging Chase out of his uncomfortable reverie.

'The truth is I'm glad you're here, Chase. Don't take it wrong, but I think Aunt Ermy might resent me and Ellie less if she has you to dislike. Ellie isn't precisely the type of biddable females Aunt is used to.'

Chase smiled despite himself and rubbed the sore spot on his thigh. That was a mistake, as the memory of their near tumble down the stairs woke other aspects of his anatomy. Her mercurial transformation from ice maiden to scolding hellcat was a very enticing combination, dowdy or not.

'You just might be luckier than you deserve, Henry.'

Henry stood and stretched.

'I know. She's a good 'un. Well, goodnight, Chase. I must rise at dawn for some absurd reason to do with sheep and pastures.'

'You won't object to Miss Walsh helping me in the East Wing?'

Henry yawned and wandered towards the door.

'No, she will enjoy rooting through Uncle's rubbish heaps. She likes books and things.'

'Aren't you worried I might take advantage of her?'

Henry's laughter trailed back from the hallway and was swallowed by another jaw-cracking yawn.

'She can keep you in line, believe me. G'night, Chase.'

Chapter Four

❦

Two steps into the passage connecting the East Wing to the rest of the Manor, Ellie understood why the servants were so reluctant to enter the previous Lord Huxley's domain. The passage walls were lined by glass-fronted cabinets crowded with a bizarre and unsettling collection of masks, jars, figurines and other artefacts.

Like a child witnessing something she knew was forbidden, she was drawn inexorably by a collection of jars filled with viscous fluids and what appeared to be lizards or snakes or…something.

She approached cautiously and rose on tiptoe to make out the contents of a particularly large glass jar with a purplish mass inside. It looked horrid, but her disgust wasn't sufficient to counter her curiosity and her hand rose towards the latch securing the cabinet door.

'Careful.'

She jerked away from the voice directly behind her, her hands flying out to stop her descent towards the cabinet, and an arm closed about her waist, pulling her back.

'Trust me, you don't want to bring that lot crashing down on us. I've already torn one pair of trousers because of you and I don't want to sacrifice another.' His breath was warm against her ear and temple as he held her against him and again she felt the unravelling of heat, her body exploring the points of contact with his as it had yesterday. It was foreign and unwelcome, but too powerful to reason away.

Like other unwelcome realities of life, she allowed it to present itself fully before she set about beating it back. Piece by piece. She began by prying his hand from her waist, which was perhaps a mistake because his hand felt just as warm and strong under hers as it felt against her waist. She dropped it and moved away, focusing on the disgusting object in the jar.

'What *is* that?'

'That is…or rather was an Egyptian cat. A mummified one. My cousin thought it might be interesting to see what would happen if he rehydrated a mummy.'

She moved away, feeling a little ill.

'That is horrid. Why is it purple?'

'The gauze around the mummy was decorated with indigo. It is a rather dominant colour.'

'Why on earth would they do that to a cat?'

'Cats were considered sacred in ancient Egypt. One of their gods, Bastet, even had the form of a cat and not far from where we lived in Egypt there was a cemetery dedicated solely to felines. Did you know it was said that if a house cat died a natural death the members of the household must shave their eyebrows?'

She touched the tip of her own eyebrow and he smiled. She took another step back.

'That sounds rather extreme.'

'No more than many religious practices and far less violent than some.'

'True. What will you do with this relative of... Bastet?'

'I think I shall donate her to the Museum. Along with her amphibian friends.'

'Amphibian? Are those frogs?'

His smile widened at the revulsion in her voice.

'Huxley was in his biblical phase at the time and was fascinated by the ten plagues of Egypt. Luckily, he confined himself to mostly frogs and locusts and avoided boils and the like. Would you care to see the locusts?'

She backed away yet another step, shaking her head, all too aware she was giving him fodder for his teasing, but the sight of that gelatinous feline was defeating her attempt to remain cool and collected.

'Here,' he said, moving forward. He twitched a

string and a blind descended over the cabinet, hiding the most offensive sights from view. 'Huxley wasn't immune to their grisliness, though they did serve to keep other members of the Manor away. I'll have them packed and removed first thing. Meanwhile you can help me in the study. There is nothing more terrifying there than reams of scribbles and more salacious Latin tomes.'

She followed, both resentful and grateful for his casual acceptance of her queasiness. She did not like being considered weak in any way.

The study was surprisingly small after the imposing passage, though the bookcases and the cherrywood desk were covered with haphazard stacks of books, bound notebooks, and papers. Chase went to stand by the desk, frowning as he leafed through one of the notebooks.

'How may I help?' she asked, clasping her hands before her.

'Do you wish to? Or was this merely a ploy to escape from Aunt Ermy's despotic influence?'

'She clearly hates it when you call her that. But then I reckon you are aware of that. *And* delight in it.'

'Delight is a word I prefer to save for more suitable subjects. My irreverence keeps her at bay and that is all I ask.'

'Are you always so blunt?'

'It saves time and effort.'

'For you, perhaps.'

'That is the whole point.'

She sighed and turned to survey the desk, frowning at the chaos.

'What is it we need to do?'

'*You* need to do nothing but hide until Ermy tires of toying with you, but I must begin working on this paper labyrinth. Go refresh your memory of *Ars Amatoria*. It is somewhere on the far shelf with the other immoral ancients. Just don't tell Henry; he won't thank me for colluding with your efforts to keep him on a short leading string.'

'I am not Fenella, you needn't expend so much effort trying to shock me, Mr Sinclair. If you wish to keep *me* at bay, you have only to ask.'

'Do you really wish to help?'

'I may as well be of use. And this place clearly needs a great deal of work if it is to be approached properly.'

'That sounds intriguing. How would one approach it *im*properly?'

She really should know better than to encourage someone like Chase Sinclair, but she could not stop her smile.

'You are giving a fair example of just that, Mr Sinclair. I do wish to help, if you feel I can be of use.'

It was the first time she had seen him smile without calculation or mocking and she wished she had not prompted the change. It was like the morning mist clearing outside Whitworth, revealing soft fields sparkling with wildflowers and dew—a moment of clear beauty, suspended and unique.

Even for a rake he was disconcertingly handsome, his face worthy of a renaissance sculpture, all sharp angles and hard planes, its harshness softened only by the fullness of his lower lip and the lines of laughter and mockery at the corners of his steel-grey eyes.

She was surprised Drusilla and Fenella weren't infatuated with this unfairly endowed specimen of manhood, or perhaps they had once been and his light-hearted teasing cured them—he might look like a fairy-tale hero, or perhaps even a villain, but he certainly did not act like one. Heroes tended to take themselves seriously, but Chase Sinclair did not appear to take anything seriously, least of all himself.

But as she waited for his response, she again felt the presence of an inner shadow, as if another person entirely was moving behind the handsome façade, considering how to wield it to his advantage.

'Very well,' he said at last, placing his hand on a stack of slim leather-bound books on the desk. 'These notebooks contain my cousin's accounts of his travels in Egypt. All the years I knew him he always kept them in order and in custom-made trunks, but as you can see that is no longer the case.'

Ellie glanced from the stack on the desk to the shelves he indicated and realised they, too, were populated not only by books and curios, but also stacks of brown-leather volumes.

'My goodness, there are hundreds of them!'

'Possibly. I would like to send them to my sister at Sinclair Hall, but first I want to put them in order, so I can ascertain if any are missing and hunt them down in this paper bog Huxley created. I wonder what Mallory was up to allow matters to deteriorate like this. He was always a stickler for neatness.'

'Are you speaking of Mr Mallory? His secretary?'

'Yes. Do you know him?'

She smiled. 'Why, yes. Well, not very well. I met him on two occasions when he visited Henry's father before he passed away. He did strike me as a very competent and serious young man. I do hope the notebooks are dated, at least?'

'The notebooks aren't, but the entries are, so with some you may have to leaf through them to find a dated entry. If you prefer not to…'

Ellie planted her hands on her hips. It would be a relief to do something useful to keep her mind off her woes.

'I shall be happy to help. I shall need some pen and paper so I can keep a record of the ones I have and perhaps separate them by year or month. And I think I will insert a sheet of paper at the beginning of each with its date and some reference to the notebooks which precede and follow it as I find them. Once I complete that stage, I will compile a catalogue so we can see which volumes are missing.'

She turned to see if her plan met with his approval, just in time to see his smile tucked away.

'Did I say something amusing, Mr Sinclair?'

'Not at all. You are the very model of good sense, Miss Walsh, and I commend your plan of attack. Mallory would approve. Pen and paper you shall have.'

'What shall I do with these strips of paper?' Ellie asked as she picked up one of the notebook with two notes dangling like pennants from between the pages.

'Leave them. No, in fact, if you find anything, bring it to me.'

'Oh, look!'

Chase looked. It was the third time that expletive had burst from Miss Walsh's lips in as many hours, accompanied by a look of delight that was beginning to grate on his nerves. Not that it was not a charming sight—her mouth softening into her rare smile and her eyes widened and lit with joy, turning them from mere brown to warm honey flaked with dancing sparks of gold and the tiny glimmer of green around the iris.

For the third time Chase found his attention

wholly captured by her excitement. This time he tried for dismissiveness.

'What have you found tucked inside his notebooks now? Another mouldering pressed daisy? An ancient Egyptian shopping list, perhaps? For ten yards of mummy wrappings and a sheaf of papyrus?'

'No. This was under the notebooks and it looks quite old.' She approached the desk, holding a small leather-bound book with the gentleness of a lepidopterist balancing a rare butterfly on her palm. He took it just as carefully, memories flooding back.

'You are right; it is very old. It is a book of hours given to my cousin by a friend of his, Fanous, an abbot at a Coptic monastery near his house in Qetara.'

'It is exquisite.'

It was indeed exquisite. A monk had probably toiled for months over the detailed illustrations and squiggly Coptic letters. The picture was of a man and a woman in medieval garb standing hand-fasted and heads bowed, either in joint prayer or in mutual embarrassment. He could almost feel the tension between them and he breathed in, surprised at his unusually sentimental interpretation of the image.

'It is a wedding, I think,' she said, her voice low and serious. 'Look here in the corner, that is the priest and those tables might signify a wedding feast. Those look like greenish pumpkins.'

'Either that or rotund babes. Those two clearly look as if they have anticipated their wedding vows.'

Her mouth quirked almost into a smile and she tucked a strand of light-brown hair behind her ear as she leaned over him to turn the page.

Unlike Dru and Fen she didn't dress or curl her hair, just dragged it back into a mercilessly regimented bun that did nothing to enliven her looks. But the deeper she delved into the notebooks, the more she unravelled. Her bun was slowly loosening its hold and though she kept tucking the escaping strands of hair behind her ears, they rarely stayed there, adding character and life to her face.

'See? These are their children, helping with the harvest.' Her voice was low and warm, lost in the imaginary world she concocted from the colourful illustrations. This is probably how she saw her little world with Henry—a safe, bucolic haven surrounded by gambolling lambs and sandy-haired babes or honey-eyed little girls with determined brows and far too much intelligence for comfort. Reality, as he knew only too well, was unlikely to be as pleasant.

She turned another page and caught a slip of paper before it fluttered to the ground. It was covered in Huxley's scrawl and before he could take it she read it aloud, a frown in her voice.

'*"Fanous as Jephteh? Who else knew him?"*
Does that mean anything to you, Mr Sinclair? Or
this list of letters? *"J... M... P... S... C... E...at
bull & pyramid"*. How peculiar. It almost sounds
like the name of an inn…you know, like the Horse
and Plough, or the Lamb and Eagle.'

Her eyes were alight with interest and Chase
took the note, adding it to the growing stack he'd
been collecting. Nothing so far appeared to shed
any light on Huxley's request. He was beginning
to wonder if Huxley's last letter was merely the
sign of a decaying mind and odd fancies. The un-
tidiness of the study and Folly appeared to support that possibility.

Mallory should be able to clear up this conundrum, but according to Pruitt he left just two days
before Huxley's death to destinations unknown
which was also peculiar, to say the least. Not that
he suspected Mallory of anything improper. Huxley had taken him on as secretary when he was
still a young man and he was as straight as an
arrow, but it was still strange he'd disappeared so
abruptly and not yet returned. Chase hoped the
message he'd sent to his Uncle Oswald to have
someone trace Mallory would settle that problem,
but meanwhile all he could do was continue sift-
ing through his cousin's remains and hope something pointed him in the right direction.

So far the only items of interest were these peculiar notes such as the one Miss Walsh had just

found, though they, too, probably meant absolutely nothing. Yet something about the letter and the peculiar disorder in the study bothered him.

And it was, unfortunately, not the only thing bothering him.

At the moment the more potent disturbance was Miss Walsh herself. Her excited 'Oh, look!' was bad enough when directed at him across the expanse of the desk. But having her a mere hand's length away was proving more distracting than he would have thought possible.

Not that she appeared to share his discomfort in the least. She was wholly engrossed in the note, her finger gently tracing the letters so that he could almost feel the rasp of her finger on the paper.

He held himself still, resisting the urge to take advantage of the little book to lean closer to her. This close he could see where the well-worn muslin fabric curved over her breasts and hips. Even in that dowdy dress it was evident she had lovely breasts, not too small, not too large. His hands heated at the thought of how well they would fit in his palms, wondering whether they would be cool or warm, what colour her...

He cleared his throat, focusing on the fragile book. His imagination was always fertile, but it usually waited for more suitable subjects for its flights of fancy.

He reached for the scribbled strip of paper and,

though he had not actively intended to, his arm brushed hers. He drew back, feeling stifled.

'I'll take that. And we had best return to our task if we are ever to finish.'

Her curiosity and excitement extinguished immediately, and the schoolmistress was back—calm, blank and faintly disapproving. He could have kicked himself for his petty rejection. He was definitely off form.

'Shall I have Pruitt bring us some tea? My temper can be measured in direct opposition to my hunger.' It wasn't much of an apology, but her mouth relaxed a little as he went to tug at the bell pull.

'You remind me of Hugh.'

'Who is Hugh?'

'My brother. We could tell the hour by his temper when he was a boy. If we had not fed him by five we did not need the clock to chime the hour. But once fed he was an angel for precisely another three hours. Mama always said it was because his mind was so hard at work. He is quite brilliant.'

'I don't have that excuse, unfortunately. How many of you are there?'

'Five. Myself, Susan, Edmund, Anne and Hugh.'

'You are the eldest? Never mind, don't bother answering. Of course you are.'

'Why of course?'

'I recognise the symptoms. You are natural shepherds—everything into its proper slot.'

'Ah. Did your brother herd you?'

'Not for many years. Lucas knows when to abandon a lost cause, a very useful characteristic in an older sibling.'

'I wish he would tell me how. My siblings inform me I am terribly managing.'

'Perhaps I should have a word with them instead. Teach them a trick or two to herd the shepherd. Behind your back, of course.'

'I don't believe they need your help, Mr Sinclair. They are enough of a handful without your dubious advice. Now, as you said, we should return to these stacks or we shall never be done.'

Her shift in humour was so swift he was caught off guard.

'Did I upset you? It was just idle nonsense. I would not really do that, you know.'

She shrugged and returned to her armchair. Chase took the book of hours and leaned across the desk to place it by her hand.

'Keep this. My cousin would have liked you to have it.'

She shook her head and pushed the book back towards him. It was another dismissal, but it made him all the more determined to restore her to good humour. He didn't like the ease with which she slipped back into her shell and he certainly didn't like being the cause of it.

'Take it. Please.'

He could see her weakening, but her eyes darted to the stacks of books on the table.

'I could not take something so precious, but perhaps… No.'

'What is it you would like?'

'I see he has two sets of the Desert Boy novels—the one on the table and the one on the shelves over there. Perhaps I could have one… They are my siblings' favourite books and I thought…'

'You could have both if you like. One for your family and the other for you to have here at Huxley.'

'Oh, but I won't be—' Her words stopped as if dropped off a cliff. Then she gathered herself. 'One set will do, Mr Sinclair. My siblings will be very grateful.'

He watched her, unable to shake a sense of unease about her. And so he did what he always did when he was on shaky ground—he went digging.

'How old are your siblings?'

Wistfulness warred with reserve on her expressive face. Even her features were a study in contrasts—her eyebrows and long eyelashes were several shades darker than her hair, accentuating the faintly exotic slant of her eyes, and her lower lip was a lush counterpoint to a thin and very precise upper lip. She wasn't traditionally pretty, but there was something fascinating about her face, a play of contrasts that caught and held the viewer's interest; like a painting he didn't understand but instinctively liked.

'Susan is twenty-two and Edmund almost eighteen, and Anne seventeen and Hugh is fourteen,' she replied, her voice still curt.

'Are you worried about them?'

She kept her gaze on the book, her long fingers riffling through the pages.

'They have never been without me before. And then there is Aunt Florence.'

'Your aunt is minding them? Then surely you need not worry.'

'They are probably minding her, rather. She is a darling, but she can be as bad as my mother for daydreaming. I do not know how useful she will be if anything happens.'

'Perhaps you underestimate them. I find it hard to believe siblings of yours are not also intelligent and resourceful. They must grow up eventually, you know.'

She finally looked up.

'Next you will say I am mollycoddling them or…or something worse.'

'No, I will say you probably need time away from them more than they need time away from you. Though I would have recommended a rather more relaxing venue than Aunt Ermy's domain.'

Her mouth wavered between annoyance and amusement.

'That does leave quite a few possibilities in between,' she replied and he smiled at her lowering of arms.

'Just about anywhere else, in fact. So, where would you go if you could go anywhere?'

Her gaze became wistful again as they settled on the Desert Boy books. 'I wish I could disappear into the leaves of one of these books. Or perhaps…there.' She turned to the framed picture on the wall. It was one Sam painted for Huxley many years ago—a view of the Nile from the cliffs above Qetara, the sails of the feluccas blushing in the sunset and the shores stubbly with papyrus reeds.

'I hesitate to ruin your daydream with anything akin to reality, but Egypt is hardly relaxing. Sam, my sister, nearly sat on a scorpion while painting that. She probably would have if poor Edge hadn't spotted it and pushed her away.'

'Goodness. Who or what is poor Edge?'

'He's the nephew of Huxley's antiquarian partner, Poppy Carmichael, and a good friend of ours until we all left to join the army during the war. His name is Lord Edgerton, to be precise, but Sam enjoyed vexing him by devising less-than-complimentary variations on his name and her favourite was Lord Stay-Away-from-the-Edge because he was always telling her to be careful, so we all began calling him Edge. He loved ancient Egypt and the antiquities as much as Poppy and

Huxley. Show him a tomb and you'd lose him for the rest of the day. He had a habit of saving Sam when she tumbled into trouble, which was often, and thereby thoroughly putting up her back. In short, that picture is a lovely lie.'

'But you love it. Egypt.'

'Yes, but not for its relaxing qualities. Some of my best memories are from the years we spent in Egypt. Huxley was my mother's cousin and it was through him that she met my father. When my father…died…we stayed with my grandmother in Venice, but one day Huxley appeared and swept us all off to Egypt. My mother's family tried to object because she had been quite ill, but, since he was our guardian along with my paternal uncle, he carried the day. Until I joined the army, I spent my time between Venice and Egypt which were both a definite improvement on Sinclair Hall. But hardly relaxing.'

He cringed a little—his answer was more revealing than intended and her clever honey-brown eyes focused on him with curiosity. They were more honey than brown, a tawny swirl that made him think of the sweet-honey-and-nut baklava cakes Mrs Carmichael used to bribe them back to the house come evening.

He could see the questions bubbling inside her, but then her mouth turned prim again, curiosity reined in.

'Well, perhaps that is what I want, too. Exciting can still be relaxing if it is different from what one knows.'

'That is true. Perhaps you shall go to Egypt one day after all.'

She laughed, but there was such resignation in the sound he felt an instinctive surge of pity.

'Don't dismiss the possibility. Who knows? Perhaps a distant relative will demand you accompany her and her seventeen pugs on a voyage to the orient.'

'Seventeen? Must it be seventeen?'

'It must. In fact, you will set out with seventeen, but there might well be a few more by the time you arrive.'

She burst into laughter.

'A pug harem. It sounds even more tiring than managing Whitworth.'

'Adventure is often tiring. But if it is calm you seek, I could find you a post acting as governess to the heir to Shaykh Abd al-Walid, Prince of the White Desert.'

'Being a governess isn't at all calm. Before my... We once had a governess and, believe me, the poor woman was run ragged between us.'

'This is not a household of sardonic and argumentative Walshes hiding under prim veneers, but a single, indolent and very plump little boy who can be appeased with sweetmeats and who naps most of the day.'

'He sounds rather like a cat.'

'Not like my sister-in-law's cat. Inky is the size of a bear cub and, though she has a sweet tooth, she is definitely not indolent.'

'Then I shall stick to my plump charge, though I doubt even someone as silver-tongued as you could convince a prince to employ someone as unqualified as I.'

'You underestimate me, Miss Walsh. I have more skills than my silver tongue and as a servant of the Crown I can be…convincing.'

The laughter in her eyes was suddenly tinged with speculation.

'*Are* you a servant of the Crown?'

'Aren't we all?' he riposted.

As if she sensed his evasion, her eyes fell from his and she went back to her seat, sinking into it with an abruptness that made her skirts billow for a moment.

'This is all amusing, but rather silly. I am unlikely to leave Whitworth so there is no point in dreaming of Egypt.'

'You mean Huxley.'

'What?'

'You said you are unlikely to leave Whitworth.'

Her cheeks turned as pink as the sunset in Sam's painting.

'Of course. I meant…it was a figure of speech. I am still not accustomed… You know what I meant. In any case, they are both a long way from Egypt…'

The squeak of the gallery door interrupted her and Chase pushed to his feet in annoyance as a footman entered with a generously stacked tea tray.

No doubt the servants were told to keep them supplied with refreshments so they did not leave Huxley's wing unless absolutely necessary, he thought.

Ermy's campaign to separate Miss Walsh from Henry was clearly underway.

Chapter Five

⁓⁓⁓⁓

Stop staring, Ellie. Yes, Chase Sinclair is a well-favoured man, but that is no reason to discard one's dignity. Keep your eyes on your task. Well favoured, hah! He's beautiful. Just look at him.

For the hundredth time in the last several days Ellie did just that.

And for the hundredth time she forced her gaze back to her task, thoroughly disgusted with herself.

He was leaning over some papers, his hand deep in his dark hair, his forehead resting on his palm. The sharp lines of his profile were already etched in her mind: the groove at the side of his mouth that curved when he smiled, the fan of his lashes, long and dark and curving just a little at the end. How ridiculous was it that she knew precisely how a man's eyelashes curved?

Even Susan, who leapt from infatuation to infatuation as if they were stepping stones across a stream, could not be so silly.

Though to be fair, after what she'd dealt with these past five years, Ellie considered she was long overdue some foolishness. It was only unfortunate that her first infatuation, if that was what it was, had to alight on someone like Mr Sinclair. But that, too, wasn't surprising. She had never spent so much time alone with any man other than family or Henry and his father, and she had certainly never met anyone as impressive as Chase Sinclair. She disliked the thought that she was joining the ranks of probably all-too-numerous females infatuated with this admittedly impressive specimen of manhood.

She couldn't' even blame him for it. He wasn't even doing anything to merit his dubious reputation. For a rake he was sadly un-rakish and she could see now why Dru and Fen treated him with such ease.

The worst was that she felt comfortable with him. Aside from her stupid propensity to stare at him, she did not feel in least awkward in his presence.

It felt as natural and as right as being alone and that was…peculiar.

He made her laugh with his nonsense, inventing ever more creative scenarios to account for her sudden travel to Egypt—moving on from pugs and plump princes to becoming a famous artist commissioned to paint a portrait of Muhammad Ali's favourite horse. On another occasion she'd been beguiled into an ascension of a hot air balloon and was swept all the way eastwards, only to become stuck on the tip of the pyramid.

She'd even managed to concoct a few plots of her own, but they were never as exotic as his, running aground on objections before they even made it out of her mouth.

In between work and nonsense, he ensured there was always a supply of tea and didn't even complain when she couldn't resist reading sections aloud from the notebooks she was slowly but steadily putting into the correct order.

In short, he treated her with his own peculiar combination of irreverence and respect which, had she not been foolish enough to conceive this girlish *tendre* for him, would have made her completely comfortable in his company.

But it only made it worse.

She would just have to ensure she gave him no reason to suspect. And, even more importantly, gave Lady Ermintrude no reason to suspect it. Ellie did not want to give her the satisfaction of knowing her machinations in forcing her into Chase's company had borne fruit. In any case he would likely leave soon, she reminded herself sternly.

Although he did not appear to be hurried, Tubbs, his valet, had already packed all the cabinets in the Ghoulish Gallery—gone were the gelatinous amphibians and carved beetles and statuettes, and this morning two trunks appeared in the study, clearly ready to receive the books and papers they were reviewing.

And Chase would not be the only one leaving soon—she knew she must face the harsh reality that, with all the best will in the world, Henry had overestimated Huxley's financial position. His plan to save Whitworth was proving just as unrealistic as pugs and hot air balloons. It was time to face the truth.

But she wasn't ready. Not to leave.

Ready or not, Ellie Walsh—you *will* return to Whitworth and try to save what can be saved just as you *will* recover from this foolishness, she told herself resolutely, opening the next notebook on her stack.

Or perhaps not.

It certainly didn't feel like any infatuation Susan described to her. There were no stars and sighs and she didn't think he was perfect and above all mortals. But she did feel that saying goodbye to these days in the study would be like leaving herself behind, something true and real that was only just beginning to form.

It felt…wrong.

The words on the page in front of her blurred. She placed her hand over them as if afraid the threatening tears would burst their dam and inundate the world. But she breathed them back inside and turned the page. At least she could escape inside the foreign but strangely familiar world of Lord Huxley's notebooks, if only for a while.

She glared at the first sentence as she noticed Chase's name. She did not want to read about him at the moment. She debated picking up another notebook, but already her mind was ploughing ahead and she gave in.

'Damned if I know how he does it. It wasn't the first time Chase smoothed over matters with the authorities. Tessa says it's a gift and curse, the way the boy can wrap people round his thumb without even appearing to.

'Just like that time with Awal. By some means as yet obscure to me Chase talked Poppy into hiring Awal for the whole season even after Poppy swore up and down the Nile he had no use for a half-blind peasant come begging for al-Jinn Chase to help him. He even convinced Poppy it was his idea. If Chase ever lost his inheritance, he could make back his fortune with that silver tongue.

'I told T. I would worry if Chase used it for his own benefits, but he only appears to do so when someone else is in trouble. T. said that worried her most of all and I must say she has a point. It's the Sinclair curse—all those extremes of dark and light take their toll.

'Poor Tessa. Sometimes I sorely regret she met

Howard through me and other times I'm grateful—these three wretches have certainly enlivened my life. When they aren't adding to my white hairs. This business with Khalidi's cats was a step too far and, though Chase said the idea was his, I detect Sam's fell influence. Chase is usually more refined in his machinations.

'Still, he should have stopped her rather than taken a hand in such an outrageous endeavour. Khalidi would have been well within his rights not only to keep Edge in gaol, but toss Chase in with him and have the rest of us banished from Qetara. I'm only glad Lucas was in Cairo or he'd no doubt have joined the fray. I told T. she ought to ring a peal over them, they are too old for such nonsense. Abducting cats! What next?'

She turned the pages, but there were no more references to the abducted cats, so she searched the stack for the notebook preceding this, to no avail. Although at least it confirmed one of her assumptions.

'Oh, bother!' she exclaimed.

'What have I done now?'

She looked up swiftly to see Chase watching her, the glinting smile in his eyes. It was like a flame flaring up too close to her face—she pressed back in the armchair, her hands tightening around the notebook to stop them from an instinctive need to press against the heat in her cheeks. His profile was bad enough, but faced with the warmth of his smile, that invitation to share, she became as soft and shapeless inside as a lump of kneaded dough.

'Whatever it is, if it has struck you dumb, it must be bad. Should I apologise?' he prompted, still with the same warm amusement.

'It's the c-cats,' she stammered.

'Cats?'

'The ones you abducted.'

'I...what?'

'That is just it. I don't know. It doesn't say. And I cannot find the one before. And I really wished to know what happened.'

'You do realise you are making no sense? Have you been tippling Huxley's brandy behind my back?'

'I don't imbibe, Mr Sinclair,' she replied, trying to sound sensible, but her mouth was already curving upwards in response to his teasing. *I don't need brandy to make a fool of myself,* she thought morosely.

'Never?'

'Spirits are expensive and we rarely entertain at Whitworth.' She didn't add that the only visitors were creditors, local matrons trying to interfere in their lives, or Henry, and of these only Henry was encouraged to linger. The teasing warmth in Chase's eyes was giving way to speculation and she looked away and turned the conversation back to the notebooks. 'I wanted to know the story behind his account of you and Sam abducting this Mr Khalidi's cats, but the notebook before this seems to be missing.'

Laughter drove away the expression that had made her uncomfortable.

'Lord, I had forgotten about that. That was when Edge, Lord Edgerton, tried to rescue a damsel in distress and ended up in gaol.'

'Was your sister the damsel in distress?'

'Sam wouldn't thank you for considering her a damsel in distress. At least not back in those days. No, this was Fatima, Khalidi's daughter. Edge was a rather handsome fellow but not quite aware of his charms.' He glanced up. 'Here is your chance for a sarcastic comment, Miss Walsh. Along the lines of "the same cannot be said of a certain vain Sinclair".'

'A certain *aggravating* Sinclair. Stop being so clever and tell me what happened.'

'Very well. Khalidi was a wealthy merchant who often did business with my cousin and Fatima was his eldest daughter and silly enough to tumble head over heels in love with Edge. When she learned he was leaving Egypt to join the army in Portugal, she escaped her home one evening and came to cast herself at Edge's feet.'

'How romantic!'

'That's what Sam thought, but Edge is one of the least romantic fellows you could meet. You should have seen his face when the poor girl burst into our dining room at Bab el-Nur and professed her love. He could be spectacularly obtuse and hadn't even realised she fancied him. I always thought that was why his lovers were older, more experienced women; they must have made it absolutely clear they...' He cleared his throat and continued. 'Well, when he tried to explain he did not think of her in those terms, she burst into tears and threw her arms around him and of course that was the moment Khalidi and his head guard Abu-Abas barged into the house with a band of his men.'

'Goodness. Couldn't your cousin or your mother explain what had happened?'

'Unfortunately, they were away that evening, I can't remember where. But while I was trying to explain it to Khalidi, Abu-Abas ordered the soldiers to detain Edge. Again, unfortunately, Sam tried to stop them and managed to land on her behind to which Edge took offence and gave Abu-Abas a bloody nose and we were in the middle of a melee. By the end of it Edge was carted off to gaol.'

'Oh, no! Poor Lord Edgerton.'

'Since I was left to try to prevent Sam from disembowelling Abu-Abas, believe me, I would have preferred to take Edge's place. She was spitting mad and terrified of what they might do to Edge. She thought it was her fault, which, to be fair, it was.'

'Oh, the poor girl. I would have been terrified as well if something like that happened to one of my brothers. But what has this to do with cats?'

'Well, they refused to release Edge because *hawajis*, or foreigners, weren't very welcome in Qetara at the time and so Sam concocted a plan to put pressure on Khalidi by abducting one of his beloved cats.'

Ellie groaned. 'That sounds like a plan Hugh would concoct.'

'My sympathies. It was definitely not one of my better efforts. We brought a special reed box and sneaked into Khalidi's house and found two of his most indolent felines. Unfortunately, we took a wrong turn on our way out and found ourselves face to face with Khalidi and his family. Sam panicked and dropped her side, which woke the cats and they started yowling.'

'Oh, no—were they hurt?'

'Not a hair on their pudgy bodies was harmed, I promise. But naturally we opened the lid and they darted out like bats from a cave and made straight for Khalidi and set to purring.'

'Were you dreadfully punished?'

'I certainly expected to be. But before I could say a word Sam began a speech in Arabic.'

'Susan to the life.' Ellie laughed. 'What was the speech about?'

'I can't remember precisely, something about Edge being as thick as a plank and having no interest in Fatima, and that she would find a thousand ways to plague Khalidi just like in the Bible if he didn't release Edge immediately. Luckily Khalidi began laughing.'

'Thank goodness.'

'I certainly did. He ordered Edge released, but he did exact punishment. He'd seen a sketch Sam had made of Fatima and demanded she draw each of his precious cats. There were more than a dozen of them so it took a while, but she didn't complain. He is a close friend of ours to this day.'

'And Edge? Was he hurt in the prison?'

'Edge is also fluent in Arabic and apparently he lectured his gaolers on the abysmal conditions and the likelihood that their negligence would come back to bite them on the…would expose them to disease, so they were only too happy to see the last of him. He didn't speak to Sam for weeks, though, which was a more serious punishment for her than having to sketch Khalidi's cats.'

'Do you know, it is quite strange. From your uncle's notebook it is clear you were far more active than you portrayed. He says it wasn't the first time you smoothed matters with the authorities.'

'My cousin was prone to embellishments.'

'He appears a very reliable raconteur to me. Was he embellishing about Awal as well?'

'If he was writing about owls, then he was definitely embellishing. Or hallucinating.'

'Don't make game of my pronunciation. He

writes you convinced Poppy to hire someone named Awal even though he was half-blind.'

'Awal? He was near-sighted, but he had the hands of a watchmaker. Once we found him spectacles, he became one of Poppy's finest workers—if anything needed mending Awal could do it.'

'I presume it was you who found the spectacles for him.'

'My honour was at stake—I had to prove Awal wasn't the useless layabout they claimed.'

'I see; it was purely self-interest. Not kindness towards someone in need of employment.'

'I don't deal in purity. And you are making a mountain out of a molehill, Miss Walsh.'

'Of course I am. I apologise for making such dreadful insinuations about you.'

'So you should be. I've called men out for less.'

His tone was humorous, but Ellie knew it for the smokescreen it was. She was struck by an image of a tall, dark-haired boy of sixteen, halfway to being a man. She could understand why his mother worried about Chase the overly responsible boy and why he'd diverged to choose the rake's path in the end. She would be tempted to do the same given the chance to safely escape her own responsibilities.

'I can't help it. These tales are far too entertaining. Someone should compile his diaries into a book. I believe travel memoirs are very popular and certainly tales of Egypt are quite the rage at the moment, thanks to the Desert Boy books.'

'I don't wish to dash your fantasies to the ground, but to the best of my knowledge there are no magical sprites in Egypt.'

'I know that, but the descriptions are so...vivid. Surely they are based on true places?'

'Actually, I believe they are, for the most part. And I agree, they are very vivid. I know most of the places described there.'

'You have read them, then?'

'Of course, I could hardly not when...' he paused and shook his head a little, as if surprised at himself '...when my sister Sam enjoys them so much. Huxley did as well. He was convinced he must know who wrote them and it vexed him no end he could not guess who it was.'

'Would he likely have been acquainted with the author?'

'Quite likely. He spent most of his winters there, both before and after his marriage, and was even there when Napoleon invaded. He knew most of the foreign nationals who spent time in Egypt, friend and foe. He was convinced it must be someone he knew and it irked him no end that he didn't know who.'

Chase leaned back in his chair, staring at the ceiling, as if the mouldings held the key to some secret.

She stared at the strong line of his throat, the

taut muscles and the shadowed hollow beneath his jaw. Her mouth watered, her cheeks began burning… She pressed her hand to her sternum, wondering if she was becoming ill.

His chair snapped back into place and she jerked upright as sharply as if she'd been slapped. What was *wrong* with her?

'There's another idea,' he said lightly. 'You shall travel to Egypt in the guise of a literary Bow Street Runner set upon the path of the elusive author of the Desert Boy books. What do you think?'

'It is an improvement on being a companion to seventeen pugs. But aren't Bow Street Runners men?'

'Simply because they are does not mean they must be. Or if you would rather not be associated with Bow Street, you could go to Egypt as Madame Ambrosia, fabled occultist, who has received communication from her soul mate on the Other Side about the location of his treasure-laden resting place tucked beneath the step pyramid of Saqqara. All you need is a wealthy patron to finance your voyage.'

She tried hard to keep her mouth prim. 'I see you are determined to persist in inventing one-thousand-and-one absurd ways to travel to Egypt. But since I don't even know what an occultist is, this one is even less probable than the others.'

'Occultists are fortune tellers who cloak their

nonsense in talk of communication with the dead. It is actually quite clever—it gives you endless scope for invention.'

'Well, with all due respect to your Madame Ambrosia, I find it had to believe anyone would be willing to pay my passage to Egypt on the word of a dead person.'

'You will find people are willing to pay for the most absurd things. Why, I know a fellow who has four snuffboxes for every day of the year.'

'One thousand, four hundred and sixty snuff-boxes?' Shock chased away her discomfort, her mind running ahead to calculate precisely what she could do with the monetary equivalent of that abundance. At one guinea per snuffbox...

'You are very handy with numbers.' He laughed.

'I would hope so, since I am responsible for Whitworth's accounts. And your friend is a prof-ligate fool.'

'I never said he was my friend,' he replied meekly. 'Merely someone I knew in Vienna. He had a room for them, too.'

'A room for snuffboxes? A whole room only for snuffboxes?'

'A whole room. Cabinets all along the walls, crimson-velvet-lined shelves and a footman whose only role in life was to lovingly polish each snuffbox in turn. It was like walking into a jewel box. I could hardly see for the glare of gold.'

'That is just…just obscene! Why, at one guinea per box that would be enough to feed and house and clothe a family for years and years. All for snuffboxes! And if he was not a friend of yours, what were you doing in his room admiring his snuffboxes, Mr Sinclair?'

He looked a little less amused at her contempt.

'If you must know, he wasn't there at the time and I wasn't interested in his snuffboxes, but what was in the room hidden behind those purposely distracting shelves. I have no more use for snuffboxes than you. And they were probably worth far more than a guinea a box, so you can heap more scorn on our profligate heads while you are all afire with missionary zeal.'

Ellie's anger fizzled at the sting of hurt in his voice and also with curiosity.

'I didn't mean *you* are profligate, Mr Sinclair, and it was wrong of me to snap at you. I was merely imagining everything I could do with fifteen hundred guineas. And what was in that hidden room? And what were you doing there while he was away?'

'Nothing and nothing.' He shrugged and stacked the papers he had been reading, putting them to one side.

The room sank into silence and Ellie searched for something to say.

'What does al-Jinn mean?'

He turned to her but his gaze was as suspicious as before.

'Why?'

'Your cousin writes Awal called you al-Jinn Chase. Is that how you say mister in Arabic?'

'No. It means…spirit or demon…it's just a nickname. It doesn't mean anything.'

'Oh.' She wanted to ask more, but he spoke first.

'Out of curiosity, what *would* you do with all those guineas if you had them, Ellie?'

He smiled suddenly, as if embarrassed at his ill temper, and she couldn't help smiling back. She was so tempted to tell him everything and perhaps he would think of a way to save them… She shoved the thought away. She was not his problem.

She knew what she *would* do with such a sum. But what would she *dream* of doing?

'I would sail to Egypt and discover a great temple filled with gold and riches and publish an account of my adventures which would be outshine even the Desert Boy books.'

'A commendable plan. May I offer myself as a humble guide on your journey? I can be quite useful in a pinch, you know.'

'So I can see from your cousin's notebooks. You may come as my trusty squire. There, you may add that to your list of One Thousand and

One Absurd Ways of Travelling to Egypt. Number four hundred and sixteen.'

The image she was weaving was so appealing she could almost see it roll out ahead of her as another path in life—one in which she walked side by side with this unaccountable, irreverent, sinfully seductive and often heartrendingly perceptive man. She looked down at her clasped hands, fighting the burn of tears.

It was almost over; the best week of her life.

Her sensible side tried to refute that foolish sentiment. How could the best week of her life exist while her family's future was collapsing? Only an infatuated fool could believe that.

And yet it was.

Which meant that was probably precisely what *she* was.

She returned her attention to the notebook, turning the pages and seeing nothing at all.

Chapter Six

Chase watched her sink back into the notebook.

There it was, that dissonance he noted time and again from the first day in the Folly. The conviction that something in her words, something in her, was false. It flickered in him like a candle too near a draught and not even his increasingly disobedient libido could distract him from it.

He didn't like dissonance. It bothered him.

In fact, far too much about her bothered him.

Just now it was the return of the melancholy that sometimes crossed her face like a falling star—sudden, sharp, and gone. If he wasn't watching her so closely, he would miss it. And the awful thing was that he *was* watching.

Far too closely and far too often.

He didn't even know why he was staring. She wasn't beautiful… Well, at least that was what he had thought. It was peculiar, but her face seemed to have changed since their first meeting, because her eyes were undoubtedly beautiful. Not just that clear direct honey with the dark-brown rims and gold and jade flecks around the pupils, but the way they shifted with her expressions, tilting at the corners when she smiled.

Then there was the hint of two wary dimples that teased when she did. He would very much like to see if those dimples bloomed into fullness if she let loose the laughter she held firmly at bay.

And her mouth...

He rubbed his chest, feeling as if he'd swallowed a cup of molten honey. Her mouth was not an intelligent focus for his attention.

The only intelligent focus for his attention would be to admit he was no closer to understanding Huxley's message. To admit he'd failed.

It happened—he just wished it hadn't happened on this particular quest.

He took out Huxley's letter from the drawer again, smoothing it out as he re-read it, but it made no more sense to him today than it did the day he received it. Perhaps as everyone here said, Huxley's mind had become feeble towards the end, caught in old memories and fantasies.

It was time to face his other responsibilities as well. Time to take Sam to Egypt and put this strange interlude at the Manor behind him. A couple of months exploring old haunts and old friends up the Nile and he would likely forget all about the peculiar Miss Walsh.

His chest tightened, an ache spiralling out towards his shoulders, and he arched them back to relieve the sudden tension and make room for air. But there was no relief, only a savage sense of dislocation, of being locked out of choices he took for granted. He sat there, palms flat on the desk on either side of the papers he was not reading, waiting for the world to settle again.

Except it didn't.

'Is something wrong, Mr Sinclair?'

Chase's mind jerked back into reality.

'What?'

'You probably didn't realise, but you were staring. I do that sometimes when I am deep in thought, but it is a little disconcerting.'

'I apologise. I was merely...deep in thought.' Chase was ashamed to feel a faint burn of heat on his cheeks.

'I don't mean to pry, but is it about that letter? You take it out several times a day and look quite troubled... Is there anything I can do to help?'

Before he could stop himself he shoved the letter across the desk.

'Read it. Aloud.'

She placed her hand on it, but her eyes were on him, worried.

'Are you certain?'

'Yes. No. I don't know.'

She turned the letter over.

'I shan't read it if you are not certain, but perhaps if you explained it to me. Sometimes it helps to talk things through and suddenly the solution appears. That is what I do with Susan, my sister, when I am stumped by something.'

'Not with Henry?'

He hadn't meant to sound quite so harsh and she flushed and began pushing the letter back towards him. He placed his hand on hers, stopping her.

Another mistake. The urge to curve his fingers into the warmth of her palm, pull her towards him... He detached his hand and sat back.

'Just...read it. Please. It is a letter Huxley sent me just a few weeks before his death. Unfortunately, I was not in England at the time and received it too late. I have been hoping something in this room or in the Folly would explain it, but thus far I have found nothing conclusive. I am beginning to think there is nothing to be found, that it is merely the wanderings of an enfeebled mind. I can hardly stay here indefinitely, but still... Perhaps hearing someone else reading it will make a difference. Would you?'

She nodded slowly. She'd returned her hands to her lap when he let her go, but now unclasped them and took the letter, her long lashes veiling her eyes. He turned to look out the window so he would not watch her as she read.

Her voice was different from when she'd read aloud from Huxley's notebooks—deeper, more

hesitant—and yet so true he could almost feel
Huxley standing beside her, whispering the words
to her.

My dear boy,
When you receive this letter, please come to
Huxley. There is something I have but re-
cently uncovered that I must discuss with
you. I do not wish to put it in writing in case
it is read by another, for it is not my tale to
tell, and indeed I think it will be best you
not share this revelation with anyone except
perhaps with Lucas, as it can do more harm
than good—I am unclear on that.

I have it all here and will take you
through it when you return from what-
ever problem Oswald has dispatched you
to solve. I do hope you are taking care? I
know it is not my place to worry, but I feel
Tessa's hand upon my arm as I write these
words, so forgive me.

In any case, it is important that you come
see me before you travel to Egypt, as Os-
wald assures me you and Lucas and Sam
are planning to do. Not just to discuss my
discovery—I have one last, but very impor-
tant, quest for you, Chase. I am failing, but
I know you won't fail me. You never have.
Your loving cousin, George

'I have failed you now,' Chase muttered in response and Miss Walsh looked up from the letter, but did not speak.

He turned away from her gaze. What the devil was wrong with him to be sharing this with her? She was not even a relation. Just his cousin's betrothed. Henry's betrothed. This woman would marry Henry and live her with him and have a family with him...

He shoved to his feet and went to the window, pushing apart the curtains and resisting the childish urge to tug the thick blue fabric down from its fastenings.

'I am honoured you trusted me with this, Mr Sinclair. You needn't worry I shall speak of it to anyone.'

He didn't turn.

'I'm not worried about that.'

'Good. How much time do we have?'

'What?' He glanced over his shoulder.

'How much longer do you have before you are dispatched to solve one of this Oswald's problems? When one has a task it helps to know how long one can commit to it.'

He turned.

She sat with her brows drawn together and her hands clasped before her, looking even more like a schoolmistress than usual. Not that it stopped his treacherous mind from noticing the way her arms pressed her breasts together. It was a sore pity she was condemned to wear such plain, shapeless dresses. If he were Henry, he would delight in taking this woman to one of London's finest *modistes* who would know just how to showcase her modest but elegant body. She would look best in long flowing lines and vivid colours…and without anything at all…

'I think it best we separate this conundrum into its components,' she continued, ignoring his silence, and he called himself to order. 'No doubt you have already done so, but it would help me to think through it. I shall need pen and paper, of course.'

'Of course, Miss Walsh.'

'And the tea has gone cold. We really should have a kettle on the hob here. I always have one in my study. It is much more sensible than sending for a footman every time one wishes for tea.'

'Much more sensible, Miss Walsh.'

Her dimples flashed and a weight levitated off his shoulders.

'And if you persist in calling me Miss Walsh in quite that way, I shall begin calling you The Right Honourable Charles Sinclair in my best imitation of Lady Ermintrude.'

'Horrifying. If I must not call you Miss Walsh, I shall call you Cousin Eleanor when we are not in company.'

She wrinkled her nose.

'Only Aunt Florence calls me Eleanor, or Henry when he is worried or excited.'

A shaft of hot resentment speared him and he quelled it. He should be grateful for the reminder. Not that it would matter one iota even if she weren't betrothed to his cousin. Lust-based fantasies were all well and good, but that was all they were. He had no wish to become entangled with any responsibilities beyond those he already shouldered. Therefore, it was time to pull the reins hard on these nonsensical thoughts. This young woman would soon be his cousin-in-law and he should treat her as such.

'What do your siblings call you?'

'When they aren't calling me horrid names? Ellie, but...'

'Then Cousin Ellie it is.'

'I did not mean...oh, very well. Cousin Ellie is respectable enough.'

'Unfortunately.'

'I beg your pardon?'

'Nothing. So, how were you thinking of cracking this conundrum? I am wholly in your hands.'

I am wholly in your hands...

Ellie's hands tensed and tingled and so she pulled the inkwell and blotting pad towards her and placed a sheet of paper on it. A problem to solve that had nothing at all to do with her family's impending doom was precisely what she needed to distract her.

She dipped her pen in the ink and began.

'Point number one. Lord Huxley mentions this is something he recently uncovered. Which means it likely happened since he fell ill and was confined to the Manor. So whatever he uncovered is here in some form unless it has been taken away by someone, which would rather take us down another path, yes?'

She glanced over at him, which was a mistake because he smiled.

'Yes. Point number two?'

'Point number two…point number two… Oh, yes—he says, *"I have it all here."* Which implies it is not one thing, but some plural. That rather rules out a single object. It is something, or rather some things, he possesses and which he intends to show you when you arrive. However, these things led to a revelation which *can* be expressed in written form, which leads us to point three.'

'Naturally. Which is?'

'Which is that this revelation would affect someone he cares about. I find it curious that he is ambivalent whether it would harm or help. It appears he thinks it might do both. This implies the revelation is not in itself good or bad, but its effects could be either. Does that seem sensible to you?'

She was in her stride now. She hardly even noticed his smile.

'Eminently. Point four?'

'I notice he says you and your brother should know, but does not mention your sister. Is that merely because he considers her inferior to you and your brother in intellect?'

'Good God, no. She's as sharp as a whip and Huxley would be the first to admit it. He had endless admiration for her intelligence and talent. If anything, he was closest to her and to my mother since they continued to live with him when Lucas and Edge and I joined Wellington in Portugal. However…he might feel protective towards her since he knew what she has been through all too well.'

'Being widowed?'

'You will have to excuse my bluntness, but being widowed is the best part of my sister's marriage. She should never have married Ricardo. But that is unlikely to be relevant to Huxley's message.'

'Perhaps. So for some reason he excludes her from this discussion. That may or may not be interesting. Shall I proceed?'

'I hope you will. This is most edifying. And very orderly.'

'Thank you. On to point five. He says *"this is not my tale to tell"*, implying it is someone else's tale. He does not use the word secret, which might or might not mean something. Why are you smiling?'

'It occurred to me you really must meet my sister-in-law. She appreciates method.'

'Well, I wish *you* would appreciate it. I am trying to be helpful here.'

'I do appreciate it...'

'But you have considered all these points previously.'

He hesitated.

'Not that point about Sam.'

'I imagine that is because you are accustomed to shielding her.'

'Only in recent years, but, yes.'

Ellie nodded and looked around the room.

'I have it all here,' she murmured. 'He would have written this letter in this very room, no doubt.'

'Probably.'

'And if you have found nothing...perhaps that is because it is right there and you are not seeing it, or perhaps because something is missing, like the notebooks.'

'What do you mean, like the notebooks?'

She straightened at the snap in his voice and rubbed her hands on her skirt. The alertness she'd sensed hiding behind the easygoing rogue was back at the surface again, giving her a glimpse of that other man, a stranger.

'I...there are gaps. You can see in the list you

asked me to compile. I meant to point it out, but I was not quite certain. The notebooks are very similar, but you can see they come in batches of slightly different coloured leather which makes cataloguing them easier. I presume they came in dozens because I have not found more than a dozen in one particular colour.'

'When did you notice this?'

'I…yesterday. The notebook I was reading ended on a mention of a planned visit to a bazaar, I think it must have been with your mother, because they were in search of something to send you and your brother in Portugal. But it ended just as it began and though I searched through all the stacks, I could not find the next one, nor see any more of that particular colour. I have been meaning to ask you if they could be in the Folly.'

'No, I had Tubbs, my valet, bring everything here the first day I arrived. Despite the jumble, there wasn't that much left there. It was all in the box you already inspected. And nothing in his private chambers, either. Everything should be right here in this room.'

She faltered as he came round the desk. He was even larger looming over her, the fabric of his pantaloons stretched as he leaned casually against the desk, the wooden edge press into his thigh, accentuating a sleek muscular line.

Her cheeks stung with a sudden memory she hadn't even realised she'd retained, of that leg against hers as she'd toppled on to him in the Folly—her knee had struck the floor between his legs and it hurt, but it was the foreign, sure sensation of his body under hers she remembered most vividly, his muscles moving as he shifted, the strength of his arm around her. It made no sense for those sensations to return now, just when she was becoming comfortable in his presence, but now the air in the room felt as heavy as before a storm, pressing her into her chair.

She cleared her throat and kept still, watching his long finger trail down her notes. It paused at the bottom and he scanned the room, as if expecting the missing volumes to jump to attention. Despite the surface chaos, there really were not many places anything could be hidden and she had watched him search them all during the first day in the study.

'I cannot imagine him losing so many notebooks. He treated them with more care than most parents extend to their children. What on earth was he up to? This makes no sense at all,' he said to no one in particular, his fingers rubbing the thick paper.

Her nerves danced to that subtle rasp and she shivered. He turned to her so swiftly she could not school her face in time and he must have seen something because his abstraction was gone in an instant.

'What is wrong, Ellie?'

So much was wrong she did not know where to begin. The urge to unburden everything to this stranger was so overpowering, she pressed her fingers over her mouth. It wasn't only Whitworth that weighted on her now, but these feelings he was forcing on her unawares. They made a mockery of her wistful dreams of some day finding a man who would want to build his life with her.

Those dreams had been impossible enough burdened as she was with her family's problems. To make Chase their object was wrong on so many levels—he was the proverbial rolling stone and it would hardly be a plain spinster well past her prime and saddled with a troublesome family who would turn his whole world view on its head. Perhaps one day some woman would achieve that feat—someone beautiful and charming and seductive and as far from Ellie as the moon was from a clump of dirt in the field.

What was wrong?

Oh, God, everything.

'I'm tired.' It sounded childish and she tried to smile. 'I wish I could sail away…into your sister's drawing or into a Desert Boy book. I often stared at those marvellous illustrations and imagined I was there…'

She sighed and her shoulders slumped, the brief glimpse of dreamy Ellie beaten back by melancholy once more.

Chase wanted dreamy Ellie back so he did something he never, ever did—he offered up his siblings as sacrifice.

'I don't know who the author is, but it just so happens I know who drew those illustrations.'

'You do? Who is it?' Immediately the light was back in her eyes and he gave silent, but grateful apologies to Sam.

'Sam.'

'Sam? Lady Samantha? Your *sister*?'

'The same. But you cannot tell anyone. I should not have told you myself.'

'Oh, my heavens, she is marvellous. Perhaps that is why her drawing caught my attention so. You must be so proud.'

'I am. But she prefers not to have people know so I would appreciate if you do not share that information.'

'Of course I shan't, though Anne and Hugh would probably faint from excitement if I did. So how does it happen that you do not know who the author is?'

'The publishers contacted Sam directly, saying the author asked for her in particular, but insisted on remaining anonymous. This is why we are convinced it must be one of the antiquarians who knew Lord Huxley, because only they were likely to be acquainted with her talents. Sam says she would almost rather not know. It adds to her sense of mystery and magic when she sketches.'

'I dare say, but I admit I would be dreadfully curious.'

'We are, believe me. At some point we even wondered whether it was Huxley, but when we asked him he said he was as curious as we. I think in his heart of hearts he wanted to be more than merely a scholar and was quite envious of the author's talent and lived in dread he would discover it was one of his antiquarian rivals.'

'Well, I think he is a marvellous raconteur. One day you will read from these amazing notebooks to your children and be grateful for the gift he left you.'

She touched the edge of the notebook he held, her finger just a breath away from his, though she did not appear to notice. He did. He noticed her words as well and his shoulders curled in on themselves in an instinctive recoil, but he kept his voice calm.

'I will not have children, but Lucas probably...'

'Oh, but you must!' Her exclamation apparently surprised her as much as it did him and she straightened, flushing a bright poppy red.

'I must?'

'I meant...not that you *must*, of course, merely... Surely you wish to have children some day?'

'No. Unlike you, Miss Walsh, I prefer not to have other people depend on me.'

'That is not quite apparent from your cousin's notebooks.'

'If I am good at fixing other people's problems, it is only because they aren't mine. I find life easier to live if I never risk wreaking destruction on people I care for. There is a monumental difference between offering someone occasional assistance, and assuming chief responsibility for a child's well-being and upbringing. You cannot compare the scope for doing harm in either case.

'Of course you couldn't, but having children, a family, can give you so much. To give all that up merely to evade risks, or to have an easier life... You *cannot* mean it.'

She was staring at him as if she had never seen him before. Resentment started bubbling up in him.

'One can have a perfectly worthwhile life without children. Huxley did.'

'I have no doubt that is true, but Huxley had you.'

'Huxley liked having us around part of the year, but he was not accountable to us and the only person he ever tried to save was my mother and he failed at that just as I did. I like my life just as it is, Miss Walsh. I see no need to inflict myself on a future generation of Sinclairs. You should know all about the dangers of imposing fatherhood on the wrong specimen. I imagine your life would have been substantially easier with a different father.'

'Hardly. Neither I nor my siblings would have existed.'

'Don't split hairs, Miss Walsh. You know what I mean. My father might not have deserved his reputation as a rake and a scoundrel, but he still wasn't exactly the man to see you through life's challenges. My mother lived and died thinking the man she cared for above all else was too weak to be depended upon and it shut her down and nothing I…anyone of us did could atone for that. Believe me, we tried.'

'It was not your role to do so, Mr Sinclair. You were her child, not the other way around.' Her voice was softly compassionate and he gritted his teeth against the need to reject her facile statement.

'You are a fine one to speak. What the devil do you think you have done with your siblings?'

'That is different. When my parents died we relied on Henry's father for guidance and, believe me, had he lived I would have been only too happy to continue my dependence on his good judgement. He was a most wonderful man. Kind and steady and reliable. It was a pity he had no more children after Henry, but he never loved another woman after Henry's mother passed.'

'A paragon of all virtues.'

Her brows twitched together.

'No man is a paragon of all virtues and I see no need to be so mocking. But that is not the point.

The point is that since his death my siblings had no choice but to depend upon me.'

'And now on Henry.'

She brushed her hand over the leather cover of the notebook, her lashes shielding her eyes as if sealing him off from whatever emotion tied her to her betrothed.

'And now on Henry,' she repeated.

He turned a little too abruptly, scraping his thigh on the edge of the desk. She glanced up and he turned to the windows overlooking the lawns. There wasn't much to see—fog obscured the treetops and turned the world hazy and dismal. A fitting reflection of his mood.

'I think that is enough for today, Miss Walsh. I doubt your Henry is out in this weather. Perhaps you should go find him and remind him of his duties.'

Chapter Seven

Ellie entered the yellow saloon early and was pleased to note Lady Ermintrude had not yet descended. Everyone else was already present, though. Drusilla sat embroidering on the sofa, while Henry stood watching Chase and Fenella play backgammon by the fireplace. Henry smiled at her and she smiled back. Drusilla's shoulders hunched over a little more.

On a burst of inspiration Ellie moved closer to the young woman.

'It is Anne's birthday soon, Henry, and I wanted to buy her something. Perhaps a shawl. Do you know where I could purchase something along those lines?'

'I haven't the faintest notion, Ellie. Can't you find something here to give her? Maybe one of Uncle's gewgaws?'

'That is a marvellous idea, Henry. Perhaps one of his jars of locusts.' Ellie met Drusilla's gaze and for a moment a complicit smile passed between them before Drusilla's face froze again and she bent back to her embroidery.

'There is a draper's shop and a silk warehouse in Deptford. I think that will be more appropriate.'

'Thank you, Miss Ames. Henry, perhaps you could find some time to accompany me this week?'

'Lord, not to the draper's, Ellie. I will die of boredom.'

'That is not very kind, Lord Huxley,' Dru said with a little snap in her voice. 'Your company would ensure Miss Walsh receives the proper attention in town. It would be considered unusual for her to go there without anyone from the Manor.'

Henry flushed and Ellie dropped her head, taking another tiny step out on to the plank.

'You are very kind, Miss Ames, but I know how busy Henry is. It is not right I take him from his duties when he has so much to attend to... Perhaps, if it is not too much of a bother, you and Miss Fenella might come with me?'

Henry heaved a sigh so heavy with resignation it bordered on a groan.

'Oh, very well. In fact, I could use a breather from all these da—dashed sheep. I see the blasted animals every time I close my eyes. Sheep, sheep and more sheep with a couple of lambs thrown in.

Couldn't Uncle have chosen to raise a less boring animal?'

Drusilla jerked to her feet, her tambour frame tumbling to the floor.

'You should not scoff at sheep so, Lord Huxley. They are a wonderful animal. Gentle and useful and they like being together and are so very good natured and… Why is it that everyone thinks big rough animals like bulls or bears or… or even horses are superior to something peaceful and soft? If you had ever held a lamb in your arms you would know better…'

Her blush was so extreme it obliterated her freckles, her voice breaking, and she hurried out of the parlour. Henry stood in stunned silence as Fenella hurried after her sister, casting Henry a fulminating look.

'Go apologise, Henry.' Ellie gave him a little shove towards the door.

'Apologise? What on earth for? I only said…'

'Go.'

'But, Eleanor…'

'Now.'

He filled his lungs and with a groan plunged after Dru.

'That is generous, but is it wise?' Chase asked behind her once Henry was gone.

'Is what wise?'

'Ordering your betrothed to go soothe another woman, especially when said woman is more than

a little enamoured of him. Is this a test of his resolve? Or perhaps a test of your power?'

She picked up Dru's frame, examined the perfect stitches and placed it carefully on her basket.

'You are not as clever as you think, Mr Sinclair.'

'Now, that is insulting since my own expectations are not very high. But there is one area
where I compensate for my lack of intelligence
with experience.'

She snorted.

'Are you seriously intending to lecture me
about your experience with women?'

'No, with men.'

'I see. The rumours about you are wrong then.'

She had expected to offend him, but he merely
laughed.

'Minx. You are saucier than you let on. I was
speaking of my experience of, not with men. Most
men, especially young, active and easy-going men
like Henry, would rather avoid an emotional scene
and, should they find themselves in the middle
of one, they are willing to do practically anything to calm the waters. Sending someone as
soft-hearted and *lamb*-like as Henry after a tear-
ful young woman who even he must know by
now has something of a *tendre* for him is a situation fraught with danger. So, if this a test, don't
be surprised if he fails.'

'Thank you for your excellent advice, Mr Sinclair, but I find I do not require any more of your pearls of wisdom about the inferior sex.'

'I never said women were the inferior sex.'

'Neither did I.'

'I stepped straight into that ditch, didn't I?' He laughed again, but his amusement faded as she looked away.

'Ellie...'

'Where is everyone?' Lady Ermintrude demanded from the doorway. 'It is five o'clock!'

'I believe Drusilla found a tear in her flounce,' Ellie replied promptly, nudging the embroidery basket under the sofa with her foot. 'Fenella went to help her mend it.'

'And Henry?'

The clock just began to chime the hour and Ellie cast a glance in Chase's direction, searching for a plausible excuse. He gave a faint shrug.

'Henry is on a chivalric mission, Aunt. Miss Walsh's favourite shawl has gone astray somewhere between the East Wing and the yellow saloon.'

'That is most inconsiderate of you, Miss Walsh. I will not have supper set back for such trifles. I hope you treat your possessions with more care in future.'

'Of course, Lady Ermintrude. I am very sorry.'

She was saved by the hurried appearance of Fenella and Dru, followed by Henry. All three looked rather heated and Ellie jumped into the breach.

'Did you find my shawl, Henry?'

Henry might not always be quick on his feet, but he had had ample training in his years of association with the Walshes and after a glance at his glowering aunt it took him only a moment to readjust.

'Sorry, Eleanor. It's bound to turn up somewhere, though. Good evening, Aunt.'

'Is it? That is debatable, Henry. Now if you have all quite finished with your trivial pursuits, I would very much like to proceed to supper.'

Chapter Eight

Chase pushed away from the desk. This was the third time he'd tried to read through Huxley's correspondence with the librarian of the British Museum and not a word was registering with his disobedient mind.

He needed air.

He pulled back the curtain, relieved to see the rain had stopped and the sky was freckled with clouds, mirroring the sheep dotting the field beyond the lawn. The sun broke free of a wispy cloud and turned the lawn to a carpet of emeralds and diamonds. Chase unlatched the window and filled his lungs with the crisp air.

'I need to breathe some air free of dust motes and parchment. Has Henry taken you to the Tor yet, Miss Walsh?' he asked without turning.

'Since I don't even know what that is, I presume he hasn't.'

'Shame on him. I never knew the boy could be

worked this hard. We called it the Tor, but it isn't truly a tor like the ones in the West Country—in fact, I don't think that term applies in Sussex. It is that craggy hill over there beyond the field. But it has a fair view over the fields to the sea on a clear day so we might be lucky if the clouds don't close in on us again. We might even be able to spot your industrious betrothed trailing behind the land agent. If you wish to join me, put on some sturdy shoes and I will meet you by that stile in ten minutes.'

He didn't wait for her response. If he did she would talk herself out of it. As it was he was only half-convinced she would join him and even less convinced it was a good idea. The solution to this growing tendency to stare at his cousin-to-be was to keep his distance, not take her alone into the fields.

Chase waited at the stile, wondering if Ellie would drum up the nerve to join him and wishing he hadn't extended the invitation. His only excuse was that her all-too-frequent transitions from schoolmistress to lost little girl were wreaking havoc with his equilibrium.

If he'd had an ounce of sense, he wouldn't have invited her.

If she had an ounce of sense, she wouldn't come.

The surge of heat as he saw her come up the

narrow path from the Manor's modest gardens was an indication of precisely how little sense he had.

He was surely both too old and too young for such complete lapses of judgement over a woman who was not only betrothed to his cousin, but who often treated him like an amusing but occasionally annoying younger sibling.

There had to be some sound reason for this madness. Perhaps it the almost unnoticed passing of his thirtieth birthday, or the effects of watching his older brother so happily married, or…something. Because he could not remember the last time his body rushed ahead of his mind so absolutely, leaving it coughing in the dust.

His only comfort was that this urge would eventually peak and pass, and perhaps in another dozen years he would look back on this interlude with amused compassion for a youthful folly. It was not as if he would do anything about this unwelcome fascination. He did have some sense of honour after all. He might be uncomfortable, but he was safe.

He leaned on the wall and watched her approach. The wind had settled a little, but it still whipped the skirts of her dull brown coat about her legs, tangling between them as he would have loved to do. Then she stopped by the stile and smiled.

He pressed his gloved hands on the uneven stones. Hard.

'What a good idea this is,' she said, brushing the fluttering ribbons of her bonnet away from her cheek. 'I feel more human already. Fresh air and a hint of sun is a marvellous way of putting the world in perspective. I didn't know there were tors in Sussex.'

'There aren't. It is merely a hill, but that was a little tame for us so we dubbed it the Tor.'

'I like that. I think I shall name the duck pond near Whitworth Loch Walsh, then I can be Madame Ambrosia of Loch Walsh. Do you think we could see where Henry is from up there?'

He held out his hand, but she clambered over the stile without his help and he watched the fabric of her skirt shift over her legs and hips.

Lucky skirt. Lucky Henry.

'Do you know, Mr Sinclair, I have been thinking about the notebooks and...'

He held up his hands.

'I appreciate your help, Ellie Walsh, but I suggested we walk to clear our heads, not clutter them further. Sometimes the best way to approach a problem is to put it aside and allow it to stew. So while out here we will talk of anything but my cousin's conundrum. Agreed?'

'Agreed. I shall add it to my problem stew and put a lid on it. For now.'

They reached the top of the Tor too quickly

for his pleasure, but her gasp of appreciation was compensation enough for her speed.

'It is beautiful!'

He looked out over the stretch of green fields fading at the edges into the sky and the sea.

'Some people find the view too plain.'

'It can be plain and still be beautiful. Beauty isn't merely to be found in rose gardens.'

Her words reflected his thoughts about her too closely for comfort, but he merely smiled and kept his gaze on the view.

'Look! There is Henry! My goodness, what a lot of sheep there are.' She gestured out over the fields that stretched out on the other side of the Manor.

'Careful, don't lean over that ledge. The stones are still slippery from the rain.' He caught her arm as she leaned past the outcropping of boulders to get a better view of the figures on horseback moving along the low stone walls and she laughed up at him over her shoulder.

'I'm not a child, Mr Sinclair. You shan't have my broken leg on your conscience. Can we reach the top of the Tor?'

'Not while it is still damp and certainly not in those shoes. It is all rock from here and some of it is loose. My brother Lucas nearly broke his neck there one summer trying to prove how sure footed he was.'

'Are you two very competitive?'

'Lucas and I? Not at all.'

'That is rather surprising. Henry said there are only two years between you. In my experience siblings so close in age are often competitive.'

'Well, perhaps we were when we were very young, but our mother was never strong after… once we left England and we did not wish to upset her, so competition was a luxury we rarely indulged.'

Her frown caught at him again. It was almost as hard to resist as her smile.

'Were you very young when your father died?'

'Ten.'

'I am so sorry. Hugh was eight—sometimes I think he felt my father's death most violently. He could make no sense of it.'

'There often isn't any sense to be made.'

'No.' Her hand rose as if to take his and he pushed his own hands deeper into his pockets. Two swallows swirled past, very close, their sleek forms tangling in an airy dance.

'Henry said your father died in a duel.' Her voice was tentative, knowingly stepping out on to a plank. He should push her back as he did everyone else.

'Yes. Sometimes I wonder if it would be easier if he had died in a different way. Something mundane like a fever or falling off a horse,' he said to the view of the sea.

'I think so. Well, not much easier, but there

wouldn't be that…shadow. Something lingering. When Hugh learned Father drowned in a ditch of rainwater he had dreams of being trapped under a ceiling of water, alive but not able to find his way through.'

'Sounds like a version of purgatory. Does he still have those dreams?'

'Not recently. When he was younger I would often wake and sit by him at night so I could be there when they happened. I remember wishing there was someone who could take my place. I hope the dreams haven't returned now I am away…' Her voice wavered into silence and he moved closer.

'Sam suffered from bad dreams as well as a child. She was quite young when it happened, but through the years she heard gossip about the duel and my father's alleged betrayals and… unfortunately she has a very vivid imagination.'

'Poor girl.' Her brows twitched together abruptly, dimming the vivid compassion in her eyes. 'You have used that word before regarding your father—*alleged*.'

He smiled. The girl had a lawyer's mind to snag on such details. It really was no concern of hers, but he wondered what it would feel like to share this new reality with someone other than his close family.

'We recently discovered the duel and the scan-

dals were not of his making. I'm only sorry my
mother died not knowing the truth.'

'How horrible. For all of you.'

'Still better than the previous version where he
was a coward and a cuckolder. My mother never
recovered from those revelations.'

'I am truly sorry for her, but glad for you and
your siblings. Still, even if you are relieved he
was not at fault, the discovery must have made
you relive it all over again and grieve for this different man.'

'At least this time we could grieve for a man
we actually remembered. It meant a great deal to
Lucas and Sam.'

'You are doing it again.'

'Doing what?'

'Removing yourself from the equation. Surely
it meant as much for you as it did for them?'

'I feel everything less keenly than my siblings.
I'm the valley between two mountains. There
are no soaring highs or crashing lows here, I'm
afraid.'

'Just your boring, middle-of-the-road rogue.'
Her eyes were laughing, but they also held an
expression he had seen innumerable times on
his Uncle Oswald's face—his words were being
weighed for messages he was not even aware of.
It annoyed him when Oswald did it, but having
this prim bluestocking do it felt like an invasion
of his private sanctuary and not through a door-

way, either, but by a bludgeoning of walls. Before he could think of a way to divert her she looked away.

'It is good you have each other.'

'Yes, siblings are quite useful when they aren't being a complete nuisance.'

Her eyes brightened with laughter, accepting his withdrawal. 'They can be, but I don't know what I would do without them. I was always sad for Henry that he had no siblings. For his father as well.'

'You loved him.'

'Henry's father? Oh, yes. Very much. He was a wonderful man and our families were very close. We all miss him dreadfully.'

'More than your own father?'

The warmth in her eyes faded a little.

'We miss him, too, but he was a different presence in our lives. If anything, it was rather as if he was our uncle and Mr Whelford was our true father. He was everything that was most admirable in a man, while my father... I think the test was how little we were willing to make demands upon him. He was often away in London and I remember as a child sitting in church during Mr Whelford's sermons, trying to negotiate pacts with God to arrange his speedy return home, promising all manner of good behaviour and assurances. My promises became quite elaborate until I realised they were rather pointless since my father always did as he pleased and was highly unlikely to be swayed by anyone's wishes, divine or not.'

'So you stopped praying?'

'I changed my tactics and resorted to cunning instead. As Mr Whelford told us every week— the Lord helps he, or she, who help themselves, so when my father did return home I tried to make myself indispensable so he would stay.'

Her smile flashed again and he leaned back against the outcropping of boulders, the cool stone a solid pressure between his shoulder blades and a welcome counter to the warmth elsewhere. He should put an end to this discussion—each guileless admission was sinking him deeper and deeper.

'What did that entail?' he asked.

'Oh, anything and everything I could think of. Mending pens and helping him with his correspondence including disposing of unwanted bills, reading aloud, turning the pages when he played the pianoforte for us. He was a very fine musician and Mama had a lovely singing voice. They always looked happy when there was music. I have no talents whatsoever, but I became general factotum. That seems to often happen to the eldest sibling.'

He nodded.

'My brother is a little like that.'

'I thought he was a desperate rake before he married?' Her smile took the bite out of her words.

'Not desperate. He merely chose which rules he wished to follow. But once he chose them, he followed them to the letter.'

'Do you like his wife?'

'Olivia? Very much. You remind me of her a little. She also is good at cataloguing things.'

She flushed and turned back towards the view.

'That is hardly a virtue.'

He smiled, remembering the near-disastrous results of one of Olivia's lists of Lucas's qualities, but stopped short of informing Miss Walsh he liked her for very different reasons as well.

'It is a quality, not a virtue. Shall I list your virtues? I don't know if we have enough time before supper, though.'

'Do not be foolish, Mr Sinclair.'

Predictably, her confiding warmth faded at the first sign of his gallantry. It was damnable that he kept forgetting she was practically a stranger. It didn't feel like that, but she was. He shrugged.

'Come, I want to stop by the Folly on our way back and see what remains to be done there. Or I could see you back to the Manor first, if you prefer.'

'No, I should like to see it one last...once more.'

* * *

'Your valet is very thorough,' Ellie stated as she inspected the room. It was empty but for several large wooden trunks and the now-bare desk. 'Was there nothing here that was of use to you?'

'Nothing, I'm afraid. And not a notebook in sight. Huxley must have moved his more valued possessions to the study when he became ill. When he was younger he often worked here and would sit out on the roof at night and watch the stars over the sea.'

'Can you see that far?'

He smiled at the light that returned to her eyes.

'Would you like to see?'

'Yes, please.'

Chase led her up the narrow stone stairs that hugged the wall, swinging open the hatch to the roof. The breeze caught them immediately and he followed Ellie as she did a circuit of the embattlements. Then she stopped abruptly and he turned to see what caught her attention.

From this vantage point they could see past the gardens to the wall marking the fields. They were dotted with clumps of sheep and at one end two horses grazed and next to them, on a bench, sat Henry and Dru. Henry's sandy curls were very close to Drusilla's straw bonnet with its black ribbon. There was a lamb on Drusilla's lap and Henry's hand was stroking the animal. Chase's hand went instinctively to turn her away from the sight, but he stopped it.

'Straight out of a Flemish painting. Perhaps you should remind your betrothed that petting the livestock can be misconstrued.'

'I think it is a good sign they have made their peace. I told Henry that since Dru is practically as knowledgeable about the estate as the steward, it makes sense for them to work together rather than forever goading one another.'

'I hate repeating myself, but I meant what I said yesterday, Ellie. Henry might be following your advice, but poor Dru is likely to misread his gesture and I wouldn't put it past Henry to be swayed by these tender moments himself. He is very impressionable.

'No reply, Ellie? Are you really not in the least concerned he will be touched by the obvious attraction that she tries and fails to hide? Especially when you treat him more like a brother than a lover from what I can see during meal times.'

She shrugged and brushed the fluttering ribbon of her bonnet away from her mouth, but beyond the defiance he thought he could see the same deep weariness he noticed in Huxley's study, as if she was losing some internal battle to stay afloat in choppy waters.

He had no right to prod her like that. She kept so much hidden from the world, he might have caused her real pain and she would not show it.

The fact that he actually wished to disillusion her about Henry only made it worse. She was a good person and he wanted her to be happy. That was all he should be thinking of. If he was halfway decent he would help her, not harass her.

'I didn't mean to upset you, Ellie. If Henry has half a brain he won't possibly prefer Dru. *Are* you worried?'

She shrugged again.

'No, I'm not. I trust Henry.'

'Perhaps that's the problem. If you aren't teasing Henry, you are taking him for granted. I would hazard a guess that you treat your own siblings with just that mix of affection and high-handedness. This is the boy...the man you are planning to marry. Have you even ever allowed him to kiss you? And don't trot out some nonsense about proprieties. You would never have agreed to help me in Huxley's study if you held such store by propriety. He hasn't even kissed you, has he?' he continued as she remained silent. 'You would have tossed it in my face if he had.'

Ellie pressed her hands to her cheeks to calm the burning heat there, wishing she could laugh away his words. He could not possibly know how often she had thought of being kissed recently and not by Henry.

She shook her head, the truth hovering on her tongue like a trapped butterfly.

But he was watching her, a slight frown between his brows. He was so unfairly handsome, so...self-contained. Like the Folly tower, set apart from the rest of the world. Was this what he did? Tease and beguile until people came to him of their own accord without ever really giving of himself?

'Is that so important? It is only a kiss.'

'You wouldn't be asking me that if he had done it. Or at least if he had done it properly. No wonder he's wandering. One good kiss and he'll follow you like one of Drusilla's lambs.'

'Is that what men do when they are kissed?' she scoffed, which was a mistake because he moved a little closer, positioning himself between her and the view, too close to the low parapet for comfort. Her hands half-rose as if to pull him back from that precarious position, but she forced them down.

'No. Shall I tell you what they do when they are kissed?'

'I know what they do when they are kissed, Mr Sinclair. I am twenty-six after all. Henry might be too much a gentleman to take advantage of me, but I am not completely naïve.'

'*Did* someone take advantage of you? Is that why you chose someone who doesn't threaten you?'

She blinked, more than a little surprised by the shift in his tone. She had not expected her little boast to spark such a burn of anger in his eyes. She had forgotten how protective he could be.

'N…no. I mean, if anything I took advantage. I was curious and…well… That was very long ago, during my first and only Season. There has certainly been no one since my parents died… And this is a most improper conversation. We should return.'

'In a moment. So why not with Henry? Did your experiment give you a distaste for the pastime?'

'I've never heard it referred to as a pastime. But to answer your question, no, it didn't. but neither did it convince me a kiss is worth risking one's reputation for. As soon as I ascertained that, I desisted in my experiments, as you called them.'

'Failed experiments.'

'I beg your pardon?'

'Had your experiments been successful, you would know precisely why one good kiss would have Henry toeing the line.'

'I presume you know what a good kiss entails, Mr Sinclair, however—'

'I do,' he interrupted. 'A good kiss is like a good book.'

She wavered. She should put an end to this improper conversation before she revealed as much as Drusilla did every time she looked at Henry, but another need, far more powerful, held her where she was—buffeted by the wind, by her curiosity and by sensations she did not even understand.

She heard the words leave her mouth before she could even process them. Opening the door. 'Why is a kiss like a good book?'

He shifted closer, creating a human shield from the gusts of sea-scented air, and the tendrils of hair that had been stinging her face fluttered down. With his other hand he brushed away one that settled on her cheek and straightened the ribbon that threw itself up over the crown of her bonnet. They were small gestures that might have been innocent, but weren't. He'd hardly touched her cheek, but it felt branded, twice the size of its twin, as if she had the toothache. Finally, he answered and his voice was lower, thrumming like the rush of the wind around them, a little like anger but not angry.

'Imagine you find a book you've searched for for a long, long time. You want to rush through it, don't you? Immerse yourself in it, consume it whole in one sitting. But you also want to make it last, sink into each page and let it absorb you whole. This is where you feel alive and you never want it to end, because you know that when it does you will be bereft, thrust out of that perfect place where you felt you belonged, where you were temporarily whole. You want to devour, but you also want to savour and that conflict is both torture and bliss. That is what a good kiss is.'

The words sheered through her, around her, sharper than the wind. They heated her skin, but chilled her inside with anticipation and dread. She knew she should move back, away. She was breathing through her mouth, unable to even clamp her lips together. She felt utterly revealed, known.

'Is that what you always feel when you kiss someone?'

He shook his head. It was a slow movement, a little hesitant. Then he breathed in and answered, 'It is very rare.'

Into the cauldron of her confusion a new and utterly unaccustomed sensation of jealousy roared, shocking her even more than the stinging need that was chasing chill with fever inside her.

He was thinking of someone in particular—she could feel the weight of his thoughts condense into one image. It was pathetic, but she would have preferred he said it was utterly common, that it was the same with every woman he had kissed, and there must have been dozens of them if Fen's tales were true. She didn't want to know what woman brought that look into his eyes, the tension deepening the shadows beneath his carved cheekbones.

It is time to leave, said Eleanor.

'How rare?' asked Ellie.

He moved away from her.

'Come, we should return. Otherwise I will give

you reason to scold me. Besides, those clouds are gathering and the weather turns quickly this close to the sea.'

A good kiss was like a good book?

What on earth had possessed him to make such a fool of himself?

Chase was grateful she didn't speak as they left the tower and made their way back towards the stile. In his current state he would undoubtedly make an even greater fool of himself.

'Oh, bother.'

He looked up as she was halfway over the stile, reaching back to tug at her pelisse which caught on the fraying wood. She gave it a sharp tug, which dislodged it, but also her foot from the damp wood. Without thinking he caught her, but instead of steadying her he swept her into his arms, holding her to him for an all-too-brief moment, his head dipping to capture her scent, his mouth just brushing the soft hair at her temple and grazing the rise of her cheekbone, trailing downwards towards the corner of her mouth. He could feel her warm breath, sharply indrawn and exhaled, and he almost bent to capture it with his mouth when sanity returned.

Though only a moment passed before he deposited her on the other side of the wall, the sensations stretched out to the ticking of a very different clock—the shift from the warm, faint pulse at her temple under the soft tickle of hair to the curve of wind-cooled skin over her cheekbone and the faintest brush of her eyelashes against his own cheek just as he let her go.

It was a whole universe explored in the passage of a few breaths and with stark clarity he knew he would never rid himself of it. Like memories of the worst battles he'd taken part in—some experiences became indelible. Without rhyme or reason, they wove themselves into the fabric of who he was and could never be washed out.

'Mr Sinclair!' Her voice was shaky and her cheeks as red as Dru's hair as she shook out the skirt of her pelisse. 'It is not fair to make game of me.'

He stood on the other side of the wall, every parcel of skin where her body had pressed against his was still clamouring for more, and the rest of him hummed with jealous need. He was tempted to tell her the only one he was making game of was himself.

A good kiss was like a good book?

He must have taken leave of his senses. Their whole conversation was a little mad, which was in line with his recent frame of mind.

He pushed away from the wall, angry at himself, at her, at Henry, at the whole unsettled universe for not following the correct order of things.

He groped for something to say and fell back on the old crutch of mocking gallantry.

'I was merely being chivalrous.'

'You haven't the faintest notion of the concept.' She turned away and it was the disappointment in her voice that struck him most. He vaulted over the wall and caught up with her.

'I'm sorry, Miss Walsh. That was ill done of me. I won't trespass again. Please forgive me.'

She nodded, but did not answer and, he walked beside her in silence, furious at himself for his foolishness.

'It is second nature for you to do such things, isn't it?' she asked after a moment. She was calmer, but he still heard the distaste in her voice and it stung.

'No,' he answered, 'believe it or not, but if I did something like that in London, we would either now be engaged or Henry would be challenging me to a duel.'

'Are you saying it is my fault, then? Because I came walking with you?'

'No, of course not! It was just…an impulse. A very foolish one. I promise you are safe with me. Believe me, after what I saw happen to my mother I would never…'

He clenched his jaw down on the words, but it was too late. He felt as shocked as she looked at his words. He must be truly thrown off his balance to even hint at such matters out loud, let alone speak of them to a respectable young woman.

What the devil was wrong with him? In a mere week he had crossed more lines with Ellie Walsh than he had in a lifetime. He should say something, diffuse the situation, return her to the Manor and forget this afternoon ever happened, and hopefully so would she.

'I'm so, so sorry,' she said, her voice hushed.

'Don't. She didn't... Nothing happened in the end. Well, not nothing. My father was badly wounded...'

Her eyes widened at the implication and he cringed internally.

'It wasn't my father who...it was my Uncle John, but that isn't the point. God, this is utterly inappropriate. We should return.'

'Your uncle?' She sounded as shocked as he felt at sharing his horrific memory. He had never spoken of this except once with his brother when they had re-entered that dreaded room at Sinclair House in London after two decades. He never even thought of it if he could help it.

'He was drunk. He was always three sheets to the wind as far as I can remember.'

'That cannot be an excuse for...for trying to harm someone, anyone.'

'No. We knew to keep out of his way, though. Usually my mother knew to keep out of the way as well, but he came in from a night of God only knows what and found her in the Great Hall.'

'You were there when it happened?'

He hardly heard the strain in her voice. He was back in the musty darkness of the cavernous armoire, with the familiar scent of the oil used to care for the foils, his body taut with anticipation of jumping out and surprising his mother as he heard her playfully calling to him, telling him she'd already found Lucas and Sam and it was only a matter of time before…

'We were playing hide and seek and I was hiding in armoire where they kept fencing gear. She was searching for us and then I heard him stumble in.'

His mother's light-hearted chatter as she searched stilled and he froze as they all did when Uncle John was around. But he still hadn't been prepared for his uncle's leering comments about bitches in heat, his mother's choked protests, the scraping of the table on the floor.

He must have cracked open the door because he could remember the look of his uncle's dark clothes pressed against her pale-blue skirt, and the flash and clang of metal as the statuette of the wolf she'd reached for slipped to the floor.

And then, perhaps most shocking, she was screeching, a fury in her voice he'd never heard before or since and his uncle was stumbling back as she flailed at him, cursing so foully Chase hadn't understood half the words.

'I don't remember much—it was all very fast and very slow. I remember my mother hitting him and he hit her and she screamed and fought him off, but then my father burst in and my uncle… Then Lucas was in the doorway holding Sam and I think he called to me and finally I ran. My father took one of the swords and my uncle…laughed.

'He was right to laugh. Even drunk he toyed with my father until he slashed him across the arm. By then Tubbs was there and he stopped it and Lucas dragged Sam and me out on to the street. I remember because it was snowing. We left the house that day and never went back until after my mother's death. They were all dead by then.' Even with the wind rushing around them he could hear his breathing, as harsh and strained as in that dusty closet. How many times as a boy had he imagined going back to that moment and taking one of those swords and running it through his uncle's black heart. 'I should have helped her, but I didn't.'

'That is utterly unfair, Chase. You were a child, a little boy.'

He straightened. 'So what? I should have done something. I didn't even call for help. A baby would have known to cry out. Sam screamed loud enough when she saw what was happening.'

Ellie shook her head; she was cradling her fist against her chest, as if it hurt.

'You cannot hold children to our standards, Chase. It was horrible for you to witness that, but it was neither your fault nor your role to defend your mother.'

'No, it was my father's and a sad job he made of it, the poor fool. My Uncle Oswald was the one who came to remove us from the house and made arrangements for us to stay in Gloucestershire while my father recovered and then arranged employment for him in Boston. We were meant to follow once he established himself, but instead he went and got himself killed in a duel over sins he wasn't even culpable of. Typical of him. My grandfather used to taunt him by calling him Howard the Coward, but he was wrong. He wasn't really a coward, just incompetent.'

He heard the disgust in his voice, but could do nothing to rein it in. In that quintessentially English pasture, with a herd of sheep munching idly by the wall and the blustery wind flattening the tall grass, he could find no purchase to combat the seductive compassion in her eyes, as warm as cinnamon and melting honey, holding open his floodgates as effectively as a rack and thumbscrews. More effectively.

What was wrong with him? In a matter of days she'd extracted confessions from him he never would have imagined making on his deathbed. The woman was dangerous.

'Come. We should return. I only meant to apologise, not…bore on like this. You were right to be angry at me. Of all people, I should know not to cross lines.'

He started walking, afraid of what would happen if he stayed. He almost hoped she would not keep pace with him. They were now within sight of the Manor and she would be safe enough on her own. But she fell into step beside him.

'Is this also why you do not wish to have children?'

'I am perfectly happy as I am. No one depends upon me and I depend upon no one. It is a very comfortable way to live, believe me. You of all people should understand the burden of having people hanging about your neck like millstones, only for you to disappoint them.'

Her shoulders hunched and he wished he'd been more careful.

'I did not mean that you disappointed them. I was referring to myself.'

'Well, I *have* disappointed them, even if they would never say anything. I have tried everything I can think of to dig us out from under Papa's debt and perhaps if last year's harvest had gone well, I might have...' She cleared her throat and again he curbed the urge to offer comfort and she continued. 'But they aren't millstones. They are my family and I love them.'

'I love my brother and sister, too, but that does not mean I would actively choose to add to my list of dependents. My life suits me as it is. No home, no ties, no responsibilities beyond those I choose and, believe me, I only choose those I can resolve and walk away from.'

She directed him another uncertain, compassionate look and he forced a smile.

'This is altogether too maudlin a topic. Can you please forgive me? And forget I was an as—less than chivalrous?'

Her mouth hovered into a reluctant smile.

'I could hardly forget that you are an ass, Mr Sinclair, since you make such an effort to remind everyone. But I will forgive you none the less. Especially since you are a useful ally here.'

'That is the least forgiving forgiveness I have witnessed in a long time,' he answered, relieved she was meeting his invitation to return to their light-hearted banter.

'That is all I am offering at the moment.'

'Then I thank you. By the way, now that we are about to re-enter the halls of gloom and will probably have no chance to speak until the morrow, what was that thought that was burdening your overcrowded mind? About the conundrum.'

She looked away, her laughter dimming.

'Perhaps tomorrow...'

'You seemed excited enough to share it earlier. Are you still angry at me?'

'No, no...it isn't that. It is merely...it regards your mother, you see.'

'My mother?'

'Yes. I was thinking of the missing notebooks and it occurred to me there might be something that ties them together.'

'And that is?'

'It was that story about the bazaar—I noticed that the notebooks preceding a missing one often end with reference to a story involving your mother. He refers to her either by name or simply by the use of the letter T.' She faltered at his silence. 'I should not have mentioned it now, but you asked. I am sorry.'

'Don't be. I am not quite so fragile.'

'I know you aren't. But perhaps I should have followed your advice and allowed your conundrum to stew a little more before I spoke.'

'No, I am glad you unburdened yourself. Now you had best run along or you will be late and I shall have to rescue you from Aunt Ermy's tongue lashing by throwing myself into the line of fire.'

She sighed.

'Hopefully there will be no need for that. Not that a tongue lashing would make much difference to the horrors of the yellow salon.'

'The horrors of the yellow salon. That sounds like a tawdry Gothic novel.'

'The Manor is a fine setting for a Gothic novel, but we lack a credible villain.'

'I would have thought I make a fine villain. Lady Ermintrude certainly thinks so.'

'Oh, no. I am the villain in her tale. The conniving, unscrupulous and opportunistic young woman come to prey upon the hero. That is Henry, by the way, not you.'

'That was clear without your elucidation. Then Dru and Fen are the heroines, no? Not quite my kind of novel, I am afraid. What role do I play, then?'

'In every great tragedy there is always an element of comedy. You are clearly the jester.'

'And you are shameless. I would hazard a guess you would not be so impertinent if I weren't determined to be on my best behaviour after my transgression.'

'Of course. I am a dreadful opportunist. I am taking advantage of your temporary remorse—I know it shan't last long.'

Not just an opportunist but rather alarmingly adorable, he thought with regret as he watched her hurry up the stairs, grateful she had allowed him to retreat with more dignity than he deserved both from his transgression and the embarrassing outpouring that followed.

Lucky Henry.

Chapter Nine

Another day, another dismal dinner.

Ellie climbed the stairs in the wake of Lady Ermintrude and her nieces and thought of the fanciful visions she and Susan and Anne sometimes had of being invited to a grand house party. There would be scintillating discussions at the supper table and then, after the men had their port or whatever they did when the women withdrew, everyone would meet for music or charades, or perhaps even some dancing…

Usually Chase added a dash of humour and warmth to these dinners. He met all of Lady Ermintrude's quelling efforts with the subversive wit that Ellie knew infuriated *Aunt Ermy* without her quite knowing why. But tonight he'd been as subdued as the rest, swamping Ellie both with regret and guilt that she had brought back all his dreadful memories.

If only she'd not reacted like a scalded cat when he caught her on the stile.

If only she hadn't felt so right in his arms she might not have reacted like a scalded cat.

Because she still felt scalded. Several times during dinner it took an act of will not to reach up and touch the places his mouth had brushed her skin as she watched him sunk into his distraction.

Why, oh, why had he stopped just short of her mouth? If she had had an ounce of sense, she would have demanded he complete the gesture and kiss her instead of confirming all his taunts that she was as prim as a schoolmistress. Fen would probably have acted more maturely than she.

She reached her room at the end of the corridor and sighed. She should be grateful there was at least a fire waiting for her, which was much more than she allowed herself at home. A warm fire might not solve all her problems, but it was worth more than a dashing ball and a soul-searing kiss, wasn't it?

As if to answer her question, the single candle shivered in the sconce that lit the corridor and Ellie reached to pull her shawl about her, only to realise it wasn't there.

'Oh, bother,' she muttered. She wanted nothing more than to climb into bed and into the Desert Boy book she was rereading and escape the world, but years of discipline turned her around.

By the time she reached the dining room the house was quiet and she was grateful she would at least not have to face the servants in her quest.

The candles were out and the table cleared, but the dying fire still cast a pleasant orange warmth about the room. But though she'd remembered her shawl slipping down the back of her seat, it was not there. Perhaps the servants had already taken it?

'Oh, bother,' she muttered again and went down on her knees to see if it slipped below the table.

'Looking for this?'

Ellie straightened so abruptly she cracked her head against the table and gave a yelp of pain.

'Blast, I'm sorry. Here, let me help you.'

'I don't need your help,' Ellie growled through gritted teeth, rubbing the singing pain in her head. Chase took her elbow anyway and helped her up from her knees, his hand warm and firm, but surprisingly gentle against her skin. In his other hand he held her shawl and for some reason the sight of the neatly folded fabric almost swallowed in his big hand struck her harder than the blow to her head.

'Ellie? I'm so sorry. Let me see...' He turned her to him, just as gently, and she realised she was crying. She took the shawl from him and buried her face in it. But that wasn't any better, it had caught his scent somehow, warm and deep, indefinable, but him. Even her shawl had given itself to him.

She tried to call herself to order. She was Eleanor Walsh; she could and would deal with anything.

Just not right now.

She waited for him to make his excuses and herd her out the door, but instead she felt his fingers touch her hair, gently tracing over it.

'Where are you hurt, sweetheart? Is it very bad?'

'No. It's not my head.' The words were muffled by the shawl and she pressed it harder against her eyes to stop the tears, dragging in a shaky breath.

Enough of this.

She scrubbed her eyes and sniffed and stepped back. She was grateful the firelight was so dim so he could not see what a mess she was, but she kept her head down none the less, staring at the contrast between his light-coloured vest and dark coat. 'I'm sorry. That was foolish. Thank you for finding my shawl. Good night.'

'Not very likely, by the sound of it. Come, you need some Dutch courage. And you need to stop trying to pull the wool over my eyes, Miss Eleanor Walsh.'

Ellie knew it was dreadfully improper to be here with him at all, even with the excuse of fetching her shawl. But to allow him to take her hand like a child and lead her to the small salon leading off the dining room where a more cheerful fire danced would surely count as depravity in Lady Ermintrude's book. Despite his swift embrace by the stile, Ellie knew he was no threat to her virtue and not merely because of his mother. The thought that Chase Sinclair might find a frumpish spinster with her face red from crying attractive was ludicrous. She knew what he was doing and at the moment she didn't have the strength to resist his tendency to find and rescue the sad castaways of life. So she allowed him to press her into an armchair by the fire as he pulled up another chair beside it and sat.

'Drink.'

'But Pruitt…'

'Pruitt enjoys his early evenings as much as Aunt Ermy. The only one on attendance after dinner is my valet and he only comes if I ring for him. I do not need the offices of servants to pour my port or extract me from my boots and coat. Sit.'

It was hardly scandalous, but the mention of being extracted from his coat drew her attention to the breadth of his shoulders and she could not stop the thought of seeing him without his coat… without his shirt…

She focused on the glass he extended to her, still avoiding looking at him.

'Drink,' he said again. 'It will help.'

She thought of her father, merry and charming

at dinner when he arrived back from his travels those last couple of years. And then later in the evening—not so charming.

'Not for long.'

His laugh was soft and ran through her like warm water climbing back into the pitcher. She shivered and he gave a little exclamation.

'Just drink, Ellie. Trust me.'

I do, as much as anyone on earth, she realised with a burst of surprise and it woke her a little. She took the glass and sniffed at it suspiciously.

'What is this? The smell doesn't recommend it at all.'

'Whisky. Huxley's favourite, bless his fastidious if not always practical soul. It feels better than it either smells or tastes. Be brave, Ellie.'

Be brave.

That was the absolutely wrong thing to say. Ellie stared at the winking, sparkling glass of liquid amber and felt a peculiar crumbling, as if a shell she hadn't even been aware of was pierced, the cracks snaking up and outwards, too fast for her to stop. She clenched her hands into her shawl, trying to stop it.

'That's all I ever am. I don't want to be brave.'

'Yes, I can see that. You'll tell me why in a moment. But for now, take a sip.'

She laughed at his insistence, at her weakness, at everything, and took the glass. But she still sipped hesitantly which was probably for the best because even just allowing the liquid to slide against her lips and the tip of her tongue was a smoky, burning explosion. She gasped and drew away.

'This *cannot* be healthy.'

He laughed and cupped his hand around hers, raising the cup back towards her mouth.

'It has nothing to do with health, but with sanity. Try again, slowly. That's right, don't fight the burn, savour it.'

Savour it.

His hand was warm and large over hers, several shades darker than hers, the veins a faint bluish tint over the fine bones on the back of his hand and where the cuff pulled back she saw hint of silky dark hair and her mind crawled up his arm, peeling back crisp linen and dark-blue superfine.

She closed her eyes hard, but that was worse because the images lingered and expanded as liquid fire hit her tongue. It burned and danced and expanded like rising smoke, but she held all this inside her as if she was holding in her soul at a meeting with Mr Soames at the bank.

And just when she thought she might choke with it, it slid through her, painting her a fiery orange from the inside, like a flame inside a glass vase.

'That's right. Another, now.'

She didn't argue. After the second swallow

she felt her shoulders melt a little and she leaned back against the chair.

It was not done—leaning.

Proper young women sat straight, making as much use of the back of a chair as a sheep made of a quizzing glass.

After the third swallow she closed her eyes, exploring her body from within as the warm wave swept through her. Perhaps that's why they called it spirits—it felt as though she'd swallowed one of the magical spirits from the Desert Boy books, perhaps one of Leila the Sprite's magical friends—incorporeal but very real—and it was getting to know her from inside and she was merely following, discovering herself alongside it.

He took the glass from her and she missed the warmth of his hand on hers more than the whisky. She finally looked at him and for a moment she felt another shiver, but this time of awe. She kept forgetting how handsome he was. The face of a beautiful devil. Dark and sharp cut, too hard even for marble, which always looked a little soft and creamy. Granite, perhaps. Yes, a beautiful granite god.

'Now, Ellie Walsh, tell me what is afoot.'

'Afoot?'

'What made you cry?'

She rubbed her head—it stung and there was even a bump.

'I bumped my head.' It sounded childish, even

to her, and he smiled, which was not a good thing because that set off another wave of spirit heat as the whisky used her innards and veins as a race course.

'I have a feeling bumped heads don't usually defeat you, Ellie. I'm rather good at telling when something is rotten in the state of Denmark and, aside from Lady Ermintrude's soul, something is definitely not quite right here. I trusted you with Huxley's letter—why can't you trust me with your problem? I'm a decent confidant, you know. I won't spill.'

She remembered Henry's words about Chase the day he arrived and knew it was true. He might be a rake, but he was also much more than that.

'Is this because of our conversation earlier? About Henry and Dru?'

She shook her head and his eyes narrowed and she saw the same calculation she'd seen from the first day.

'Yet I saw you watching them again tonight. And you must have seen what I saw.'

'What did you see, Mr Sinclair?'

The corner of his mouth rose a little at her defensive taunt.

'I saw tension, confusion…and attraction. And then I looked at you and I saw… I'm not quite certain what I saw, but not what I would expect to see on the face of a woman engaged to be married and in love with her betrothed. And yet here you are, thoroughly miserable, and only stopping yourself from crying your heart out by sheer force of will. You are either a brilliant actress or...'

'A liar.'

Oh, God, she'd said it. She squeezed the shawl harder, trying to stop the words.

'This is such a mistake. I knew it the moment I said yes.'

He met her beseeching gaze with all the stillness of a wolf hovering just within reach of a sheep munching at a clump of clover. She felt the predatory force of his eyes, but even knowing she was falling into his trap she couldn't, didn't want to stop.

'If I hadn't been so desperate... But there's no point. I have to tell Henry I cannot do this.'

'Cannot marry him?'

'No, not that. We never intended to marry. He was afraid Lady Ermintrude would try to entrap him into marrying Dru or Fen like she'd tried last time he was here.'

Something cracked through his façade. Confusion and a wariness that hadn't been there before.

'Do you mean Henry suggested you come with him to Huxley and *act* as his betrothed?'

'Yes. His idea was that I would eventually jilt him and leave him inconsolable. He never intended to marry me at all.'

'Miss Walsh. It has been an exceedingly long day...week...and I am also not at my best. Would you have me believe Henry asked you to act as his betrothed and then believed you would melt away when it suited him? Only an innocent fool would take such a step without knowing he was risking putting himself squarely in a parson's mousetrap.'

That knocked some spirit into her and she leaned forward in anger.

'He is not a fool and he knows I would never entrap him. I told him it was a terrible idea, but he convinced me and… I had my own reasons as well.'

His face went blank again.

'And they were?'

She knotted her hands together in the shawl and looked away.

'That is my business.'

'I see. Did you think that coming here as his betrothed might convince him to make the sham a reality? Is that why you are so miserable now that you see he is falling in love with the very woman he was trying to avoid being forced to marry?'

What remained of the pleasant haze of the whisky was shoved back by the intensity of his attack. She tried to rally some answering anger, but felt only a deep emptiness and disappointment. She'd been wrong about him. For a moment she had felt she could trust him as he invited her to. She'd only made a fool of herself.

She stood, but he stood as well, blocking her passage between the chairs.

'Wait, Ellie…'

'No, get out of my way, you stupid, idiotic… clod.'

'No. I didn't mean to say it…that was a mistake.'

'No, it was my mistake to tell you, to think I could trust you…'

'You *can* trust me.'

'Hah! I'd as soon trust Lady Ermintrude. At least she doesn't coat her venom with sugar. She doesn't ply her prey with whisky and…and armchairs and…things.'

Maybe the whisky was stronger than she'd realised because neither her anger nor her words were performing as expected. She just felt… miserable. She didn't resist when he pressed her back into the armchair and again the words were tumbling out of her, because she needed him to understand.

'You're wrong. I'm not in love with Henry. He is like a little brother to me, even if he is a year older than I. He's not like his father, you see. Oh, he is trustworthy and kind and he means well, but he doesn't have Mr Whelford's strength of character. And Arthur knew that about his son. He was quite ill at the end and we talked a great deal and though he knew Henry would one day be Lord Huxley because he said his brother would never marry again, that he was too deep in love with the woman he had lost to ever contemplate matrimony, he also hoped Huxley would live a long life because Henry still needed to grow up a great deal. And he asked me…if I would look out for him.'

Ellie pressed a hand to her throat. The memory of Arthur Whelford's death was almost as bad as the death of her mother and that tiny baby a year earlier. He had been her final protection from the world. When he died she'd realised it was only her. It was all up to her.

'I miss him so much. So very, very much.'

She hardly noticed when he shifted her and sat her down on his lap like a child. She leaned her forehead against the firm warmth of his neck and jaw and cried into her shawl.

He'd asked for this. He'd purposely gone after her defences, coaxed and pushed and even—though he hadn't meant to—attacked.

He was despicable.

And he was paying for it.

He kept his breath as measured and calm as possible as she cried against him, but it was agony on too many levels. He wanted to breathe her in again, draw in that inexplicably seductive scent that the longer he was around her the less he could make comparisons to anything else but Ellie. It wasn't like anything else and holding her wasn't like holding any other woman.

She was trouble.

It was foolish to be glad she wasn't in love with Henry and even more foolish to feel a wholly irrational jealousy towards a dead vicar. Chase hadn't known Arthur Whelford well, but Huxley always called his brother 'the archetype of a good man'.

Everyone loves Arthur, Huxley had said once. *He's such a good, reliable fellow they can't help themselves.*

Did she realise that though she wasn't in love with Henry, she might very well have had serious feelings for his father? No wonder the poor girl was so miserable.

He let his head lean a little against the warmth of her hair, rubbing her arm gently through the worn muslin dress. She felt so frail, shaking like that as her crying subsided. But the body pressed so trustingly against him was a strong one—he could feel the firm lines of her upper arm, not those of a girl whose only exercise was the turning of *La Belle Assemblée*'s pages or flicking open her fan.

She was a study in contrasts. Conundrums had always been his weakness. Usually they appealed to his mind, but Ellie…

He took another deep breath of her and kept as still as possible as his body took that material and condemned him, gathering and rising to bear evidence against him. If this were a trial, he'd be on his way to the gallows now.

She might need comfort, but he needed distance.

'Ellie,' he whispered, shifting so he could press those words against her hair. It was warm and even silkier than it looked. God, he was going to suffer tonight. And served him right—he was bringing this on himself, but he couldn't seem to put her away from him. It was such a contrast to her disgusted rejection when he carried her over the stile and he didn't want the moment to end.

'I'm so sorry.' Her muffled response breathed warmth against his neck and he took another cautious breath.

'Don't be. This is perfectly sensible behaviour for an occultist. They are very sensitive to celestial vibrations and I hear Jupiter is in ascendance.'

A little quiver ran through her and she giggled. It was such a non-Ellie-ish response that his arms tighten around her despite himself.

'Ellie. Don't worry so. I will fix it.'

She straightened so quickly it was only his reflexes that stopped her from cracking her head again, this time on his chin.

'You will *not* fix this. This is *my* problem.'

She fumbled out of his arms and he let her go and waited while she tidied herself.

'I asked you for help with Huxley's letter. Why do you find it so hard to do the same?'

'That is different.'

'How?'

She looked down at the mangled shawl.

'It just is.'

'Infallible logic.'

'Not everything that makes sense can be explained.'

'I dare say the incomparable Arthur Whelford would understand what that statement means.'

She finally looked at him and there was a stubborn curve to her lower lip, just hovering on the edge of a pout and making his life even more difficult.

'Why do you dislike him so?'

'I don't dislike him; I hardly knew him. But I don't think it is wise to idolise him as you do. Sometimes you have to accept help from less-than-perfect sources, Miss Walsh. Or pay the price for stubborn foolishness.'

'I'm surprised you accepted help from someone as foolishly stubborn as I, then.'

'You were still the pick of the litter around here.'

She gave an outraged gasp that ended in a ripple of laughter.

'It is very ungallant to make me laugh when I am angry.'

'You shouldn't be surprised; we already established how unsuitable I am as knight errant. You already told me about Henry, would it be so awful to tell me the rest?'

'You are like a dog with a bone.' She sounded

more weary than angry so he pressed his advantage.

'Is it your family?'

'Our family home. There were debts and a mortgage when my father…died. I'd hoped with good management we might pull through in time, but then last year there was little rain and the crop was poor and Mr Soames, from the bank in Nettleton, said they can no longer be lenient. We have three months until foreclosure. Henry said… Oh, it does not matter what Henry says. He tells me not to worry, but I can tell he is avoiding facing the truth. With all the goodwill in the world he cannot save Whitworth.' She hitched her shoulders back. 'I have been thinking, though, that once the bank has Whitworth, perhaps he could lease us a cottage. We do not need much space. And perhaps he could take Edmund on to help manage the estate. It might be easier for all of us to start anew elsewhere… It is only that I hate failing Edmund like this. Whitworth has been held by the Walshes for at least two centuries.'

'That is on your father's head, not yours, Ellie,' he said softly.

'I know, but still…'

Her shoulders sank and once again he saw the pain and weariness. Without a thought he pulled her back into his arms, tucking her head against his shoulder. For once there was no fire in the contact of her body with his, just a deep, comforting warmth, as if their bodies were melting molasses, melding into each other, blurring into one.

'Poor sweet,' he murmured as he gently rubbed her back.

'I'm not sweet.' Her voice was muffled against his coat, her breath warm through the fabric.

'I can hardly say poor crosspatch, now can I?'

The momentary lull in his lust was already abating, but luckily after a moment of shocked stiffening she laughed and pushed away.

'You are incorrigible.'

'And you are…tired. Things will look better in the morning.'

Her smile wavered and he brushed his knuckles down her cheek.

'They will, I promise. Now take your poor shawl and go to your room before I do something to earn my reputation.'

She hesitated, and he held his breath, counting out the seconds of temptation. But finally she went to the door, closing it softly behind her without another word.

Chase returned to his contemplation of his port.

When he finally looked up he was surprised to see a half-hour had passed. He drained his glass and went to ring for his valet. Poor Tubbs would have to be up and out at dawn, but there was a great deal to do in a short amount of time.

Chapter Ten

$\mathcal{E}$llie winced as the door to the Ghoulish Gallery creaked. Her head ached after a night of disjointed sleep and dreams and regrets and pointless wishes. She still couldn't believe she'd behaved so... She couldn't even quite think of a word that could encompass it. She'd cried at him and on him, betrayed Henry's trust without even consulting with him first, allowed him to insult her and to make her laugh...

How on earth would she face him this morning with any degree of calm?

But if she didn't come to the study, he would know she was embarrassed. Perhaps he would even realise she was more than embarrassed...

She unpeeled her hand from the doorknob.

Either go forward or back, said sensible Eleanor. *Standing here like a pillar of salt is no solution at all.*

None of those options is a solution, not really, Ellie retorted.

Then when in doubt, go forward, Eleanor replied and released her hold on the door.

Oh, be quiet, said Ellie, but went forward none the less.

Only to find the study empty.

Only a couple minutes ago she might have convinced herself she would be relieved not to face him. Her response to his absence made a mockery of that conviction.

She felt cheated.

Soon she must return to her world, but while she was here, she wanted to hoard these new sensations, feelings, experiences—however unsettling.

Clearly he was regretting last night even more than she if he did not wish to face her this morning.

Ellie looked around the study, memorising it. Already most of the contents were packed away and only two shelves and the wall of prints remained to be cleared by Chase's valet. It was like watching leaves slowly being stripped from a tree by coming winter. Now just a few clung, but they could not prevent the approaching frost.

She could already feel loneliness creep back on her and that made no sense. Why would she feel less lonely with a man she barely knew than with her own family? She loved her brothers and sisters—she wasn't blind to their faults and she knew they weren't blind to hers, but she loved them and wanted their happiness and safety. She'd just never realised she was lonely until she wasn't.

She kneaded her fist in her hand as she stared at the empty chair behind the desk. Today she would speak with Henry and tell him it was time they both faced the truth, then she would return to Whitworth.

She closed her eyes and fixed the sight of the study in her mind—Chase sitting at the desk, head bent over the notebooks...

She wished she had his sister's skill so she could sketch the image.

As if summoned, Chase entered the study, pausing in the doorway as if surprised to see her there.

'Good morning, Ellie.'

It was a perfectly proper greeting and that in itself was enough to make her heart sink further. She knew it was a mistake to reveal so much to him last night.

'Good morning, Mr Sinclair.' She tried to make her eyes meet his as if there was nothing at all peculiar about her behaviour or revelations last night, but she couldn't. So she turned to the wall with its exotic prints of places she would never see.

The wallpaper in between was old and faded,

except for one patch. Her mind leapt to latch on to the diversion from her embarrassment.

'Has Tubbs already begun taking these down? I cannot remember what was in this space.'

'In what space?' he asked and she pointed to the gap between the frames directly opposite the desk.

He cursed softly, moving forward to touch the brighter blue of the wallpaper where it had been protected from the light. His hands were large, but finely cut, as if a sculptor had agonised over their making, judging every line, even the rise of veins over the fine bones on the back of his hand. The only imperfection was a faint scarring and roughness over his knuckles.

'My mother.'

'I beg your pardon?' She dragged her eyes away from his hand.

'There used to be a sketch Sam made of my mother and Huxley sitting in the garden at Qetara. Huxley liked it so much we framed it for him as a gift. It was always there. How could I not have noticed?'

'Are you certain Tubbs has not removed it?'

'Quite certain. It's not in the cupboards or gallery cabinets, either. Tubbs and I cleared out the last of those yesterday evening.'

'Perhaps he sent it to be reframed?'

Chase shook his head.

'I doubt it, Huxley never parted with it,' said

the drawing was his lucky amulet. Even when he travelled he kept that sketch and some notebooks in a special travel case. I noticed the case was gone, but... Are you certain the portrait wasn't here before?'

'Quite certain. I have been wondering if Lord Huxley looked like Mr Whelford, but there are no paintings of him here or in the portrait gallery. I am tolerably certain I would have noticed a drawing of him and a woman. I am sorry, Mr Sinclair.'

'Chase,' he corrected absently. 'Why are you sorry?'

'Because it was of your mother. I only have one miniature of mine and I would hate to lose it. Some days I already find it hard to remember what she looked like. Was your mother very beautiful?'

The harshness bled out of his face, his mouth curving a little, and again the world expanded and contracted about her. Chase was back. The sense of rightness at his smile terrified her. It should not matter so much.

'Not really. *We* thought she was, but I remember people saying behind her back they didn't understand what my father saw in her. She was... vivid. Less so after my father died. Sometimes it came back. She liked Egypt. When we were there I think she sometimes forgot what she had lost. But it rarely lasted.'

'She had you.'

He turned at her protest, his gaze focusing again.

'Precisely. She had to shoulder alone the burden of three difficult children because the man she adored had allegedly cuckolded a friend of his and then shot him in the back. For over a year she only left our great-grandmother's *palazzo* in Venice to take us to concerts at La Fenice, only to return to her room and cry. If it hadn't been for Huxley forcing her to bring us to Egypt, she'd likely have stayed there until she died. I never quite understood why my cousin took us on, but I know how much I owe him. He succeeded in doing for her what we couldn't, no matter how hard we tried.' He looked back at the gap on the wall. 'I should have come here more often these last few years. Damn it.'

She didn't comment at the profanity—he was far away again. Her mind tumbled over itself to find ways to alleviate the pain she'd unknowingly unveiled. The need to soothe and help frightened her—she never felt that way outside her little circle and she didn't want it to expand to include this stranger who made rooms shrink and expand and her balance totter.

He turned his back on the wall and went the desk.

'Come, we'd best finish with these notebooks. Tubbs will pack the rest of them this afternoon and take them to Sinclair Hall tomorrow.'

Ellie turned away as well, but there was no evading the implications of the emptying study. The books were gone, too, aside from the set of Desert Boy books Chase had left for her. At least she would have some memento from this strange time other than a broken heart. She picked up the top book, letting it fall open, and gave a little gasp.

'Oh no! it is all cut up.'

'What?'

'Look. Oh, this is *terrible*.'

He came and took the book from her. Three whole pages were missing and half of the next page. He flicked forward, finding several more places where similar cuts had been made.

'How peculiar,' he said, clearly not as affected as she by the vandalism.

'Why would he do this? What on earth would he do with a clipping of a description of the Silver Desert?' she demanded, her heart sinking as she checked the next volume and found more missing pages.

'The what?'

'Don't you remember? Leila and Gabriel reach the Silver Desert where there are towers shaped like mushrooms and crystal flowers growing from the ground. And here… I think this is from the scene where that evil sorcerer…what was his name? Jephteh… He is trying to hurl Gabriel from the cliffs and Leila the Sprite saves him. See?'

He didn't answer, just picked up the next book on the stack. Sure enough someone had taken a pair of scissors to this as well.

'Do you recognise the missing scene here?' he asked, holding it out to her, and she nodded.

'Yes, this is where they find a drunken camel with a missing ear wandering at night near the step pyramid and he leads them to the sacred spring.'

'A missing ear…'

'Oh, and this where Gabriel and Leila are caught in a sandstorm and fall into a cave and she is scolding him. Susan always had me read the scenes between them twice. She is convinced they are in love with on another…' Her voice petered out and she moved back. 'Do you think this is a sign of his deterioration? Surely it cannot have anything to do with your little quest.'

'I don't know. Wait here a moment. Where is that map? Ah, here.'

He pulled a rolled-up map of Egypt from one of the boxes and spread it on the desk, the Nile twisting upwards and then blooming into the veins of the river delta.

'Fetch me those paperweights on the shelves over there, would you?'

Ellie gathered the little statuettes shaped like Egyptian gods and he began placing them around the map as he leafed one by one through the mutilated books.

'Well, I'll be damned,' he said at last and she bounced a little on her heels, her dismay giving way to curiosity.

'What? What is it?'

'Perhaps this was why Huxley had all the notebooks out. He must have been looking for clues.'

'Clues to what?'

'To the author of the Desert Boy novels. He must have recognised these places as well. And not just places. That tale of the camel with the missing ear? Remember the tale I told you about Fatima and Khalidi? Well, a few years later Khalidi's favourite donkey disappeared and we all went searching and eventually found it with part of its ear missing, probably taken by a jackal.'

'That could merely be a coincidence.'

'Except that we found this donkey munching on some bushes in the middle of the most arid part of the valley which led Khalidi to discover an old underground well that was probably used once by camel traders.'

'That *is* an interesting parallel,' she conceded.

'And the scene with Jephteh?' He pointed to one of the statuettes located halfway down the Nile. 'That is an almost perfect description of the Howling Cliffs.'

'The what?'

'The cliffs just above Poppy's house in Qetara. You reach them from a path leading off the gardens and sometimes at night when the jackals

are on the hunt it sounds as though there are
hundreds of them. In fact, now I think of these
scenes together, I recognise most of them except
for the Silver Desert. But your description of
the mushroom-shaped towers could refer to the
Sahara-al-Beyda, the White Desert, near Farafra.
Very few explorers have been there, but I know
Huxley went once with Poppy and Edge and Mallory and some others. I remember Huxley telling
Sam the illustrations she made of them lacked
verisimilitude and she said it was his fault because he hadn't allowed her to join that expedi-
tion even though she'd begged to go.'

He took another volume and between them
they pieced together over a dozen events or loca-
tions Huxley had removed from the books.

'So you recognise them all?' she asked and he
nodded, his gaze moving back in time, his mouth
softening.

'I told you he was curious about the author.
Every time Sam received a new commission for
illustrations the conjecture would begin again. I
think he even wondered whether it might be my
mother because Sam said he was surprised she
received a new commission after she died.'

The animation drained out of his face, the firelight gilding his features and turning his eyes
more black than grey. He looked a little like an
Egyptian statue himself—a secretive and enig-
matic god. Ellie watched the firelight gild his low-

ered lashes and in her mind she touched her hand to the tense line of his jaw.

He picked up one of the paperweights she'd handed him from the shelves. It was not a stat-uette, but a lovely stoppered vase made of a peach-and-cream-coloured substance she did not recognise.

'It is lovely,' she said. 'See how the light shines through it. What is it made of?'

'It is alabaster,' he replied and cleared his throat. 'From Egypt. I'd forgotten about these also. My mother bought a matching pair of them for Huxley because he liked alabaster. The other one must have broken. You may have this one. If you like.'

'Oh, no, I couldn't possibly...'

Her voice disappeared as he enveloped her hands in his, closed them gently about the vase.

'Take it. Please.'

They stood there, above the map of Egypt, his hands about hers and hers about the modest little vase, as if it was as unique and precious as the holy grail.

Chase froze, dragged out of his abstraction by the feel of her hands in his. Though there was nothing terribly outrageous in his gesture, even as he did it he knew it was a mistake.

His blood hummed as if laced with whisky— expanding as it raced through his veins outward from the point of contact between them, singeing him from within and gathering into a near-unbearable pressure at his centre. He looked down at the vase, waiting for the ache to subside.

Walls built over decades could be torn down in moments.

It was one of Oswald's favourite warnings and though Chase was accustomed to rolling his eyes at his uncle's descents into philosophising, he'd seen the truth of this too often both in war and peace. A city's or a nation's defences are never quite as robust as one hoped.

He'd just never thought it applied to him.

He thought he'd understood the pull she exerted on him—lust, friendship, even caring—he could manage these, pass through them and continue. It never once occurred to him there was a line to be crossed that signalled real peril.

But with his hands on hers, he teetered on the edge of a cliff, only half-aware he must…he *must* recapture his balance before something terrible happened.

He managed to remove his hands from hers, but then her lashes rose to reveal the warmth in her gold-spiced eyes and he could not stop himself.

He fell.

The closest he'd ever felt to this sensation was when he'd fallen off a twenty-foot cliff into the Mediterranean Sea. The moonless night had provided good cover for his meeting with the Sultan's agent but also for the several of the Russian Tsar's less diplomatic representatives, and their short but spirited scuffle ended when he and one of his opponents miscalculated their distance from the cliff's edge.

He could still feel the shock of the ground disappearing from beneath his weight, the desperate denial as mind separated from body. Then came the stinging impact as he hit the water and the frantic clawing through black liquid, unsure which way was up, his lungs begging for air, his heart hammering even as his mind bellowed commands.

He'd forgotten about that moment, but now it was back—the same overwhelming shock and resistance. This could not be happening.

But it was.

If he could have moved, he would have been out of the room like a bat out of hell, putting as much space between him and the absurd conviction that everything, his life, his very being had suddenly shifted to another plane.

This wasn't just misplaced lust, this was not something that would ache a little and eventually he would look back on it with rueful fondness.

This was his fate. This would never leave him.

Like the moment his mother had looked up from the letter she held and spoken those four words—*'Your father is dead'*—and he knew nothing would ever be the same.

Nothing would ever be the same.

She wasn't even doing anything—just standing there, her smile raising a dimple on the soft slope of her cheek—and it was the most natural thing in the world for him to be with her. He was made for that moment, to watch her laugh, to give her joy, to bring her peace in a way he knew was as unusual for her as this descent into madness was for him.

It made no sense, no sense at all that he could not do what every element of his being was telling him was at the very fundament of existence— bend down to press his lips to that elusive sign of her pleasure, bury his face in the soft warmth of her hair and breathe in her scent—the coolness of lilies and the sweet, almost exotic promise of vanilla, as conflicting and complementary as the strains of her nature. Wrap himself around her and just…be. Even the agony of lust she sparked in him was a pleasure he would happily wallow in if she could only be his.

'Chase?'

He heard her voice, but he could not move because to move would be to accept this madness. Perhaps if he kept very still it would pass him by, like the riders of the wild hunt passing through a village by moonlight.

But then the distinctive squeak of the gallery door broke the silence and heralded Pruitt's arrival.

'Her ladyship requests your presence in the yellow salon, Mr Sinclair, Miss Walsh.'

Chapter Eleven

Ellie glanced at Chase as they followed Pruitt. He had not said a word since closing her hands on that vase. There was that same distant look on his face as when he was deep in thought, when the humour and warmth were washed away and exposed the taut watchfulness that revealed his uneasy passage through life.

It was a timely reminder he was no longer the bruised, frightened boy hiding in the cupboard or the young man in Huxley's notebooks who quietly but efficiently arranged the world for others.

Now he was The Right Dishonourable Chase Sinclair—charming and protective when so inclined and ruthlessly dismissive when not. She'd seen the warning signs that very first day they met in the Folly, but now it was far too late to heed them.

Tomorrow he would leave and take part of her with him. And she would have to take part of him in her memory and preserve it, like the Egyptians preserved desiccated organs in funerary urns.

Her hands burned, her throat and eyes, too, and as Pruitt crossed the hallway she hung back. Why did Lady Ermintrude have to send for them now, when she had so little time left with him?

Chase turned to her, his gaze coming into focus as he scanned her face.

'What is wrong?'

'Nothing.'

'You have no cause to worry. I imagine Aunt Ermy fantasises about casting us out into the rain and watching us melt into the fog, but she has no power over you.'

The thought of melting anywhere with Chase was far too unsettling.

'I know that.'

'Good. Now come let us see what Aunt Ermy has in store for us.'

What she had in store was nothing more alarming than an attractive and fashionably dressed young man with a wide smile and curly hair the colour of firelight. He was seated on a sofa beside Dru, but he stood at their entry, beaming at them as Lady Ermintrude made the introductions.

'Mr Sinclair, Miss Walsh, may I introduce Mr Ambleside of the British Museum.'

Henry strode forward.

'There you are, Chase! I was telling my aunt

there is no need for Mr Ambleside to waste his time here. Uncle left his collection to you, didn't he?'

'No trouble, no trouble at all,' Mr Ambleside said. 'Happy to make the trip. Lord Huxley was a noted collector. Make myself useful sorting the wheat from the chaff, eh?'

Lady Ermintrude ignored this enthusiastic interjection.

'Huxley's will specified the contents of the East Wing and the Folly go to the Sinclairs, but there are other artefacts littering the Manor which I am convinced you will be only too pleased to see assessed, yes, Henry?'

'But…'

'Precisely,' Lady Ermintrude continued. 'Now why don't you show Mr Ambleside around, Drusilla? After all, you know the Manor best, my dear girl. I suggest we begin in the Long Gallery.'

Henry's frown deepened, but he fell into step beside Ellie. Mr Ambleside walked ahead with Dru, his head bent towards her as she spoke.

'Did you see this Bartholomew baby's waistcoat?' Henry whispered contemptuously. 'Hummingbirds and clocks!'

'He seems a pleasant young man,' Ellie replied politically.

'I concur,' Chase said. 'I know the family. Good prospects. Maybe you should invite him to stay, Henry. He might be able take one of your dreaded cousins off your hands. In fact, he looks halfway to captivating Dru already,' he added, ignoring Ellie's frown.

The Long Gallery was a wide hall which Lady Ermintrude kept resolutely closed, but which could serve as a ballroom if she ever loosened her vice-like grip on the manor. Pruitt opened the curtains and a burst of sunlight caught on a series of stone friezes and burnished Dru's hair into russet and brass and Mr Ambleside's hair into mahogany as he went to inspect the carvings.

Lady Ermintrude seated herself on a *chaise longue.*

'You may take Miss Walsh to look at the family portraits at the other end of the hall, Chase. You go with them, Fenella. Henry, you sit by me. Drusilla can see to Mr Ambleside.'

'Our marching orders, Miss Walsh. Fen, come along.'

'What on earth is wrong with Henry?' Fenella asked as she followed Chase. 'He looks livid.'

'Indigestion, Fen. He is having trouble swallowing the charming Mr Ambleside. Come look at this fellow, Miss Walsh. The first Baron Huxley and just as much a sufferer of indigestion as the current one by the looks of him.'

Fen giggled, but Ellie cast a worried glance at Henry, who had left his perch by Lady Ermintrude and was hovering beside Mr Ambleside and Dru. Even across the gallery Ellie could see he was being neatly shouldered aside by the taller Mr Ambleside.

'Perhaps I should…'

Chase clasped her elbow gently but firmly.

'No, you should not. Now, Fen, tell us what ailed this bewigged fellow.'

For the next half hour as Dru guided Mr Ambleside through the Manor Ellie was convinced they had fallen into a farce, with Lady Ermintrude as the managing mama, Dru the shy but promising debutante, Mr Ambleside as the charming suitor and poor Henry the bumbling one that kept saying the wrong thing at the wrong time and growing ever more flustered and angry. To her added frustration, Chase spiked every attempt of hers to intervene on Henry's behalf. She was even more surprised that Lady Ermintrude appeared to approve of Mr Ambleside's interest in Dru.

'He must be very wealthy for Lady Ermintrude to be encouraging him so,' Ellie muttered to Chase as they finished the tour and headed back towards the yellow salon.

'Priceless. And such a handsome fellow, no?' Chase replied.

'He is too pretty.' Ellie shrugged, annoyed on Henry's behalf. Chase stopped in the hallway, his mouth twisting.

'Ah yes, I forgot your taste runs to rustic vicars.'

'Don't sneer. I don't see why you are enjoying Henry's discomfiture. It is not like you to be unkind.'

'Thank you for that at least.'

'Couldn't you rid us of that fellow before Dru forgets all about Henry? Tell him there is a...a marvellous mummy in the Folly or something?'

'Lie for you? My dear Miss Walsh. Or perhaps you plan for me to lock him there while darling Henry recovers lost ground? And in the dark of night we would hear him howl for his love and more importantly for his supper. That would add a touch of drama to your tale.'

Ellie tried not to smile.

'You haven't a romantic bone in your body. Surely you can think of something to pry him away, or at least stop interfering when I try to do so.'

'And how do you propose to do that? Dazzle him with your golden eyes and lips like new rose petals?'

Ellie's smile faltered as his gaze followed his words. He continued, his voice losing its sardonic tone, sinking deeper.

'And I object to the slur, Ellie Walsh. You might be surprised how many of my bones are romantic. Now come along before we overplay our hand.'

She allowed him to move her towards the salon, a little dazed by the seductive force of his words.

The moment they entered, Henry strode towards her.

'Eleanor! Where did you disappear to? And where is Pruitt? I rang for him hours ago!'

'Pruitt might be otherwise engaged with more important tasks, Henry,' Lady Ermintrude interjected, but for once Henry did not beat a retreat.

'Well, he should un-engage himself, Aunt Ermintrude. He is now *my* butler and he does not have more important tasks than doing as I request and so I shall tell him!'

'Henry!' Dru admonished. 'There is no reason to be rude and certainly not to exaggerate. It has not been hours; we have not been here ten minutes.'

'It feels longer,' he muttered. 'Are we done here? Surely you've seen every dusty and dank corner in the Manor, Mr Ambleside.'

'Miss Walsh reminds me there is yet the Folly to inspect, Mr Ambleside,' Chase offered and Ellie blushed.

'I would be glad for a look in the Folly, Mr Sinclair,' Mr Ambleside replied amiably, throwing a smile at Drusilla. 'Miss Ames tells me it is quite a curiosity. Perhaps you care to join us?'

'I do not think there is anything there worth your time, Mr Ambleside,' Dru said conscientiously. 'I helped Uncle Huxley prepare a package to be sent to Egypt while Mr Mallory was in town and we searched the Folly thoroughly for a note-book he wished to include. I did not see anything there that might be of interest to the Museum.'

'A package?' Chase and Ellie asked in unison and Dru blinked.

'Why, yes. He mentioned something about sending it to Egypt, I presume to his friend Mr Carmichael. Though I don't see what he could want with old notebooks and the pages ripped out of those poor books. The only thing that might have been of interest was a lovely little vase we wrapped in cloth and there was a small picture frame, though I did not see if there was a picture in it or not. It certainly didn't appear worth the cost of sending Mr Mallory all the way to Egypt, but I do hope he is careful so that lovely vase doesn't break. It looked quite delicate.'

'No one mentioned that Mallory went to Egypt.' Chase said sharply and Dru blinked at him in surprise.

'I did not know you were interested, Charles. I would not have known myself had I not helped him prepare that package and then it was only a passing comment he made. You know what he was like before he fell ill—he and Mallory would be up and gone in a moment without a word to anyone.'

'What on earth does it matter?' Henry de-manded. 'Stop distressing Dru, Chase. And you'd best go to the Folly soon so Mr Ambleside may yet catch the mail coach to London.'

The moment the words were out Henry flushed at his ill manners, but Chase merely nodded and opened the door.

'Come with me, Mr Ambleside.'

Mr Ambleside directed a smile at Drusilla and a bow at Lady Ermintrude and followed. When the door closed behind them Dru turned to Henry.

'That was very rude, Henry. He was only doing his duty.'

'Was he? It looked as though he was doing a great deal more than that! I'm the head of the family now and I am dashed if I will have pop-injays like that come in and sniff around the Manor at will, flirting and smirking and grabbing arms...'

'He only took Dru's elbow to steady her when she tripped on the loose carpet,' Fen said. 'I think it very gallant of him.'

Henry snorted and Dru took a step forward.

'I did nothing improper, Henry Huxley. *I* didn't spend hours with him alone in...' She stopped, her eyes flying to Ellie, her cheeks flushing as brightly as her hair. She pressed her palms to them and hurried out, murmuring something that sounded like an apology as she passed by Ellie. Ellie was sorely tempted to go after her, but instead she turned to Henry.

'Shall we go for a turn in the garden, Henry?'

Henry looked as though he would prefer kicking something, but he mastered himself and followed.

'Tell me,' she invited when they were alone, and Henry tugged at his hair.

'What a counter-coxcomb that fellow is! I dare say he's heard Dru is an heiress. And she! Why, she was as bad as he was! I haven't seen her smile so much since she saw me trying to skate on the winter pond years ago.'

'Perhaps Dru doesn't have much opportunity to meet nice young men.'

'That's where you are wrong. Dru has even had a couple of offers, so don't you feel sorry for her. But there's something not above board about that fellow and I'm dashed if I'll have him sniffing about and making up to her. He is a fortune hunter if ever I've seen one.'

'I doubt you have seen any and besides, Chase said he is quite—'

'Quite what?' Henry frowned as she broke off.

'Quite priceless,' Ellie repeated in a hollow voice as realisation struck. No wonder Chase been so bent on keeping her away from Dru, Henry and Mr Ambleside. But how could she guess anyone would actually bring…what? An actor…? To perpetrate such a fraud simply to excite Henry's jealousy? It was an outrageous gesture. But then, this wasn't anyone. This was Chase.

'Priceless,' Henry snorted.

She took Henry's restless hands in hers and gave them a little shake.

'It does not matter. What does matter is that we must call a halt to this, Henry. We never should have begun, but I never imagined when we did that you would fall in love with Drusilla.'

She waited for his denial, but his hands merely tightened in hers and he groaned.

'I don't understand it, Eleanor. I never liked her and she never liked me. It makes no sense, but I can't seem to stay away from her. Deuce take it, I must have been dropped on my head at birth to be such a fool. What are we to do?'

'You will tell her the truth.'

'No. Eleanor…' He groaned again.

'All of it.'

'She will never forgive me.'

'Somehow I doubt that. Once Mr Ambleside is gone, I suggest you find a private moment and make a clean breast of it, just please don't make a gift of the news to Lady Ermintrude until I am gone as well, I don't think I could bear her gloating. Could you arrange for me to return to Whitworth tomorrow?' Her voice broke a little on the thought and his grip tightened.

'I might yet find a way to raise the funds, Eleanor. Ermy isn't loosening the purse strings as I hoped and every last inch of land is entailed, but perhaps if Dru does agree to wed me she might…'

'Good heavens, Henry, you cannot ask the

woman you wish to marry to lend money to the woman she thought was rival for your affections. You shall have your head handed to you and with good reason. But I was thinking…perhaps if we lose Whitworth we might lease a cottage here on the estate…'

Henry's dark expression lifted. 'Why, that would solve everything, Ellie. I know you will miss Whitworth, but it really is a millstone about your neck. Father would have approved, do you not think?'

Ellie forced her lips into a smile and nodded.

'Oh, yes. Undoubtedly.'

Chapter Twelve

Ellie slowed outside the door of the yellow salon—the voices were low but recognisable and Ellie smiled. She could not hear what was being said, but it was clear Henry and Dru were, for once, in accord. She gave a little sigh and moved on towards the small drawing room, hoping her quarry had not yet retired for the night.

She eased open the drawing-room door and glanced inside. He was seated with his back to her, a glass of dark liquid in his hand, his boots stretched out to the fire. She sighed in relief even as her nerves leapt to attention. He turned and rose in a swift motion that reminded her again how different he was from the men she knew. For a moment she stood in silence, trying to read his expression, but the fire behind him cast him into shadow.

'Miss Walsh. Did you forget another shawl?'

Ellie shook her head, closing the study door behind her.

'No. I was curious. About Mr Ambleside. You brought him, didn't you?'

'I thought you would see through our little charade immediately.'

'So who is he? A friend of yours? He was most convincing.'

His mouth softened at her enthusiasm.

'I shall tell him so. He is my secretary, Mr Barker. I sent for him so we could discuss some business of mine and I thought he could be useful prodding some sense into Henry. It was far more effective than I imagined.'

'It was. They are in the yellow salon even now. I tiptoed past.'

He swirled the contents of his glass and she waited for him to offer her some, but he just watched her.

'It does not bother you?'

'Of course not. I am happy for Henry. But what is truly fortuitous is that we might not have heard about the package the late Lord Huxley sent to Egypt with Mr Mallory if not for Mr Amb—Mr Barker's questions. At least it solves the mystery of the missing notebooks.'

'Does it?'

'Well, only their possible whereabouts, not why he sent them or what he wished of you. What shall you do now?'

He indicated the armchair with the glass he held and she shivered at the memory of the other evening—his arms around her, his thighs firm and warm beneath hers.

'Sit. Have some.'

She hesitated.

'I don't think...'

'Good. Don't. It is not whisky this time, but port. A rather gentler path to perdition.'

She sat, barely resisting the urge to burrow into the warmth left by his body. Time was slowly melting from the hourglass and she wanted to cherish every moment in his company.

'Try it.'

He pulled a chair close to hers and held out the shimmering crystal. The thought of drinking again from the same glass his lips had touched sent a shiver through her, followed immediately by a wave of warmth, as if the spirits were already swirling through her.

Carefully she took it, touching her lips to the cool rim, allowing the scent to reach her first, full and earthy, making colours swirl in her mind. She tilted the cup a little further and the liquid touched her lips, burning a little before it even enveloped her tongue. It was different from the burn and burst of the whisky but she still shuddered as it slid into her, both foreign and familiar. A word came to her—luscious. A warm, rolling word for sinking into…a whole world of sensations waiting to be embraced outside her straitened world.

Luscious…

Lustful.

She looked up and in the guttering light of the candles he looked beautiful and devilish, as tense as a hawk ready to swoop, talons extended.

'I've never tasted anything like it,' she murmured, struggling to keep her voice light. He reached forward slowly and took the glass from her. She watched as he raised it to his lips, her fingers curling into fists in anticipation. He drained the glass and refilled it, handing it to her once more.

He smiled as she took it, his expression relaxing at last.

'Do you like it?'

She nodded.

'This is my second time indulging in spirits here. I told you I don't often…imbibe.'

'You don't often indulge yourself at all, do you?'

She tried to laugh, cradling her hands around the glass, but it sounded more like a cough, so she took another sip to mask it and warmth met warmth. Her cheeks were filling out, probably becoming rosy like a village maiden's. She smiled at the absurdity of the thought.

'At least you eat more now than when I first arrived, Ellie. Tonight you even tried the syllabub.'

On the surface his remark was innocuous, but her cheeks heated further. She probably looked like a boiled beet now. Before she could marshal her defences he shook his head.

'That's not a criticism, Ellie, quite the opposite. Every now and again you should remember to put yourself first and send everyone else to the devil. Now drink.'

She did as she was told, keeping her eyes on the glass so he would not see the tears pressing for release again. She wished they could stay like this. No, she wished for something else entirely, but that was pointless. When the glass was half-empty he reached across to touch it.

'Just a little more, but not too much, or you will be cursing me come morning.'

'Did your secretary bring you bad news?' The words rushed out of her and in the silence that followed the ticking of the clock marched alongside her heartbeat.

'Why do you ask, Ellie?'

'You appear...unhappy.'

He hesitated, his gaze moving from hers to the fire. His mouth pressed into a hard line before he spoke.

'There is another problem I am dealing with. It is complicated.'

'Does it concern your sister?'

'No. This problem is wholly mine.'

'Perhaps you need someone to fix your problem for you.'

She tried to smile, but though he turned back to her, his eyes were almost black, as if the flames had transformed them from anthracite to obsidian.

'Some problems cannot be fixed, at least not from the outside.'

'Is there anything *I* can do to help?'

He pulled the glass from her fingers and for a moment covered her hand with his. His palm was cool, firm, she could feel the pressure of his callouses along the back of her hand.

She had large hands, but his swamped hers, his fingertips curving into the edge of her palm, his thumb touching the base of her wrist. His touch was light, but it stung, heat crawling over her body like smoke snaking out from under the door of a burning room, and her sympathy vanished like dew in the desert, replaced by wholly selfish thoughts. Her pulse galloped against his touch like a bolting horse, but he said nothing. His lashes veiled his eyes, but she read tension in his cheekbones and the answering pulse beside his jaw. She waited for him to act, but then his hand released hers and he stood.

'You can go to bed.'

She rose as well, her mind both numb and raw. By this time tomorrow she would be back at Whitworth. This could be the last time she saw Chase Sinclair. She would not see him again. Ever.

A rumble, very like a snarl, filled her head before she recovered her senses.

'Goodbye, then, Mr Sinclair.'

It made no sense.

'I shall see you in the morning, Miss Walsh.'

Heat chased clammy cold over her skin, pinching at her cheeks and nape and leaving her shaky at the reprieve. How utterly pathetic that with everything she had yet to face, postponing their inevitable farewell could do this to her. She stepped backwards as if she could somehow put distance between herself and her weakness. Then she turned and made her feet carry her out of the room.

Chapter Thirteen

May hot dreams warm your cool heart.

He'd cursed her that first day. Laid a spell on her. And it had come true in spades.

Ellie was no stranger to miserable nights. Plenty of hers had been ruined by worries about mortgages and the future or by sick or nightmare-ridden siblings. But she wasn't accustomed to the kind of dreams that took possession of her that night. She wanted to blame the port, but there was no tucking away the vivid images her mind conjured.

They began realistically enough—she entered the drawing room and Chase offered her his glass… But what followed was wholly different, wholly unholy… She went to him, trailed her fingers along his jaw, the tense line of his lower lip, exploring every beautiful, uncompromising line of his face, all the while feeling the steel-sharp flames of his eyes stripping her, his hands mapping her, his mouth brushing the soft hair at her temple, moving lower…

But even in her dreams she was a fool because what did she have to go and do but speak the words she held so tightly inside her and suddenly there was nothing but the dull grey of dawn and the realisation that today she would say goodbye to Chase and tomorrow she would wake in her own bed in Whitworth and begin the rest of her life.

She needed air.

She tied her bonnet with a sharp tug, wincing as the ribbons caught the delicate skin beneath her ear, precisely where she'd dreamed of his lips caressing her.

When she reached the stile she cursed her recalcitrant mind for bringing her here. She stood anchored in the high grass, watching a cluster of sheep sheltering under a twisted oak a few yards away. Part of her wished her life was like theirs—surely sheep didn't wake worrying if today would be the day everything they owned would disappear, or wake burning with need for a man who would probably be embarrassed but resolutely kind if he found out he was figuring in her lascivious dreams…

'I would offer to help you over, but that landed me in trouble last time.'

The sheep raised their heads from the grass at her startled cry. He must have come across the field because she hadn't heard his approach. He was not wearing a hat and his hair was disordered by the wind and his cravat only loosely knotted. He looked like a man returning from a night of revelry, or stepping directly from her overheated dream. But he was all too real and solid, the scent of his soap and skin reaching her like an embrace. When she remained silent he leaned his hip on the wall by the stile, crossing his arms.

'You are out early.'

'I am on my way to the Tor.'

'Alone?'

'Yes. I wished to see the sea before I leave. It might be years before I see it again.'

He did not answer, but when she turned towards the stile he followed and, though his hand rose, he didn't assist her. She wished she hadn't reacted so missishly the previous time. Today she would not object at all to feeling his arms around her, that sweep of his mouth on her cheek…

How was it even possible today was the last day she would see him?

Denial of such a possibility was buzzing inside her even though she knew she had no future with someone like Chase Sinclair. In fact, she had not much of a future of any kind. Tomorrow she would be facing the harsh realities of her failure and Chase would be on his way to Egypt.

It was utterly unfair.

She was Eleanor Walsh, spinster, twenty-six

years old, and she was so, so tired of being a shell of herself.

Her hands burned with rebellion and her lungs were tight with fear. He made her body and mind rage like a poison, unsettling everything she had so carefully built, but even if she wanted to hate and resent his effect she couldn't. It was too strong, too…wonderful.

In the past week she'd gathered more memories of pleasure and joy and been more herself, just Ellie, than in the past dozen years. In his company she rediscovered who she was and she wanted more.

She wanted to *feel*.

She wanted the kiss he'd spun out of air and words.

He owed her.

They reached the ledge of the Tor and stood looking out towards the greyish-blue line of the sea blending into a murky, breezeless sky. It would probably rain all the way back to Whitworth. A fitting beginning to the rest of her life, but she was not there yet.

'I want something from you before I leave.'

'Name it.'

She laughed at his immediate response. It was so like him. She could probably ask him for the money for the mortgage and he would give it to her without a second thought. But what she wanted she was not at all certain he would give as freely.

'I want a kiss. A real kiss. I want you to show me what it is like.'

'I...*what*?'

She kept her eyes resolutely ahead. If she looked at him, she would lose her nerve.

'Is it such an outrageous request? Surely you have kissed so many one more can hardly make a difference?'

'Blast it, Ellie. You know full well it is an outrageous request! And for your information I am a great deal more fastidious than you're implying. I've certainly never kissed women who were... I mean...you know what I mean.'

Yes, she knew what he meant. Women who were plain and proper and past their prime. She'd never before wished with such a fever to be beautiful, or seductive, or anything that would make him regard her as more than a friend.

She didn't know what to do next, but she'd already stepped so far out on to the ledge, she *couldn't* withdraw now.

'It is merely a kiss. I am not asking you to sell your soul to the devil. Today I must return to Whitworth and I doubt I shall have another opportunity to...experiment. I know I am not what you are used to, but... Does it matter so? Could you not try?'

* * *

Chase noted Ellie's fisted hands, her half-wistful, half-defiant expression, but mostly the lost look in her eyes. He'd seen it often enough in the eyes of young men in the moments of fleeting calm before they marched into battle. It was a look that stretched back into the past as if gathering their whole life into one sensation, knowing it might be their last chance to embrace who they were.

It was not a look that should be in a young woman's eyes and it cracked his resolve far more than her defiance. He wanted to gather her to him and shield her from everything.

Himself included.

He wished he could tell her she had no reason to worry about her home, but that wasn't part of his plan. The last thing he wanted to do was give her cause to resent his interference.

'Ellie. You don't know what you are asking.'

He took her hands. Her fists were vibrating with tension and he couldn't bear it. He wanted to give her whatever she asked for, however wrong. She turned her hands to clasp his.

'Yes, I do. I am asking for a kiss. What else is there to know?'

Another layer of heat sheathed itself around his lungs and began spreading. The images from his dreams that night flared along with his body—he'd dreamt of licking amber-coloured drops of port from her skin, watching them slide with agonising slowness down the side of her neck, over the slope of her collarbone and towards the valley between her breasts…he could almost hear the soft whisper of liquid on skin as they'd continued their descent…

He wasn't hot, he was close to combustion. He wanted to take off his coat…her pelisse…stretch her out on the mossy ground…

He tried to remind himself that it was cold and damp and there was nothing alluring about being covered with mud and moss. But not even mud could ruin his vision of Ellie unveiled, waiting for him…

Hell and damnation. Stop it. Now.

But his will was melting through his fingers like ice on a hot brick as his mind gathered ammunition to defend the indefensible.

She'd said it herself—she wasn't a girl any longer, but a mature woman of twenty-six. He might even discover that there was nothing at all special about kissing her. There was no better antidote to fantasy than fact. For both of them.

He touched his fingertips to the ridge of her cheek, where a wisp of hair clung and shivered.

'Take off your bonnet.'

She untied it, but the straw snagged on her hair and instinctively he reached up to slip the tangled lock free. He didn't let go, though, running the freed hair between his fingers, drawing it down to its full length, his fingers just a shiver of breath from her breast. It was silky and warm and he brushed it over his lips to capture her scent—lingering on the exotic sweetness of her scent. God, he was hungry for her.

She stepped forward, her stubborn chin accentuated, the long line of her neck a creamy invitation to follow it beneath the outmoded pelisse as in his dreams. She should be dressed in the finest muslins and silks and spread on the finest sheets.

If she was his he would... But she wasn't. She was a self-contained little island still hankering after her image of perfection embodied in Henry's father. She might toy with the idea of adventure, but she was the kind of woman who probably longed for an upright, virtuous man who would fulfil her dream of stability and safety. His only role in her future was to free it to find the kind of life she so obviously wished for. Once he did that she would begin to see the world, and her prospects, quite differently. And very likely regret this moment.

He dragged in a breath, forcing it past the aching tension in his lungs. Then he tightened his hands on her arms, pushing her away.

Except that she didn't do as she ought. Her fingers dug into his coat and she raised herself on tiptoe as she had that first day in the Folly. But this time she wasn't trying to take back her property, just destroy him. All she did was tip her head ever so slightly, fitting her parted lips against his. He didn't move, but with each breath the blood rushed and fled where they touched, like a leaf buffeted in the wind. Even his heartbeat was shifting, becoming nothing more than a reflection of her warmth flowing in and out of him. It felt so good, so right, that he feared something terrible would happen if he drew away; everything would suddenly, cataclysmically, stop.

'What now?' she whispered, her voice wobbly, tickling his sensitised lips. One hand eased, moved upwards over his chest, shifting the linen of his shirt against his skin, his muscles contracting in its trail.

He tried to answer, but couldn't. Instead he did the only thing he felt capable of at that moment. He sank his hands into her hair, curving over the shape of her scalp, and kissed her.

Not the way he wanted to—that was too dangerous—but as if they both stood on a sheet of ice and any reckless movement might destroy them both. He teased her lower lip gently between his, coaxing it into pliancy before skimming her controlled upper lip with the tip of his tongue. She gave a soft murmur of pleasure, rubbing her lips against his and, without thinking, he let his hands slide down, curving over her behind and bringing her closer. Her body jerked against him and he stopped immediately, cursing himself and her. He didn't want it to end, not yet. Not ever.

But instead of drawing away, she shook her head, deepening the friction against his hands and mouth.

'No, I didn't mean to move. I couldn't help it,' she whispered. 'Please don't stop.'

A groan of agony and gratitude rumbled inside him. He *should* stop. They'd barely begun and already he was as hot as Hades and as hard as the Tor, not to mention his conscience was beating all the drums to call him back. But he couldn't. He was shifting the course of her future, but so was she.

She shuddered, moving closer, her hands rising, tangling for a moment in his neckcloth as if she would remove it, before threading into his hair. It sent streaks of pleasure over his scalp, trailing like a rain of brimstone down his body. He had been hot before, now he was on fire, and for no better reason than a half-chaste kiss.

He abandoned reason and sank into the kiss, drinking her in until she was shivering with the rhythm of his lips and tongue, her breath catching on his name as he finally drew back so they could breathe. But he didn't completely let go, toying with her lips, reluctant to break contact even to allow her to recover. He mapped them, seeing them without looking, bringing to the surface all the images he had been gathering this past week—he kissed her smile, the prim line she condensed her mouth into when she was trying not to answer Ermintrude's verbal jabs, the little dip in her upper lip where she touched her tongue when she was nervous, the way she plucked at her plump lower lip when pondering a puzzle…

He hadn't even noticed he'd registered those details, but now they rushed at him, a whole knowledge of the mouth moving against his, seeking his, seeking him. He met every one of them: tasted, coaxed, soothed, took. His hands did the same and he only stopped their roving when she squirmed closer to him, shooting sheer agonised lust in every direction from his arousal.

Disastrous, supplicating words stuck in his throat—he could almost hear his voice speaking them. But it was their condemning echo that forced him to break the kiss—this wasn't right.

You have no right.

Still, he couldn't quite let her go, so he held her there, his mouth pressed against the rapid tattoo of her pulse at her temple, breathing her in, his breath coming back to him, hot and fast and shallow and bringing with it her lily-cool scent of early spring, still carrying the winds of winter, but signalling the coming warmth and brightness of summer. She even smelled like a conflict.

And it was his job to defuse them.

'God. Ellie… This… Damn it.'

* * *

Ellie surfaced into his struggle for control, his arms already stiffening about her, the words hard against her sensitised skin.

She clasped his head, turning so that his denial was smothered against her mouth, and kissed him. It wasn't as practised as his. She pressed too hard, she could feel the pressure of her teeth against her lips, her nails edged into the soft skin at his nape.

Not yet. Please...

She only realised she'd spoken aloud when he answered her muffled cry with a rough sound, almost a growl, his hand splaying into the small of her back, as his mouth closed on hers again. She heard her own whimper of relief beneath the thudding of the pulse in her ears, her lips parting to welcome him back as if she had been waiting for him for years.

'I need to taste you, Ellie. Open for me.'

His words rumbled through her, harsh and low like distant thunder, and she obeyed. His tongue sought the heat of her mouth, a counterpoint to the hard pressure against her stomach that even in her inexperience she knew was a sign of arousal. Everywhere he touched stoked pleasure upon pleasure. His hands were mapping her, painting her into this new world, the side of her thigh, over her hip to cup her buttock and bring her closer still, then flaring up her waist until the heel of his palm brushed her breast.

She whimpered, trying to turn towards that elusive caress. She felt her breasts tighten as he stroked, his motions far too languorous for the fevered kiss, the contrast transforming her skin into a tingling fabric stretched over hot coals. When his thumb finally brushed the layers of fabric over the hardened peak, she pulled her mouth from his, turning her face into the curve of his neck at the burst of agonised pleasure.

She had never imagined it would be so exciting. That it would make her body press back of its own volition, her hips trying to meet and match that pressure, her core filling with an uncomfortable, yearning pulse.

Her hands tangled in his dark hair, her nerve ends alive with joy at finally being able to touch, to take. In a moment now he would show her where this was going, show her the beauty she knew was possible.

'Chase.' Her voice was deep and dark and not at all her own, but she hardly heard it except as an echo of yearning. 'Chase. Please…'

His curse was lost in a harsh indrawn breath and she felt her name rumble through him, his hands move roughly over her back, and she loved it. Loved the sensation of the fabric dragging against her skin, the pressure of his fingers shaping her into being, and when they sank down and gathered her behind, raising her against his body, she wrapped her arms around his neck and rose on tiptoes because she needed to be as close as she could be, breathing him in, her mouth touching the beautiful lines and the warm silk skin of his neck she'd so wanted to taste.

And she'd been so right—he tasted of her own personal heaven. She could even taste the words he was speaking against her, but then he moved, his fingers sliding into her hair, sending a burst of pleasure over her scalp and down her spine as he raised her face to his and kissed her, pressing her back against the boulders.

The world melted, there was no cold stone behind her, no rising sea breeze mixing with their scent, no faraway thunder rippling through the air—only Chase kissing her as though he needed her to survive. She melted into the sensations, not caring that she whimpered when his tongue touched hers, lighting her from within, drawing a heated surge upwards that she knew he could answer, that all she had to do was follow and he would finally show her.

She clung to him like a limpet, utterly without thought or shame. So when he suddenly shuddered and stopped she just pressed harder, but now his arms were stiff as steel around her.

'Enough. Ellie. We must stop.'

His voice was harsh and a mixture of shock and shame finally woke her. She sank back on to her heels, her hands falling from his neck. He detached his own arms and moved away from her, rubbing his jaw as if someone had just struck him.

She hadn't even noticed it had begun to rain, slow, sluggish drops tapping on her head and shoulders. He took her bonnet from where it lay on its side by a puddle on the rocks, one faded pink ribbon floating on the glinting surface.

'I'm sorry. It's wet.' His words were terse and she could hear his shame, remorse and outrage at himself.

She tied her bedraggled bonnet and searched for something to say, but nothing came.

A rumble of thunder galvanised them into action and he reached out to take her arm, but she hurried past him. When they reached the bottom of the Tor he caught her arm.

'Wait, Ellie. We must talk. I should not have done that.'

'You have nothing to apologise for. It was my choice. I told you to do it,' she replied, hiding behind the sagging straw of her bonnet.

'That is no excuse. I rarely do as I am told and I certainly have never…' He took her hands and she stared down at the hands holding hers. They were much larger and darker, and she noted that the knuckles on his right hand were rougher and that the small finger on his left hand was stiffer than the others, as if it had once been broken.

'Ellie, Listen… Oh, hell, there's Henry.'

His voice was another vibrating torture on her nerves, but before she could drag herself back into sanity, he dropped her hands and all expression left his face. She turned to see Henry riding towards them, leading a saddled mare. Behind her Chase spoke rapidly.

'Ellie. We are both leaving today, and there are some matters I must attend to which cannot be put off. But I promise it will all come right in the end... Damn and blast Henry,' he muttered as Henry reached them and dismounted.

'Trust you to go walking in the rain, Eleanor. The maid said she saw you walking towards the Tor, so I came to fetch you. The carriage will be ready in an hour and you must eat something before you go. Sorry, Chase, I didn't know you were out as well. You'd best hurry back.' He raised Ellie on to the mare in one easy motion before she could even think and then swung up himself and prodded the horses towards the Manor.

Life held greater challenges, much more serious ones than a broken heart. So why did it feel as though this pain outstripped anything she had felt before? That every yard opening between them was draining her of breath and warmth. That by the time she reached Whitworth, she might be nothing but a dried, hollowed husk.

It made no sense at all.

Chapter Fourteen

'Out of the way, Inky.' Chase removed the cat from the table and deposited her on the floor. 'You're letting her run wild, Sam. Olivia and Lucas won't thank you when they return and find their monster cat has become uncontested Queen of the Hall.'

Sam wiped her brush on a rag and sat back with a sigh. The blue drawing room had been their mother's refuge, but Sam had it cleared of everything, making room for two enormous tables and a specially commissioned slanting desk where a sketch of a mosque was waiting for its final touches.

'I don't think they will mind that as much as my indefinite presence here.'

Chase leaned against the table, measuring his response.

'Has Olivia given you any reason to feel unwelcome?'

Sam's blue-grey eyes rose to his. They used to be so expressive, but like Sinclair Hall they'd fallen into disrepair and now they just reflected a rueful weariness. Chase still hoped that, like the Hall, their old grandeur could be resurrected.

'Not at all. She has done her best to convince me I will always have a home here, but just looking at the two of them... I told Lucas I would like to have Rose Cottage. He's not happy about it, but perhaps you can convince him when you see them in Egypt.'

Chase rubbed his palms against the table edge.

'I can see why he might not be happy about that. You do know Rose Cottage was where Grandfather and Uncle John kept their stable of mistresses?'

'Over twenty years ago, Chase dear. The place is practically a ruin now, but it is close, it is large and there is no one living there who must be displaced because I'm too frightened to start my life again elsewhere. Would it be so very bad? I mean, would it cause gossip for Lucas?'

'Everything causes gossip for Lucas. For all of us. It's like swimming in gossip soup; every movement makes ripples in it.'

Sam laughed and leaned down to scratch Inky, who'd positioned herself with her rear raised defiantly in Chase's direction. Chase sighed and glanced at the illustration Sam was working on.

'You have the minaret on the wrong side.'

'What?'

'The minaret—it is on the south-west corner of the Abu Hasan mosque. That is Abu Hasan, isn't it?'

'I…yes. I forgot. Do you remember whether the arch was round or scalloped? I wanted the drawing to show Gabriel from the Desert Boy coming to seek advice from the mystic Al-Masri and I was hoping there might be a drawing in the *Description de l'Égypte*, but there isn't.'

Chase was about to answer when he stopped himself. The moment of truth was upon them.

'You'll just have to see for yourself. When you come with me to Egypt.'

Sam put down her brush and selected another, finer one.

'I don't think that is a good idea after all, Chase.'

Inky pawed the air next to Sam's knee, but was ignored and came to stand by Chase, eyeing him with her unsettling round grey eyes. Chase smiled at the feline and crouched down to pay tribute.

'Inky, do me a service and tell my sister that she wouldn't know a good idea if it jumped on to her lap and bit her. You may feel free to demonstrate my point, too.'

'They are on their honeymoon, Chase.'

'Yes, I noticed that as well. But I have a solution so you needn't expose yourself overmuch to Lucas and Olivia's turtle-dove act. I shall find you a companion. Someone nice and interesting so the two of you can go off and ignore the love-birds and that way they won't feel constrained to play nursemaid, either. It's a perfect solution.'

'A perfect solution? To saddle me with some old biddy who will complain about the heat and the flies—'

'No,' he interrupted. 'Someone young who you can take around and show her how marvellous Egypt is. You used to love it when people visited and you could take them to the bazaars and the pyramids and to the temples at Qetara.'

'You are so transparent, Chase.' Sam sighed and he clenched his jaw, but clung to his temper.

'So, you will leave me to make an awkward third all alone?'

'You at least can do as you wish once you reach Egypt and you probably will do precisely that. No doubt Oswald already requested you see to un-tangling some political knot while you are there.'

'Actually, I haven't spoken with Oswald since I arrived at Huxley and I will do my best to avoid him before my departure so that is unlikely to be the case.'

Sam snorted.

'Oswald probably knows precisely where you are and what you are doing and what you ate for breakfast and what lovely lady you have in keep-ing at the moment and you know it. I'm surprised he can even spare his key dispenser of oil upon troubled political waters for a jaunt to Egypt. Now that he has all but lost Lucas, he must be short of able hands.'

It was close enough to the truth, so Chase didn't bother denying it.

'I have no lady in keeping at the moment, thank you, and this trip to Egypt is purely personal and will remain that way, whatever our esteemed uncle's agenda. If there is one thing I learned from Oswald it is that everyone is expendable. Other than himself, of course. I have given him and the Crown the last ten years of my life and upon more than one occasion almost given them the whole of it. I think I deserve a couple of months of freedom to celebrate that decade of service. So I can assure you I won't disappear and leave you stranded with the lovebirds. I am going because I failed Huxley while he was alive, but I intend to fulfil his last wish. *We* owe Huxley that.'

'It still isn't necessary we both go. Huxley is dead, Mama is dead, everyone but the three of us are dead. I'm content here, Chase. Why must you always try to make things better? Better isn't always better, you know. Sometimes just staying where one is can be the most sensible thing to do.'

Sensible.

Sensible Sam. It was just wrong.

Sensible Sam and sensible Ellie.

Utterly, unacceptably wrong.

'I'll only be a burden there.' Sam repeated,

staring at her drawing. 'I shall have to start again on this. I cannot believe I forgot it was on the other side.'

'The colour is wrong, too.'

'It is?'

'You've been away too long. If the best you can do is copy from the likes of Burckhardt and the *Description de L'Egypte*, how much longer do you think the Desert Boy author is going to give you these commissions?' Chase said.

Watching the fear creep over his sister's face, he could see these concerns were already in her mind. He was being mean, but he couldn't help it. He felt mean.

'Sam, I need your help. Why can't—?' He broke off, sheathing his temper.

Sam turned, looking at him fully for the first time since he arrived that afternoon.

She'd been a plump child—as enthusiastic about food as about everything in life, but since her marriage she'd been steadily fading. She looked unwell, even paler than usual. Lucas and Chase had hoped her widowhood would release her, but, if anything, she'd sunk further since returning to England.

He *hated* seeing her like this. It was like watching their mother all over again. But he knew all too well that he could not save her.

He fixed problems, he did not save people.

Just as he'd fixed at least one of Ellie's problems yesterday, but that did not mean he'd saved her from the role she'd assumed in her family's life.

'I was wondering about that since you arrived, Chase. Something is wrong, isn't it? Has something happened? It isn't Lucas and Olivia?'

'No, of course not. As far as I know they are either still in Venice or on their way to Egypt.'

'Then what? Something *is* wrong. I may have become pitifully self-absorbed, but I can still tell when you are trying too hard. Just like you did with Mama. I am not like her, you know.'

'I know.'

He looked down at his boots. Inky's white-tipped tail was brushing idly at them, her eyes moving between them as if following their conversation.

'I don't think you do sometimes, Chase. But that is not the point. The point is there is something wrong with you. There is, isn't there? Are you ill... Chase, are you in trouble?'

He held out a hand at the rising concern in her voice. He had hoped to get through this without bringing himself into the equation. But perhaps that wasn't possible.

'I suppose I am. In a way. I was hoping to do this without...burdening you, but...'

'It isn't a burden if you need my help, Chase. I won't assuage your conscience by being something I do not think I can be, but I would do anything in my power to help you and Lucas, you should know that.'

Chase went to warm his hands by the fire.

He was actually afraid to speak of it, he realised. As if laying it before Sam might make it twist out of his control. Or worse—she might reflect what he least wanted to hear.

'You'll be angry with me.'

'Well, that's nothing new. You always think you know best. It is very annoying. Especially in a brother. Tell me why I shall be angry with you.'

'I want you to come to Egypt in part so I can convince someone else to come to Egypt. I'm exploiting you.'

'Someone else. Is it related to Oswald?'

'No. God, no. I wouldn't involve you in that. What the devil do you think I am?'

'Far too nice. Oswald never told you I was quite useful to him in Venice, did he?'

That knocked Chase out of his melancholy.

'What? I'll skin him alive. Don't tell me Lucas knew of this.'

'Of course not. It was a long time ago. Just some help keeping an eye on a few dignitaries who frequented the Montillio Casino. So, who is this someone else?'

'It is a little complicated. Henry Whelford is… was…well, possibly still is but only…in any case he became betrothed.'

'Oh. Is he the "someone else"? What has he to do with Egypt?'

'No, the "someone else" is his betrothed. He is about to jilt her for Dru.'

'Drusilla Ames? I always thought she was sweet on Henry. But Henry would never jilt anyone. He is far too honourable. Why, his father would leap out of his grave at the very thought. And what on earth does this have to do with you?'

Nothing and everything.

He ran his hands through his hair and told her in the basest terms about Ellie's situation, the betrothal plot, and Ellie's help in his attempt to uncover the meaning behind Huxley's letter.

'And yesterday I went with Barker to Nettleton and he paid a quick visit to the bank that holds her mortgage...' He paused, daring a glance at Sam to see what she made of his confession so far. At least he had her attention, but he wasn't certain what thoughts were behind her wide-eyed stare.

'Her mortgage,' Sam prompted.

'Yes. Well, I had Barker purchase it from the bank for me. There were other debts as well. He told the banker to inform her they'd sold the liabilities to another institution and to deliver a letter stating Whitworth...that's their family home... has been reassessed or something and that the long and short is that they are no longer under threat of foreclosure if they meet a new and more reasonable schedule of payments. I could hardly have them forgive the debt outright—that would have set all the bells pealing. Which still leaves her with a problem.'

'The new and more reasonable schedule of payments.'

'Precisely. Which led me to think…should she receive a certain salary for a position that would provide her and her family with the means to honour those payments, especially in the event the estate itself continues to face challenges?'

'I see. A position. Say, with a certain widow in need of a travelling companion?'

Chase waited for her to kick down his house of cards. It was so flimsy, he was surprised she didn't just laugh in his face, but she merely looked down, brushing at a stain of paint on her skirt.

'Tell me what she is like, my future companion.'

Chapter Fifteen

⁓⁓⁓

Chase swung off Brutus and studied the house before him. Estate management was not his forte, but even he could see it was being held together with spit and goodwill. The windows were warped, the paint was chipped and what might once have been a lawn was being methodically but not very neatly tended to by a pair of goats that raised their heads to glare at Brutus.

Brutus glared back.

Chase slung the reins over the gate and approached the next, and far more daunting, stage in his plan.

He had barely raised the knocker when the door opened and a head of grey curls, some still tied in strips of cloth, poked out and began a slow journey upwards from his boots.

'Good afternoon, is—?' Chase's polite enquiry was interrupted mid-way.

'Well! You are a very tall young…well, not-so-very young man. And well favoured, but that is beside the point. Your height, however, is not.'

'It isn't?' Chase took a step back to get a better view of the woman. She looked to be in her sixties, but with a surprisingly youthful face. He searched his memory and smiled. Aunt Florence.

'It is *precisely* the point, my tall fellow. I was searching for Hugh, but you are better. Here, take this.'

Chase automatically extended his hands and received an earthenware pot with a rather limp stalk of green.

'Slugs,' the woman announced.

'Slugs?'

'Precisely. They adore basil. You may place it there on the top shelf. This is south facing, you see.' She pointed to a wooden shelf to the side of the entrance which already held an assortment of mismatched pots. Chase went to place the pot on the top level.

'I see. You are hoping that even the most intrepid slug will tire before he scales those heights.'

'You are clever. I dare say you are married as well. Tall, well favoured, intelligent men are rather rare on the ground. Unless you have been clever enough to evade matrimony.'

'And if I have?'

'Then you may come in after you save our basil. Were you thinking of coming in or have you come to dun us? So many people do nowadays, but I warn you it will do you very little good. We are quite, quite destitute and likely to remain so for the foreseeable future. Eleanor will add you to the list, though, if you wish. It is, however, long.'

'Actually, it…'

'It is my brother's fault, of course. But we shan't speak ill of the dead, at least not in public. It is Tuesday, is it not?'

'Wednesday, I'm afraid.' Chase brushed the earth from his gloves and returned from his basil-saving mission.

'Are you afraid of Wednesdays? How peculiar.'

'Miss Walsh, I am sure this charming discourse is very effective in discouraging unwanted creditors, but I assure you I am only here as a friend of the family.'

She tugged at one of the strips of cloth, setting her curls dancing. 'How do you know my name?'

He smiled at her descent from batty to wary.

'Inference. I am utterly harmless. I merely wish to speak with Miss Walsh… The other Miss Walsh,' he amended as she opened her mouth to speak. She looked him up and down again, but there was a different quality to this inspection.

'That is a blatant untruth, young man.'

Chase blinked, taken aback for the first time since she shoved the basil pot at him.

'I assure you…'

'You may be many things, sir, but harmless is not one of them.'

'I…'

'Who are you speaking to, Aunt Flo?'

A young woman with red-brown curls and a smattering of freckles poked her head around the door. He saw the family resemblance immediately, though this young woman was shorter and plumper than Ellie. Her eyes widened as she inspected him, but the wariness remained there and she didn't give any more room in the doorway than her aunt. It reminded him of his days brokering a truce between feuding tribes near the Khyber Pass. These people were accustomed to living on disputed territory.

'He says he's a friend of the family,' said the aunt.

'Which family?'

'Precisely. But he did help with the basil. The slugs, you see.'

'It was my pleasure to do so, Miss Florence Walsh. Miss Susan Walsh.' Chase bowed to both women in turn.

Susan Walsh's eyes widened further, showing a very bright blue.

'He did that to me as well,' Florence Walsh said. 'It is very suspect. And yet he assures me he is harmless.'

'That was perhaps an unfortunate choice of words. But I stand by my statement that I am a friend of the family.'

'Are you *certain* you have the right family, sir? Walsh is a common enough name.'

'Quite certain. I am here to speak with yet another Miss Walsh. Miss Eleanor Walsh, to be precise. My name is Charles Sinclair and...'

'Chase?'

Miss Florence Walsh stood aside as Ellie opened the front door fully, her hand braced on the door jamb.

Chase had been enjoying himself with the two other Misses Walsh, but that one word was like having the cold muzzle of a gun make contact with his bare back. He went very still, every nerve end on alert, every sense strained to its maximum to prepare for danger and action. The only difference was the heated pulse that began hammering insistently and the conviction that whatever happened, no matter how much this might be a mistake, he was absolutely on the right track.

He might not be harmless, but Ellie was decidedly harmful for his equilibrium.

'Ah. Miss Walsh. Your sentries seem to think I am not to be trusted.'

'They have excellent instincts. Mr Sinclair.'

The wash of heat that spread through him at seeing her receded at the distinctly cool note in her voice. He wasn't certain what response he'd expected at turning up on her doorstep, but not to hear the same tone as at their first meeting.

The other Misses Walsh planted their hands

on their hips in unison, but Chase was no longer in the mood to be amused.

'That may be the case, but I would like a word with you, Miss Walsh. If I may.'

'And I with you, Mr Sinclair. Sue, please could you take that aptly named brute of a horse round back? I'm afraid our stables aren't up to his standards, but then I doubt Mr Sinclair will be staying long.'

Chase flexed his hands.

'Surely your groom...'

'We haven't a groom. Or a footman. And I think Cook might swoon just at the sight Satan's steed here. You needn't worry for Brutus. Sue is excellent with animals.'

'I not worried for *him*...' Before he could strike back at Ellie's jibe, Susan took Brutus's reins and began leading him off.

'Come along, Brutus, you lovely thing, you.'

To Chase's shock, his valiant steed dropped his head and followed Susan Walsh like a chastened schoolboy.

Ellie turned back into the house and Chase followed, not quite as complacently. He was tense and annoyed, but he still absorbed the shabby but neat interior. There was a single side table by the door, but other than that the narrow hallway was empty and the walls bare. Ellie led him to a room at the back which evidently had once been a large library. He looked around at the mostly empty shelves and at the large desk stacked with ledgers. There was no fire though the day was chilly, but there was a thick and rather tattered blanket draped over the chair by the desk. He closed the door and focused his attention on Ellie as she took something from the desk and sat down on one sofa, motioning him to the other. He remained standing, leaning his hands on a chair.

'So. What is all this hauteur in honour of, Ellie? Or is this how you greet all your guests?'

She held out a sheet of paper.

'I received this from the bank in Nettleton this morning.'

Ah.

'Bad news?'

'That depends. It informs me the bank has sold our mortgage and certain debts acquired from various merchants in Nettleton... But I am quite convinced I need not inform you of the particulars, Mr Sinclair. Because no sensible institution would acquire what they must know are debt of such poor quality and offer such reasonable terms unless they had an ulterior motive.'

Chase rocked the chair a little, considering his options. The temptation to dissemble was strong, but he knew lying to Ellie would come at a price. But then so would being honest.

'Is it so very obvious?'

His admission melted the ice in her eyes, but only to reveal the fury behind it.

'Obvious! I return from Huxley to face my fate after pouring out all my woes to you. After you manoeuvre Henry and Dru into each other's arms with that Mr Ambleside of yours. After you wave me on my way and tell me everything will come right in the end, which was possibly the most infuriating statement anyone has ever said to me and I am including our many creditors. And a day later I receive…this.'

The paper shook in her hands. *She* was shaking.

He tightened his hold on the chair. He wanted to go to her and take her hands, say something idiotic like 'everything will come right in the end'. Again. And she would probably hit him, box his ears with something much harder than that piece of paper.

'You had *no* right. This is *my* responsibility.'

'Technically it is your brother's.'

Well, that was a mistake.

Her eyes narrowed, the brown as hard as the Russian Steppes after a frost. She no longer looked pallid or drawn, she looked livid and ready to wage war against the hordes of hell.

'Precisely. *My* brother. You didn't even consult with me. You just swooped in and made everything right… I struggle for years and years and years and all you have to do is send in your man and your money like…like a magical sorcerer. How dare you!'

'Ellie…'

'I will pay you back. Every penny. Every blasted farthing. However long it takes.'

'Ellie, calm down…'

'No, I will not calm down! Don't you dare tell me to calm down! You think every problem can be solved with money and manipulation. Because that is all this is, Mr Sinclair. You smooth things over as swiftly as you can, arranging the world to suit you by whatever means possible, just like my father. The devil take principles if one can buy one's way to freedom.'

That stung and he stepped back, his anger finally rising to match hers.

'Would you really prefer your principles over the welfare of your family? Principles are costly, sweetheart.'

'It can be even more costly if you do not have them!'

'Well, obviously I don't, according to you, so I need not worry. I apologise for saving your family from ruin. Or should I be apologising for proving you cannot manage on your own? That you might actually need help from someone? Or especially from someone as unprincipled as a Sinful Sinclair?'

'My objection has nothing to do with your family, but with your methods. You knew I would never agree, so you stepped around me. You have put me in a…a devilish position, Mr Sinclair.'

'So I have. But you are in it and so am I. So I suggest you stop sulking and perhaps we can re-solve it together.'

'How dare you? I am *not* sulking. This is my home we are speaking of.'

'I'm well aware of that. Apparently I now own part of it.'

She surged to her feet, her expression waver-ing between shock and outrage.

'You are despicable!'

'Because I told my man of business to resolve this issue? It took me twenty minutes to explain the situation to him and cost me little more than that brute of a horse out there. Why shouldn't I have done it?'

'Because…because now I am in your debt.'

'No, you are not, your brother is. You think I am arrogant? Well, you outshine me, sweet-heart. You are merely the overly managing older sister who is too proud to admit she can't whip the world into line just as she does her little fief-dom here.'

She gave a strange little gasp and turned her head to glare at the window.

The carved moulding on the chair was biting into his palm and he eased his hold. She had every right to be upset and he had no such right. It was foolish to feel disappointment, hurt. And even more foolish to strike back.

The wood beneath his palm was shiny and

dark, worn by many hands resting on it. Her family, her home. All she had.

'It's done, Ellie. You are right, I acted hastily. But I did it in good faith.'

'I know you did.' The words were forced out. 'And I didn't mean those things I said. I know you aren't... But I cannot let it stand, can't you see that? We will repay you. Everything. But it will still take longer than your...terms.'

'Yes. Well. It need not. You see, I did have an ulterior motive. And that is why I am here.'

'An ulterior motive?'

She turned slowly, but the colour sweeping up from her neck was swift and definite. He clung to the chair again as a wave of heat swept through him, too, in the completely opposite direction. At least the chair was well placed to mask the effect she had on him. He didn't know whether to be offended or admit he was so tempted to employ any means to finally feed this insistent desire.

'It's about Sam,' he said, almost desperate to put something between him and his worst instincts. At least it caught her off guard.

'Sam? Your sister? Has something happened to her?' Her transition from anger to concern was too swift for him.

'No, no. I mean, not exactly...'

'Tea?'

They both turned as Aunt Florence's grey curls, now cloth-free, poked round the door.

'I have a tray here with a fresh pot.'

She disappeared, reappearing bearing a wooden tray with a teapot and two delicate cups adorned in pink-and-yellow roses. 'I brought out Mama's good set,' she said with a quick apologetic smile at Ellie as she placed the tray on the table beside the sofa.

'I can see that, Aunt Flo.'

'You really should light the fire Ellie. It is quite frozen in here, isn't it, Mr Sinclair? Well, I shall leave you to continue your discussion.'

Chase took the hint and went to the fireplace, taking off his gloves. There was not much kindling, but he took the tinderbox from the mantelpiece and set about lighting the fire, grateful for the activity. When the first flames licked at the twigs he stood and brushed his hands.

'Which one of us was she checking on?'

'Both. No doubt everyone is in the kitchen, trying to make head or tails of your visit. They know something happened at the bank today and naturally the appearance of a strange man here is further cause for concern.'

'Haven't you told them?'

'Only that we have more time. I did not know what to say. I knew something was wrong when Mr Soames called on us, but I never guessed... Until I heard your voice and then... Well, once I made the connection it was rather obvious, just like Mr Ambleside. What is it you wished to say, about your sister? And ulterior motives? I would rather know the worst as soon as possible, if you don't mind.'

He rubbed his jaw, the stubble rasping against his palm. To think he'd risen at the crack of dawn to reach Whitworth at a reasonable hour only to come under more attacks than he'd had to cope with since he was caught in the middle of a tribal war in Afghanistan.

'And I would like to have some tea, if you don't mind. I've spent nigh on five hours on a horse and I'm tired, thirsty and being turned to ice when all I wanted to do was serve you a good turn...' He held up his hands, bringing himself to a halt. It was all true, but that wasn't what had him teetering on the edge of an abyss he didn't want to look into. He needed something a hell of a lot stronger than tea.

She swallowed and went to pour the tea.

'You must think me dreadfully ungrateful,'

The tea was hot and sweet and it reminded him of the tea they made on campfires during the war—coarse but precious in its rarity, a link to another life, to safety.

'I think you're frightened,' he said.

The delicate cup wavered in her hand and she gave a little squeak as tea sloshed over the rim on to her dress. The brownish patch spread on the dull muslin, clinging to her thigh. He pulled out his handkerchief and handed it to her, waiting for her to do what anyone would do—take the handkerchief, blot at the moisture, be annoyed or embarrassed. She didn't even put down her cup, just stared at the stain.

'Ellie?'

Nothing.

He placed the handkerchief on the stain, took her free hand and pressed it down on it. It was bad enough touching her hand—blotting her damp thigh was beyond him at the moment. She finally surfaced, clasping the linen and patting at the tea.

'I don't have any whisky or…or port to offer you. We don't keep any.'

'I don't need any, not yet anyway. We are not celebrating quite yet. But I do need you to drink your tea and listen to what I am proposing. It is nothing awful, I assure you. This isn't one of those pacts with the evil sorcerer like in your favourite novels. No handing over your first born or being forced to eat your sprouts…'

Her lips curved upwards.

'That would be awful. I hate sprouts.'

'You can give me yours then, I'm actually partial to them.'

Her nose wrinkled and he resisted the urge to run his finger down it.

'Sprouts aside, are you ready to listen?'

She finally met his eyes.

'Yes. What did you mean, about your sister?'

'I told you we were to go to Egypt?'

Her hand closed about his handkerchief and she nodded once.

'Yes. I was certain you would be on your way already.'

'That was the plan.' He winced at the murky territory of half-lies he was entering. He was truly losing his skills; he never used to mind blurring the truth. 'Sam, however, is baulking at the fence. I told you she is very wary of leaving Sinclair Hall, but that the one thing that still occupies her are her illustrations. I have very callously pointed out that if she doesn't soon go and refresh her memory of the places which inspire her illustrations, she might put her commission at risk.'

'Chase…'

'Yes, I know. I am a horrible brother. However, it had its effect. She is inclined to agree, but she doesn't want to play gooseberry to my newlywed brother and his wife and I can see her point. Olivia, Lady Sinclair, is lovely, but she and Lucas are rather disgustingly in love and even Inky, their cat, finds them rather too much at the moment. Their first night at Sinclair Hall, that monstrous feline deposited a dead mouse in their bed to show her displeasure at their new living arrangements.'

Ellie's smile widened, her lips parting and the firelight infusing some gold into her eyes.

'Perhaps this Inky saw it as a housewarming gift?'

'Perhaps. It *was* still warm, according to Lucas.' Chase grinned at her laugh. 'Whatever Inky's internal monologue, the fact remains that Sam is worried.'

'But *you* will be with her.'

'Yes, but I'm merely a brother and she is convinced I might be distracted by other concerns... *family* business concerns,' he emphasised as the narrowing of her eyes indicated precisely what she thought might distract him. 'I happen to represent my uncle's interests in various areas of the world and it is true that I might have to absent myself on occasion. So I suggested we find her a companion. Someone who could go about with her to visit all those places she wishes to inspect for her illustrations and who might have the patience to explore with her and perhaps sit and read while she sketches. Olivia and Lucas might be willing to do these things with her, but she will never ask it of them. A paid companion, however, would be another matter entirely.

'Chase—'

'It is a perfect solution for both of you,' he interrupted before she could voice objections. 'That way I needn't saddle her with a complete stranger who will probably faint at the first challenge Egypt is likely to throw at her. You said you wanted to go there and I know full well you meant it.'

'Yes, but... This isn't a game, Chase. All those...

Madame Ambrosia the occultist and the pugs, and the governess to the future King of the Purple Mountains or whatever, those were jests…just foolish nonsense. You cannot be serious. Besides, this is no solution to the problem you… A companion's wages would not even make a dent in what we owe you.'

He surged to his feet, putting some distance between her and his need to shake some sense into her.

'This is my sister I am talking about! Do you think it makes any difference to me if it is ten pounds or ten thousand? There are only two people on this earth whose welfare is my concern and one doesn't need me and I am failing the other. I would give my last farthing if I thought it could…'

He shoved his hands through his hair and went to the window. It overlooked what might also once have been a pleasant lawn, but was now a large kitchen garden planted around a twisted apple tree already covered in buds. Bathed in soft sunlight it looked inviting, hiding the effort he knew must go into maintaining this sagging home and estate. Why the devil did she have to be so stubborn?

He'd just lied, but it wasn't the lie that was choking him, it was the reality behind that lie— there were no longer two people, but now three in his circle of care.

He heard her come to stand on the other side of the window, but didn't turn.

'We started that garden with Mr Whelford,' she said. 'He knew he was ill and he knew he could not help us settle our debts, but he could help me prepare to live with them.'

He looked away from the garden. He did not want to hear about Arthur Whelford's many virtues at the moment.

'I'm well aware my pecuniary gesture doesn't sit on the same heavenly level as Whelford's moral support.'

She sighed and returned to sink on to her chair, rubbing at the tea stain. 'That is not what I meant. I merely wanted to explain… How could I leave them?'

He leaned one hand on the windowsill and took another cautious step on to thin ice.

'They were alone while you were at Huxley.'

'Well, yes, but that was only to be for a few weeks and it was a mere carriage ride away. This would be… I don't even know how long.'

'Two, maybe three months, depending on the voyage.'

Maybe a voyage was not a smart word to use quite yet. Her fingers worked the handkerchief even more briskly at the stain. The poor muslin would likely disintegrate any moment. Not that he would mind…

He forced his gaze back to her face. Her teeth

were pulling at her lower lip, leaving it reddened and damp, and he cursed silently and resumed his station behind the chair.

'At the risk of offending you as I once did, I would hazard a guess they managed quite well without you. Judging by my welcoming committee outside, at least two of the Walsh clan are more than capable, especially now you no longer have any pressing financial concerns.'

As if on cue, the door opened once more and this time it was Susan who entered with a tray.

'Aunt Flo thought you might like to try the first of the season's strawberries. They are a little tart, but lovely. And Hugh and I brushed down Brutus and put a blanket on him in the stable, Mr Sinclair, so you needn't worry. Will you stay for supper? Cook says she can wring Gaspard's neck if we are entertaining.' She grinned at Chase's expression. 'Gaspard is our goose. But I think Cook's pie is just as good as a roast goose and will be ready far sooner. She's from the West Country, you see.'

'I would prefer no one's neck is wrung on my behalf. I am staying at the Green Man in Nettleton and they can feed me.'

'Not as well as Cook's pie.'

'Were you in charge when your sister was at Huxley, Miss Walsh?' Chase asked Susan before Ellie could send her away. Susan cast Ellie a look and Ellie shrugged.

'Well, not in charge. No one was in charge, not like Ellie is. Edmund and I looked after the books and went round the tenants, and Anne helped Aunt Flo and Cook in the kitchen and the gardens and saw to Hugh's lessons.'

'Thank you for the strawberries, Sue,' Ellie said. 'And tell Cook the pie will be quite sufficient.'

Susan left with obvious reluctance and Chase smiled at Ellie's glower and took one of the strawberries. They were still a little hard, but surprisingly sweet. Rather like Ellie.

'Delicious. Try them.'

'I picked them. Mr Sinclair…'

'Chase. You know I'm right. Your siblings will not only survive, but probably thrive. Not despite you, but because of you. I will have my priceless man of business Mr Barker keep an eye on them and report to us and ensure nothing terrible happens to them. Come. Aside from everything else, don't you wish to see Huxley's quest through to the end?'

She clutched her hands before her.

'What if your sister dislikes me?'

'She won't.'

'You don't *know* that. I'm not…exciting or fashionable or anything a companion should be. I will bore her within five minutes.'

'You certainly don't bore me and I'm a far flightier fellow than Sam. Besides, you forget she has spent almost three years now immured at Sinclair Hall and right now her only companion is a very complacent and opinionated cat. You don't have much competition.'

'But...'

'Ellie. All I am asking is that you give her a mere three months of what I profoundly hope will be your very long life. You will travel to Egypt with a woman who needs help and a man who has run out of ideas how to help her. You will see the pyramids and temples and curse the flies and sand and travel on a *dahabiya* up the Nile. Not only you will never forget this trip and provide your siblings with marvellous letters to look forward to and tales to enjoy upon your return, but you will have thoroughly earned every last penny of your companion's wages. Can you honestly turn your back on my proposal and live with the regret?'

Her hands were bunched into fists on her thighs and her eyes were shooting jade and gold darts at him and he knew he had won this battle.

She stood, tossing his crumpled handkerchief on to the table like a gauntlet.

'You are thoroughly, unashamedly devious, Chase Sinclair. And you call *me* managing!'

Chapter Sixteen

'Our course is set for an uncharted sea…' murmured a voice behind Ellie as she looked out over the endless teal blue.

Her hands tightened on the ship's railing as her nerves sang and danced with the wind and the waves. She'd hoped the internal cacophony Chase's presence sparked in her might calm a little after two weeks spent in relatively close proximity on HMS *Seahawk*, but she'd been sadly wrong.

Not that she saw much of him, not with Lady Samantha falling ill the very night they sailed from Portsmouth. At first Ellie was convinced it was the sea sickness she herself had been so worried she would succumb to, but the ship's surgeon quickly declared it a bad case of influenza exacerbated by exhaustion.

Without even discussing the arrangement, Chase took night duty while Ellie spent her days in Sam's cabin, often reading to her from Sam's collection of Desert Boy books while Inky curled up on the bed, alternately napping and staring at Ellie as she read with a disconcerting one-eyed squint, like a suspicious chaperon trying not to nod off.

Ellie's fears that Sam would resent being dependent upon a stranger soon faded. She was surprisingly easy to talk to, perhaps because Ellie felt she knew the young woman from Huxley's notebooks, or perhaps it was that strange Sinclair charm that enticed trust even when there was no evidence to back it.

As for Chase, she only met him between their shifts, or sometimes on deck when they came up for air. And every time she saw the worry on his face she wanted to put her arms around him and tell him it would be all right. She knew she'd only just met his sister and was seeing her at her worst, but she saw what Huxley depicted so clearly in his notebooks—Sam was strong and stubborn— she would cling to the cliff face even with rocks tumbling down about her.

But Chase never gave her an opening. He'd changed again since they embarked at Portsmouth—he might still tease and charm and continue his embellishments on *A Thousand and One Absurd Ways to Travel to Egypt* when their paths crossed, but she might just as well have been Fenella. The message was eminently clear—

whatever had happened at Huxley, remained at Huxley.

It was sweet torture being with him and being kept firmly in her place, but she didn't regret one second of her time with him. Ellie's revelation from Huxley's study held—she might be confused, frustrated, worried, but she wasn't lonely. His mere presence filled spaces in her she hadn't even known existed. Sometimes she felt she knew him better than the new person she was becoming in his company.

'So, what have you done with the pugs this morning, Madame Ambrosia?' Chase said as she remained silent. 'Did you feed them to the sharks?'

'No, the captain put them in a longboat and cast them out to sea. He said if their carousing with Inky kept him awake one more night, we'd likely run aground. The last I saw of them they were asking directions of a mermaid.'

He smiled at her latest embellishment, resting a hand on the railing next to her.

'You are becoming quite adept at this. There is hope for you yet, Miss Ellie Walsh. How is Sam this morning? Did she sleep?'

The wind blew his dark hair against his forehead and her hands twitched with the need to brush it aside. She hoped she didn't look as exhausted as he, weariness deepening the shadows under his eyes and deepening the creases by his mouth. But then last night was the first night he'd spent in his own cabin and not in the hammock strung in Sam's.

'Better than you by the looks of it. In fact, she was still asleep when I left. And she ate a good dinner which is an excellent sign.'

'Yes. I was beginning to worry I had made a grave error, forcing her to come. I've never seen her so ill. There were nights I considered forcing the captain to put us ashore…anywhere.'

'I know. She said you offered to, but she told you not to.'

He rubbed at the dark wood of the railing and Ellie resisted the urge to cover his hand with hers.

'I never meant for your companion's role to turn into that of a nursemaid. I haven't thanked you for being so patient with her. With me. I know I haven't been very entertaining…'

'You cannot be serious, Chase. I came to act as companion…'

'But not as nursemaid.'

'That is part of what being a companion is, is it not? Compared to my siblings, tending to her has been a holiday. I've done little more than read to her and talk. She is an excellent listener. Is that a family trait?'

'But Sam has no ulterior motive when she listens. Unlike me she is genuinely interested in people.'

She sighed. 'Of course, how could I have forgotten you have an ulterior motive for everything you do.'

He did not answer and she wished she hadn't succumbed to being snide again.

'That was foolish of me, Chase. I have been meaning to show you something, but I felt it was not right while Lady Samantha was so ill.'

'Show me something?'

'Yes. May I?'

For a moment he just stood looking down at her. It was like being on the Tor again, pinned by his gaze as the world receded. The emptiness around them only made it worse—the sense that only he mattered, that her compass would seek him for ever.

Then the ship angled into the wind, the deck shifting beneath her feet, and he held out his arm.

'Show me.'

'Look.'

Chase looked at Ellie. She was unwrapping an object from a strip of flannel, but all he saw was her smile and once again his heartbeat shot forward like one of Napoleon's cannonades. When would his body remember he was thirty and not thirteen?

This was his first time in her cabin. It was smaller and substantially tidier than Sam's and he tried very hard not to look at the narrow, neatly made bed and think about what it might look like when it was not so neat, or empty.

Her scent caught him immediately, soft and soothing, and addictive. Every evening he'd come to replace her in Sam's cabin they'd discussed Sam's progress in the corridor and he would fill himself with that scent like the Bedouin filling their water gourds at the desert well.

The thought that one day he would have to do without it, without her, was becoming increasingly an impossibility, less reasonable than mermaids and sprites and turning back time.

'Chase?'

He caught himself, forcing his gaze to the alabaster vase in her hands.

'You brought the vase with you?'

'When I took it out at home, the stopper fell off and I found these inside. They might be nothing, but I did not wish to read them without your approval.'

She turned over the vase and several rolled-up strips fell on to the wooden table.

'Read them, Ellie.'

'Are you certain?'

'Of course. This is as much your quest now as mine. Read them.'

'Very well. Here… This one looks like the note in the book of hours. *"Saqqara most definitely. Timing of stay in White Desert should settle the question definitively. Have Chase ask Poppy."'*

She looked up but he motioned her to unroll the next.

'This is a reference to a book, see? It reads: *"Yes—this. Page ninety-seven, paragraph three. It strikes clean to my heart. I wonder if it could have been that all along."'*

As she unrolled the third small scroll he noted it wasn't paper, but papyrus. The ink, too, was older, a little faded, and the handwriting was not Huxley's, but a more precise and legible hand.

He reached for it, but not before she read the words aloud.

"'One vessel for all you gave and one vessel for all I could not give. To carry that part of my soul that will always be yours in friendship and gratitude. Tessa...'"

Her voice faded on the name and she let go and it rolled back into shape. Very carefully she put them back inside and held the vase out to him. He shook his head.

'Keep it. I gave it to you.'

'But I cannot. This meant something to her. To him. The other two notes might refer to his search for the anonymous author, but not this last note. And not the vase—it was obviously something precious to him if he sent its twin to Egypt with Mallory. It belongs to your family. Please take it.'

Once again he closed her hands around it and this time it was worse. The temptation to go down on his knees right there and beg was so powerful it choked him.

But his mother's words stung hard. *Friendship and gratitude*. He'd gained those from Ellie, he knew that. But he wanted more. A life's worth more than that. And it terrified him that like his mother's unsettling message to Huxley, this might be all the woman he loved could give him. He would not risk what he held, not until he was certain…

'I want you to keep it with you for now, Ellie. You are an inseparable part of this.'

Chapter Seventeen

'I promised you that if we made it to Egypt, I would take you to the pyramids, Miss Ellie Walsh, and I am a man of my word. Mostly. So? What do you think of them?'

Ellie heard Chase's question, but could not answer. It was a good thing the small mare she was mounted on was of a slothful disposition, because had the horse decided to bolt she probably would have fallen off in her stupefaction.

None of the illustrations or the descriptions in Huxley's notebooks or the Desert Boy books truly prepared her for Egypt.

They'd left Portsmouth under a sodden blanket of fog and now the world looked like it had never met a cloud, let alone a drop of rain. It was barely past dawn, the sun not yet more than a sulking smear on the far side of the Nile, half-hidden by a row of date palms, but it was already pleasantly warm and the sandy plain between them and the horizon looked as hard and inhospitable as Lady Ermintrude's dining room.

And then there were the pyramids.

They made no sense whatsoever.

In illustrations they looked impressive, but it had never occurred to her to question how they were possible any more than she would question a cathedral or a castle.

But now that they stood before her she realised they *were* impossible.

In fact, almost everything in the past weeks felt impossible.

'I think I might be dreaming.'

She hadn't meant to say the words aloud, but Chase laughed and Sam turned in her saddle and smiled as well, the first unforced, purely joyous smile she had seen on the woman's face since they boarded the *Seahawk*. And as if something inside Ellie had been waiting for it, a knot inside her unravelled with an almost audible sigh.

'Is it a good dream at least?' Chase asked.

'The very, very, very best. At the moment I feel capable of living up to your Madame Ambrosia occultist fantasy and leading us all to a fabled treasure.'

'Lead on, Madame Ambrosia. Just don't expect me to do the digging. After that voyage I need a rest cure and so do you.'

'This is better than any rest cure. Perhaps I have the fever, too, because from the moment we disembarked nothing feels quite real and the pyramids look taller than anything on earth.'

'They are.' Chase answered. 'Napoleon said he calculated there are enough stones in that big one to build a wall nine feet high and three feet thick around all of France.'

'That is a great many stones.' She gaped. 'But how do *you* know what Napoleon said?'

'What a suspicious mind you have, sweetheart. Since he made that comment some two decades ago I assure you I wasn't a fly on that wall.'

The endearment, casual though it was, sent her heart thumping and a flush wholly unrelated to the rising sun spilled heat through her body, making her feel like a parched plant under a long-delayed rainfall.

But beyond that was the reminder of the other Chase, who dealt with secrets and quests. The one who just yesterday introduced her to his brother and his wife with cool respect as if she was precisely what her role purported—a favoured connection of Henry's and now companion to Sam. This Chase was here to help his sister and satisfy Huxley's wishes, not to fulfil her own unrealistic fantasies, and she had best remember that.

'I quite thought the moment we disembarked you would go directly to find Mallory and Huxley's box.'

She felt him measuring his answer as he patted his mare's perspiring neck.

'I wouldn't dare open the box without you after all your efforts; no doubt Madame Ambrosia would cast a curse upon me at the mere thought. But I could hardly renege on my promise to show you the pyramids and today we are invited to attend a ball at Jasperot's. I doubt another day or so will make a difference. Tomorrow we leave for Qetara and hopefully we shall find the box safely awaiting our arrival.'

'Did you tell your brother everything when we arrived yesterday?'

'Everything?' The corner of his mouth twitched.

'About the letter and the notebooks and…the rest.'

'The rest being your little sham with Henry?'

'Yes.' She flushed.

'Yes.'

'Oh. He was very nice to me, though.'

'Of course he was. We Sinclairs know full well not to condemn others for not being completely straightforward with the world. I also told him how grateful we are to you for helping Sam during the voyage. Had you not been there I honestly don't know if I would have found the fortitude not to disembark at the first port and board the first ship back to England.'

'Poor Sam, I was tempted to suggest returning to England myself, I felt so very guilty.'

'Why guilty?'

'I was hoping so hard she would not ask to

return because *I* did not wish to return. It was selfish of me.'

There, it was out. She hunched her shoulders, waiting for his condemnation.

'Good. About time you were selfish. And though I don't want to tempt the fates, this is the first time in years I've seen her look a little like her old self. So perhaps our selfishness will yet bear unselfish fruit.'

'*You* weren't being selfish.'

'Wasn't I?'

'No. Had you been selfish you would have left her safely in England and me to my fate and come to find the package on your own, so please stop trying to convince me you are something you are not.'

'Far be it from me to convince you I'm not something I am.'

She sighed.

'I see now we are safe on dry land you have donned your rogue's façade once more.'

'No, my dear, now that you are under the aegis of Lady Samantha Sinclair and not mine I no longer must be on my best behaviour.'

His eyes were narrowed against the glare and Ellie could read nothing but the usual light-hearted humour in the curve of his mouth. Then the moment was gone as Sam slowed her horse to join them.

'The pyramids are amazing, aren't they?' she

said with more warmth in her voice than Ellie had heard during the whole voyage. 'I hadn't quite remembered how enormous they are. How on earth did we make it to the top, Chase?'

'Edge and I only made it to the top because you climbed up and were too scared to come down alone,' he replied and Ellie wondered if Sam heard the strain under his teasing, but Sam laughed, her eyes more blue than grey.

'I was not! I was merely tired and resting... Oh, very well, I was a little frightened. It seemed so unbearably high and I was thirsty and...'

'And as you said at the time it was all Edge's fault for telling you not to climb it in the first place.'

Sam's smile dimmed.

'Yes. I often blamed him for my mistakes, didn't I? I was quite a trial for all of you.'

'No, you weren't,' Chase said hurriedly, but Sam merely shrugged and nudged her horse forward again.

'Blast,' Chase muttered, a frown sharpening the already hard-cut line of his profile as he watched his sister.

'Give her time, Chase.'

She wasn't prepared for the swift return of his gaze to hers and her hands tightened on her reins in shock at the searing heat in his gaze. But then he looked away and for a moment neither spoke as their horses continued to pick their way over the rough ground. They had left the rows of palms and the fields behind and now there was only rock and sand before them with the pyramids rising starkly against the pale blue sky. A trickle of perspiration ran down her back and she shifted, wishing she could wear the colourful cotton robes Hamid and Youssef wore.

'Oh, look! Is that the Sphinx?' she gasped. It said much for how overwhelmed she was by the majesty of the pyramids and the jumble of her own emotions that she only now saw the imposing statue. The only excuse for her oversight was that the stone was the same colour as the pyramids and half-sunk in the undulating sand.

'Can we go see it?' she asked and his mouth quirked and she could almost see him visibly unravelling his tension.

'Later. Hamid wants us in and out of the pyramid before someone decides we can't.'

'Why would they?'

'Because though Muhammad Ali is uncontested ruler, there are endless squabbles about who is in charge of the antiquities. Every time you want to look at a stone you have to secure a *firman* and pay at least a dozen officials from the local *Shaykh* to the regional *Kashif* and up to whoever is in the Viceroy's favour at the moment. It's a business and as confusing as hell. Jasperot arranged this visit, but Hamid wants us in and out before someone pulls their weight and says we cannot. You may thank Jasperot nicely at the ball this evening.'

'But I cannot go to a ball,' Ellie said, appalled.

'Why not? Do they throw you out in a rash?'

'They wouldn't take me in long enough to throw me out. I haven't anything suitable to wear.'

'We shall find something suitable, don't worry.'

'But...'

'You may argue with me later. For now, your only task it to enjoy yourself.'

Her horse drew to a halt and she realised with some surprise they had reached the base of the largest pyramid. She leaned back to take in the full measure of the structure, still shocked by its immensity, but now she could see that it wasn't smooth at it appeared from a distance. The large warm-coloured stones created an uneven surface though at the very top there were remains of a paving that she imagined had once covered the whole of the structure.

'How on earth did Sam climb——?' She broke off with a squawk as Chase grasped her waist, lowering her to the pebbled ground. There was nothing truly improper about helping a woman down from her mount, but when her feet touched the ground his hands softened on her waist, but did not let go. She looked up and was speared on the steel grey of his narrowed eyes, the half-smile that parted his lips jolting her with memories of the kisses that plagued her dreams.

It was the first time he'd touched anything but her arm since England and the storm of heat whipping up inside her had nothing to do with the desert sun. It was lucky her hands were still clinging to the reins because it was the tug of leather and her mare's snort that stopped her hands midway to his chest.

'So, you're glad you agreed to come to Egypt?' His voice was a rasp of velvet on her skin and the hair on her nape rose, her nerve ends stuttering with excited need.

'I still think I must have been mad, but I am so happy,' she admitted, unable to keep her joy out of her voice. She saw his chest rise and fall, his eyes skate over her face and rest on her mouth, and her lips felt parched and salty and practically begging to be licked. Her tongue pressed against her teeth as her own gaze settled on his mouth. She was not lost enough to think he might kiss her there, in full view of everyone, but it felt as though he had to. He could not prevent this from happening again.

Finally.

She must have lost a moment in time because his hands were no longer holding her and instead of kissing her Chase was handing their reins to the guide. She stood where she was, her heart thudding so powerfully she felt it could reduce the ageless structure that loomed over them to a tumble of stones. Then she heard Sam call her name and she moved.

Chase handed the reins to Youssef and watched as Ellie joined Sam and Lady Sinclair where Hamid was explaining about the pyramid. He wasn't surprised Olivia and Ellie took to each other so well and so swiftly. Olivia might be an heiress, but her life had been anything but simple and her mind was as sharp as Ellie's. Seeing the three women together, he was more than ever convinced he had been right to bring Ellie to Egypt.

Even if it meant remaining in a constant state of frustration.

He'd been smarter than he thought, erecting a wall between them during the voyage because clearly he had absolutely no self-control around her. A few smiles and a little warmth in her voice and he was ready to go down on his knees in the sand and beg.

And ready to bend the rules. Holding her like that, even with the bulk of his horse shielding them from their view, was an invitation for disaster, but at that moment he hadn't cared. Heat—animal, undeniable, possessive—overtook all else. It was still lashing about in him, like waves in a storm caught between the rocks.

He wanted to taste that pleasure on her curving lips, to lick the salty perspiration instead of her wiping it from her cheek. To taste her. Everywhere. Hell, after a month being on the same ship with her, but acting as if they were mere acquaintances, he was starving. It was like crossing the desert with a sealed bottle of water and knowing he was dying, but could not drink a drop.

All he wanted was a drop.

The tiniest brush of her mouth over his…

Liar.

You want to empty that bottle and lick the…

'Coming, Chase?' Lucas prompted and Chase scuffed his boot on the pebbled ground.

He was bursting to come, blast the woman. Another four weeks of this and he would need medical attention.

'Hamid says he has checked the passages and they are clear up to the main shaft. I could do without another visit inside, but Sam is determined to see it again and Olivia is curious so I will have to resign myself to squeezing through that spine-cracking passage,' Lucas said as Chase joined the group at the base of the stones, his careful avoidance of looking at Chase telling in itself.

'Do you think Miss Walsh would like to enter or would you two prefer to continue your… discussion out here?'

'I hope you crack your head on one of the granite blocks in there, Lucas.'

Lucas grinned.

'Just getting a little of my own back, little Brother. You were more than a little smug when

Olivia was putting me through hell. Ah, I see Sam convinced Miss Walsh. What a pity for you.'

Chase didn't answer. There was no point. All his protestations—to himself and to Lucas—had foundered the instant his hands closed on Ellie's waist. The sheer joy he felt at seeing her so...alive, so full of pleasure and excitement and knowing that he had given her this moment. He wanted to give her so much more—he wanted to give her the life she deserved.

And that was the problem.

He was still no nearer being certain he had a role in the life she deserved.

'I like her. So does Olivia, which is impressive, she is usually quite wary of new people.' Lucas's black eyes were narrowed against the rising sun, giving nothing away, but Chase knew him too well to try to avoid this conversation.

'You needn't warn me to behave, Lucas. I have no intention of doing Miss Walsh any harm.'

'I know that. At the moment I am more concerned with your welfare than hers.'

Chase looked away and Lucas whistled.

'I'm surprised the Sphinx hasn't picked up its skirts and run off the way you're glaring at it, Chase.'

Chase directed his glare at his brother.

'It was a long voyage, that is all. There were times when I seriously considered forcing the captain to take us to the nearest port and boarding the first ship back to England. I didn't know if Sam was truly ill or... Ellie said it might be that everything Sam had held inside was finally forcing its way through. I only know those first two weeks are a hellish blur.'

'I am glad you weren't alone with her, then. I feel guilty that all along I was in Venice with Olivia being thoroughly self-indulgent.'

'Nonsense. You two deserved your time together. We made it safely and Sam looks... almost like Sam.'

'She sounds more like herself, too. You, however...'

'Oh, go sit on an obelisk, Lucas.'

Hamid led the way up the uneven blocks to the passage leading into the heart of the pyramid. The last time they were here was over a decade ago with Huxley, Poppy, Edge and a few others and Chase could already see the difference—it was now a site for curious travellers, not merely scholars, officials and hopeful plunderers. There were signs of many people moving around the flattened earth and the mounds of shifting sands that covered the lower parts of the pyramids were partially cleared away so they could be approached without climbing.

Ellie didn't need his help, but Chase still placed himself behind her as she followed Sam inside. Immediately the temperature dropped and the cadence of the desert emptiness was replaced with the echoing, almost underwater sensation of the narrow tunnels.

Ellie trailed her fingers along the gritty stone walls and he saw she had removed her gloves and immediately did the same. Even if he could not take her hand as Lucas held Olivia's, if Ellie did need assistance he had a perfectly valid reason to touch her. It was pathetic and childish, but that was what he was reduced to at the moment.

No one spoke as they hunched over to climb through the shaft leading to the large inner chamber. In this position Chase could enjoy the sight of Ellie's lushly rounded posterior as she went ahead of him. He realised with some satisfaction that she'd lost the strained pallor and slenderness of only a month ago, her face and figure now gently rounder...

He lowered his eyes to the passage floor and blessed the cool air and darkness which became heavier as the light from outside was replaced by the light of the torches carried by Hamid and Youssef. Sound also hollowed out, their shoes and boots clicking and scraping on the stone floor until they finally reached the King's Chamber.

Just like the first time he entered here, he had a sense of loss. Unlike many of the beautiful tombs he'd seen elsewhere in Egypt, this chamber was surprisingly bare but for a large stone sarcophagus which stood in the middle—plain, empty, lidless and cracked.

'Perhaps if not for grave robbers this burial chamber would still be full of treasure,' Hamid said into the silence, his voice deeper in the enclosed space.

'Hardly likely,' Chase said drily. 'Had Napoleon found anything in here, it would now be in Paris.'

'Napoleon was inside this very chamber?' Ellie whispered, her fingers hovering above the cracked lip of the sarcophagus.

'He was, Aanisah Walsh,' Hamid answered. 'He stood here alone in this chamber and came out as white as a sun-bleached shroud.'

Chase shot Hamid a frown, but Ellie merely drew closer to Hamid, her eyes widening, their colour more amber than gold in the torchlight. He should have known she would be more allured than alarmed by such tales.

'Why? What happened to him in here?'

'He never said, Aanisah Walsh. Some say a vision of Alexander the Great told him he would be just as illustrious one day.'

Chase crossed his arms.

'Unfortunately that was almost the truth. The French are certainly still strong in Egypt, despite losing the war.'

Youssef nodded. 'Yes, and Drovetti is Consul-General again, though he was Napoleon's man.

These French, they like the gifts he sends from the temples so much they forgive him. They are as greedy as the British Museum, but much more willing to pay. Every day another ship departs with treasures.'

'Perhaps it is good Edge disappeared off the face of the earth. He would have an apoplexy at the thought of where we have come.' Sam sighed, shaking her head, and Hamid smiled.

'It is true. He and Effendim Carmichael did not like it when the others moved statues and took treasures, though Monsieur Jasperot is only too happy to provide gifts for the Bourbon King, and even Mr Mallory may have a hand in this now.'

'Mallory? Cousin Huxley's secretary? Is he in Egypt?' Sam asked in surprise.

'He came through Cairo on his way to Qetara, Aanisah Sam. I told you, al-Jinn Chase, yes? I heard Sir Henry asked him to oversee a shipment destined for the great museum in England when he returns. Jasperot is to excavate the tomb of the bulls near Saqqara. Remember, Aanisah Sam? The one you and Effendim Edge fell in all those years ago? Only now did Jasperot receive the *firman* to open it and he was most delighted to discover it had not been plundered meanwhile. He and Consul-General Salt arranged for Effendim Mallory to accompany a shipment to your museum. But you shall see him yourself soon.' Hamid smiled. 'It is good you are all back. It has been too long. Tomorrow we go to Qetara to visit your mother's resting place. It is sad Effendim Huxley's body could not be in its proper place there, too. But though his body may be in your country, his soul is in mine. Come, it is time to leave.'

Chase did not turn with the others or notice as someone came to stand beside him at the lip of the empty sarcophagus.

'Chase? Is something wrong?'

'I forgot.'

'Forgot what?'

He took a step back from the sarcophagus so he could not see into its blank emptiness. He should tell Ellie he needed to be utterly alone for a moment, because that was how it should be.

'My mother is buried in Qetara. In the garden of Bab el-Nur, the house owned by Huxley and Carmichael.'

It wasn't something one forgot. Perhaps forgot was the wrong word. He had not thought of it, not since the news of Huxley's death, perhaps not for longer than that, he couldn't even remember when he had last thought of that little temple at the end of the gardens. One of the original reasons to come to Egypt was to visit her grave with Lucas and Sam. But it had gone clean out of his mind until that moment.

He shook his head.

'Come. Time to go.'

Other than Youssef and the torch the others were already quite far ahead and the silence was almost absolute other than the muted scuffle of their shoes.

Which was probably why her cry caught him completely off guard.

'Chase!'

'What is it?' He turned abruptly, completely forgetting to mind the low ceiling, and slammed his head into the granite. *'Yina'al abuk wa abu abuk,'* he cursed in Arabic, gritting his teeth.

'Oh, no. Are you hurt? I'm so sorry. Here, let me see.'

'Hell, I'm not six years old...' He breathed deeply. 'What made you cry out?'

'Nothing. I mean, it just came to me. The initials in that note we found in the book of hours. Are you certain you are not badly hurt?'

'I will survive, but save your explanation and your *eureka* moments for when we are safely outside.'

When he could stand straight he rubbed his head and Ellie stopped beside him, looking charmingly contrite.

'Now, what revelation merited a cracked skull?'

Her mouth wavered into a smile, but she repressed it, which was just as well.

'It occurred to me as Sam and Hamid were talking—I remembered the initials. On Huxley's note. I'd almost forgotten.'

'The initials.'

'You must remember that note we found in the book of hours with the image of the bull and the jagged pyramid and the eight letters—J M P S C L E.'

'How on earth did you remember those letters?' he asked, surprised. That particular note had caught his attention as well, but it should hardly have had the same impact on her.

'The way I remember most tasks at home—I create an image around them. In this case a bull jumping over a scale poised on the tip of a pyramid.'

'A what?'

'The letters—*J M P S C L E*. Jump Scale. Without the *U* and *A*. And the bull and pyramid were mentioned in the same note. Arthur Whelford was very fond of word games and he would sometimes pose us riddles and we would guess their meaning. But that is beside the point. It just occurred to me that your cousin often referred to people merely by the first letter of their name. Those letters are all of you—Jasperot and Mallory and Poppy and Edge and your brother and you and Sam. You were all at that bull tomb together, weren't you? And it is the same one described in the page Huxley removed from fourth Desert Boy book. I am right, aren't I?' Her excitement wavered at his silence and he relented.

'I think you are. I had a look at the description in Sam's book and it is incredibly accurate, including the corner in which the debris was stacked and the cracked granite slab from the sarcophagus desecrated by some long-ago grave robbers.'

Even in the dark he saw her eyes light up with excitement.

'So we were right! Huxley *was* trying to guess the author's identity.'

'Probably. There is only one amendment to his list.'

'Oh, was someone else present?'

'No. But at the time Jasperot was recovering from a broken arm and collarbone. He never went down into the tomb and since the authorities had the place sealed up and it wasn't reopened until last year, there were only six people who could describe it so accurately.'

'That doesn't completely exclude Jasperot from the list—any one of you might have described the tomb to him.'

'True, but it makes him a less likely candidate. I doubt anyone described the mound of debris that fell in when the part of the roof caved in with Sam's fall as shaped like a giant tortoise, but once I read that passage I remember that is precisely what it looked like. I tend to agree with Huxley that whoever wrote those books was in that tomb with us that day and I don't believe it is Mallory, he hasn't the imagination for it.'

She frowned.

'I seem to remember he was a most intelligent young man.'

'I hesitate to undermine your fervent admiration for Mallory, but intelligence and imagination don't always go hand in hand.'

'But you cannot be certain.'

'No, but once I track him down I am convinced I can confirm he is not the author. Which leaves Poppy or Edge.'

'You have been thinking about this!' she accused.

'Is that a bad thing?'

'You didn't say a word to me about it the whole voyage.'

'It may have escaped your notice, but we were otherwise occupied and, besides, schooners are not precisely built for privacy. Unfortunately.'

'Is that why, or is it because you did not wish to discuss it in Sam's presence?'

He glanced over his shoulder at Youssef, who was standing by the exit, faithfully holding his torch aloft and trying to look completely unconcerned with his role as chaperon. Chase was very tempted to tell him to make himself scarce.

'That, too. Once we reach Qetara we will probably find out the truth, but please don't tell Sam either way. This is her one area of certainty. I don't want to upset that.'

'Of course I shan't, Chase.'

She reached out and he took her hand without thinking.

For a moment he held it in his, her warmth spreading to him, the weight of thousands of years setting them apart from everything that awaited them outside.

'Chase!' Lucas's voice reverberated up the passage and Chase dropped her hand. Blast big brothers.

Chapter Eighteen

'Off, Inky. That is mine,' Ellie admonished the cat, gently moving it off the book she had forgotten in the salon. 'You will have to find some other place to sleep away the afternoon heat.'

A slight movement in the corner of her eye made her turn. A pleasant-looking man with eyes and hair the colour of rich earth stood in the arched passage between the salon and the courtyard, frowning slightly. He was immediately familiar. but it took her a moment to realise why.

'Mr Mallory.'

His skin was already rather reddened from the sun, but it heated further.

'I beg your pardon, Do I… Goodness, you are Miss Walsh. We met at Arthur Whelford's several years ago, did we not?'

She laughed, extending her hand.

'We did. Some seven years ago. I am impressed you remember.'

'But of course I remember. We had a most fascinating discussion regarding the Parthenon Marbles.'

'You are very kind, Mr Mallory, but all I can recall was asking you far too many foolish questions.'

'Not at all, not at all. I was most impressed by your concern for the welfare of the antiquities. It was a point Lord Huxley…the late Lord Huxley and I often discussed.' He sighed again. 'I shall miss him.'

'You have heard, then…'

'Mr Carmichael received a letter from the executors regarding poor George's passing.'

'I am so very sorry, Mr Mallory. What will you do now?'

'Well, once I speak with Mr Sinclair, I must return to Mr Carmichael in Qetara to help him prepare a tribute to Lord Huxley. Then Sir Henry Salt, the Consul-General, and Monsieur Jasperot requested I accompany a shipment of antiquities to the British Museum and he has been kind enough to provide me with a reference to Mr Planta, the Principal Librarian there. The Museum is expanding rapidly and there is a great deal to be done…' He paused, tugging at his cravat. 'I do apologise for running on, this cannot be of interest to you.

'I assure you it sounds fascinating, Mr Mallory. I am lucky enough to be here as Lady

Samantha's companion and I am finding everything about Egypt fascinating. But on no account
can I allow you to leave until Mr Sinclair returns,
so please do let us sit down and you may tell me
all about Qetara.'

He looked a little alarmed by her enthusiasm,
but he joined her on the *mastaba*—a long cushioned bench running the length of the salon and
looking out the arched doorways on to a courtyard filled with lushly flowering potted plants.
His alarm grew as Inky leapt up on the *mastaba*
between them and turned her saucer-sized eyes
on Mr Mallory, placing one dark felt paw gently but with exquisite menace on his pantaloons.

'Don't mind Inky, Mr Mallory. She is Lady
Sinclair's cat and insisted on accompanying Sam
on this journey. I made the mistake of trying to
stare her down when she decided she was bored of
Lady Samantha's and Mr Sinclair's cabins aboard
ship and came to sample mine. She is still considering whether to forgive me for my imperti-
nence in trying to evict her. Isn't that true, Inky?'

Inky gave a sharp-toothed yawn and came to
deposit her substantial bulk on Ellie's lap. Mr
Mallory gave a sigh of relief at his release.

'Apparently, she forgives you, Miss Walsh.'

'Animals forgive us more swiftly than we
forgive ourselves.' Ellie smiled and stroked the
warm, purring bundle on her skirts.

'That is probably true. I wish I had that facility at the moment. I admit to feeling quite torn about leaving Lord Huxley when I did. I knew he was unwell at the end, but he was most insistent I go to Egypt when Mr Sinclair did not respond to his letters and he realised he might already be on his way there. Otherwise I would never have agreed to leave him at such a time…'

Ellie leaned forward impetuously. 'Oh, please don't tell Mr Sinclair that, Mr Mallory.'

'Don't tell me what?'

Mallory stood abruptly at Chase's question and Ellie turned, more surprised at the animosity in his voice than his sudden arrival. Mr Mallory strode towards him, hand extended.

'Hello, Chase. I am so very pleased to see you.'

Chase took his hand with a peculiar reluctance, but then the harsh look on his face faded into a smile.

'And I to see you, Mallory.'

'Relieved, too. I am only sorry I left the box in Qetara, but I felt it was safer with Mr Carmichael and after all we were certain you would go to Qetara once you did arrive here.'

'The box.'

'Yes, that is why I came to Egypt. George thought you might already be on your way here and he wanted to be quite certain you received it before you left Egypt.'

'Why?'

'I… I don't know. He did not explain it to me.

Those last few months he was not quite himself. Oh, I do not mean he lost his senses, but he knew he was failing and he became preoccupied and... unpredictable.'

'I should have come to see him.' Chase's expression did not change, but Ellie could see the shadows of pain in his eyes.

'In truth, Chase, I don't believe he wished anyone to see him. When he realised he was ill, I immediately suggested sending for you and Lucas and Samantha, but he said he preferred you remember him as he had been, not as he had become.'

Chase moved away.

'Never mind. So the box is in Qetara?'

'Yes. When will you be travelling there?'

'Tomorrow. We were considering going to Saqqara, but will likely save that for our return to Cairo. I hear Jasperot has finally received a *firman* for that tomb Sam fell into. Have you been to see it?'

'Not yet, but I shall also go after I conclude my affairs in Qetara. I am most interested to see it again. All I can remember is clouds of dust and a rather lovely wall painting of a *felucca*. Jasperot tells me he has uncovered the most exquisite mummified bulls you could hope to see.'

'I don't often have cause to link together the words exquisite, mummies and bulls, so I will reserve judgement. Is that all you remember? I was trying to settle a debate with Lucas that it sounded very like a passage in one of the Desert Boy books. You know, the one where Gabriel falls through the roof of a collapsed tomb and is rescued by Leila?'

Mallory shook his head ruefully.

'I'm afraid I don't. Perhaps if you showed me the passage?'

'Perhaps later. I see you and Miss Walsh introduced yourselves already.'

'Miss Walsh and I met several times when I came to Nettleton to meet with Mr Whelford on Lord Huxley's behalf,' Mr Mallory corrected punctiliously. 'Miss Walsh was kind enough to listen to me bore on about antiquities.'

'Were you bored, Miss Walsh?'

Ellie flushed, confused by the acid in Chase's voice.

'Not at all, Mr Sinclair. I told Mr Mallory it was more likely the other way around. I found his views on the Parthenon Marbles fascinating.'

'Charming.' Chase turned back to Mallory. 'Do you know what is in Huxley's box?'

'Well, yes and no. Lord Huxley was quite secretive about this project of his and, of course, I did not press. I know he included quite a few notebooks and some personal possessions. I presumed he was preparing a leave-taking gift for Mr Carmichael, which was why I was surprised he asked me to deliver it to you. I went to find you in London, but all I could gather from your man of business and from Lord Sinclair's butler was that you were away somewhere on the Continent, but they did not know where, or when you might return. I knew Lord Sinclair was in Venice with his wife and due to travel from there to Egypt, so naturally we assumed you might be doing the same. George decided I must take the trunk to Egypt myself and intercept you. Naturally I did not wish to leave him while he was unwell, but he was most insistent and I felt it was best for his health that I do as he wished. And so here I am.'

Ellie watched Chase, but he had retreated behind his blank façade again.

'Were there books in the package?'

'Not that I am aware of. Perhaps some clippings. He had developed a rather strange habit of cutting sections from his favourite books. When I asked him why, all he would say was that he was exploring a theory. That was one of the books, too.' He pointed to the book Ellie had rescued from Inky.

'Oh. Have you read it, Mr Mallory?' Ellie asked, treading carefully. It was just possible that Chase was wrong about Mallory—he certainly appeared intelligent enough to write the Desert Boy books. She rather liked the idea of the mild-mannered secretary harbouring a secret life as a writer of novels.

'I am afraid not, Miss Walsh. My time is often

taken up with scholarly journals and histories. In general, I do not see the benefit of squandering my time on fantastical novels, not when I could be using it more productively.'

Ellie clung to her patience. She hadn't quite remembered Mr Mallory being so very…dry. 'Having now seen just a very little of Egypt, I must say I find them impressively accurate and I certainly see nothing wrong with a little fantasy, especially when it is so well written.'

'Perhaps I should make the effort, if you think so highly of them, Miss Walsh.' Mallory smiled.

'Why don't you get a start on that now, then, Mallory?' Chase said, standing up. 'I don't want to hurry you along, but Miss Walsh should rest before Jasperot's ball this evening.'

'Of course, I didn't mean… I shall see you all there then, I hope?' Mallory stammered as she stood.

'Probably. But I will come by your hotel tomorrow in any case. I want to speak with you before you return to England.'

'Oh, but I will likely see you in Qetara as well. Mr Carmichael requested my assistance for a couple of weeks. Well, it was lovely to renew our acquaintance, Miss Walsh. I shall see you tonight and pay my respects to Lucas and Samantha as well. Jasperot assures me there will be dancing…' He cleared his throat. 'May I request the honour of a dance with you this evening, Miss Walsh?'

'I shall be honoured, Mr Mallory.' Ellie replied, trying not to smile at his formality and quite pleased to have already secured a dance at what was likely to prove a challenging evening. If only Chase would follow suit and ask her to dance... Perhaps even a waltz... Not that Chase looked like a man interested in dances at the moment.

The silence as the door shut behind Mallory vibrated with Chase's antipathy and Ellie waited, a little puzzled. Something had been wrong with Chase the moment he entered the salon. She was wondering how to frame her concern when he turned back to her, his face still a cold mask.

'Mallory may be a friend of the family, but that doesn't mean you should be alone with him.'

'Why? I'm alone with you now.'

'That is different.'

He sounded so dismissive, as if no one in their right mind would suspect him of having designs on her. 'It most certainly is,' she snapped right back. 'I am convinced he at least has a pristine reputation.'

Chase snarled something and sat down on the *mastaba*, flexing his hands on his trousers. Inky came and stretched out between them, her tail curled over Ellie's thigh and her paw cuffing Chase's hand. Without looking Chase began dutifully scratching Inky's head and all of Ellie's hurt bled away.

'Is something wrong, Chase? Did you discover something with Lord Sinclair?'

He shook his head.

'No. We went to see some acquaintances. Nothing related to Huxley.'

'Oh. Were you hoping Mr Mallory might have something more conclusive to say? I don't think you should give up hope until you see the contents of the trunk. It was clearly very important to Lord Huxley that it reach you.'

'Yes.'

She waited for something further, but he was wholly engrossed in Inky.

'I admit I think you are right in your assessment that he is not the author,' she continued and he finally looked up, still with the same edge of mockery she did not understand.

'Of course he isn't. Mallory might be a scholar, but he is as unimaginative as your beloved Arthur Whelford. And I doubt it took all that determined flirting to ascertain as much.'

For a moment the absurdity of his accusation struck her speechless. Then, like a knife breaking skin, it sank through.

'I was *not* flirting.'

'No? It certainly looked like flirting.'

'As an expert you would know, of course.'

'Precisely. I realise Mallory embodies all the virtues you hold dear, but I suggest you pace yourself with him. Unless he has changed a great deal in the past few years, he is unaccustomed to the press-gang methods you developed as head of the Walsh clan.'

'That is a hateful thing to say, Mr Sinclair.' Ellie surged to her feet. For the first time she felt the impossible miles between her and Whitworth. She wished she was back there—where she knew how to face the world and at least her heart had been safe. She turned and strode towards the door before she did or said or revealed anything she shouldn't.

'Ellie! God, I'm sorry. That was low of me. Please don't be angry.'

He caught her hand, turning her, his palm cupping her cheek. It took every ounce of her strength not to lean into that warmth of his hand, capture it and not let go.

'I'm not,' she replied foolishly, closing her eyes hard.

His laugh didn't sound amused and he took his hand away, but before she could lament its loss his arms went around her, gathering her against him, her breasts flattening against the hard surface of his chest. She breathed in, filling with the scent of warm musky skin and that magical essence that was at the core of her dreams since their meeting in the Folly.

She shuddered, a small cry of defeat rising out of her, and his arms tightened, his mouth brushing her temple, his breath grazing her cheek, the corner of her mouth, taunting her to turn and close the circle and kiss him. She might have done just that if he hadn't spoken, his voice low and harsh.

'Ellie, don't listen to me. I have no right.'

She was free again and he was halfway across the room when the door opened and Sam entered.

'There you are, Ellie. Samira brought up your gown and we want to see if the alterations she made will do for tonight.'

Ellie managed a smile at Sam.

'*Your* gown, you mean. There really was no need…'

Sam rolled her eyes.

'I haven't worn half the gowns Olivia commissioned for me from Madame Fanchot and I doubt I shall any time soon. If I had my way, I would be back in the same cotton robes I wore as a child. They were so much more comfortable in the Egyptian climate.'

'When we reach Bab el-Nur you can find an *aba* and *kamis* and be comfortable again,' Chase replied.

For the hundredth time Ellie watched his features soften as he spoke with his little sister and not for the first time she felt resentment pinch at her insides. Not that she wanted Chase to regard her as a little sister—far from it. What she wanted was quite, quite different. And quite, quite foolish.

She'd reached the door when he spoke.

'Miss Walsh?'

'Yes, Mr Sinclair?'

'You will save a dance for me as well, I hope?'

Chapter Nineteen

Jasperot's palace was one of the finest examples of Mameluke grandeur in Cairo. It stood on the eastern side of the city not far from the famed Citadel, only a tall earthen wall and a few stunted hills separating it from Cairo's cemetery, the City of the Dead. Many palaces closer to the river surrounded their homes with lush gardens, but Jasperot's was different—it was built as an homage to the Abbasid-style mosque Ibn Tulun, with the living and entertaining quarters surrounding a large inner courtyard lined with arched arcades.

In the centre of the courtyard, instead of Ibn Tulun's dome-covered *sebil* and water basin was an enormous and incongruous Roman fountain, with bucking horses and spear-touting warriors, their near-naked bodies glistening under the drizzle of water.

Right now that outrageous fountain was a

backdrop for something much more offensive as far as Chase was concerned.

To a disinterested party the man leaning solicitously over the young woman dressed in an elegant gown of pale-peach satin only added to the magic of the setting. But Chase was far from disinterested and it took every ounce of will not to stride over and physically intercede between Mallory and Ellie.

He would do nothing of the sort, of course. He'd already made enough of a fool of himself in the afternoon. His only excuse for fumbling so badly was that he wasn't accustomed to jealousy. He'd certainly never expected it to strike here, when he finally had her safe and secure in Egypt and ready to embark on the next stage of their adventure.

He'd come looking for her that afternoon to tell her about the *dahabiya* Hamid had arranged for the trip to Qetara, imagining her pleasure with the slow voyage up the Nile on the brightly painted flat-bottomed ship, watching this new world unfold. They would make good time to Qetara, which was just south of Beni Hasan, and after a short stay at Bab el-Nur, where he hoped they could settle Huxley's riddle once and for all, they would continue upriver—to see Karnak and the wonders of Edfu and Abydos and Abu Simbel...

The shock of seeing her smiling so charmingly at Mallory had been bad enough. But hearing the

two of them discuss him behind his back moved
him far too swiftly from surprise to antagonism
without a sensible thought in between.

He was trying, hard, to shake off that juvenile
reaction. To stick to his plans. It didn't help that
she looked so lovely now in her borrowed dress
of a shimmering colour between honeysuckle and
pale peach and with the silver spray of the fountain behind her making the air around her vi-
brate like the sky around a sunset. He wanted to
take her somewhere, alone, and lay his hopes and
fears bare and...

He cut his mawkish thoughts short and went
to stand by the arcades. In the far corner of the
courtyard a small orchestra was playing courtly
music that would have been at home in any Euro-
pean ballroom, but beyond the walls behind him
Chase could hear the rumble of drums from other
festivities—a wedding perhaps. There would be
lute-like *ouds* and other instruments but all he
could make out was the rapid, hollow beat of *dar-
buka* drums.

In another life he would have turned and left
this stolid parade of local and foreign dignitaries
and prowled the dark streets, catching glimpses
of those other lives and stopping for sweet mint-
infused tea in the cafes. Ellie would probably
enjoy seeing that side of Cairo. If only...

Perhaps it would be wise to leave anyway.

'For someone with so little experience in the

role you do a marvellous impersonation of a jealous lover, Chase,' Lucas said, coming to lean on the pillar beside him.

Chase's tension rose a notch. Any higher and he'd probably disintegrate into a thousand blazing shards of frustrated fury.

'Go dance with your wife, Luke.'

Lucas considered the couple on the other side of the fountain.

'Or perhaps you are quite content to have someone intercede and capture her attention and save you from your baser instincts. Are you beginning to regret choosing a gently bred woman you lust after as Sam's companion? If so, you will be pleased to hear I offered Mallory a place on the *dahabiya* tomorrow.'

'What? Lucas, you didn't!'

'Why shouldn't I have? He needs to return to Qetara as well. This is Mallory, Chase. He's known us since we were grubby boys.'

'I don't care if he gave us sweetmeats when we skinned our knees, blast you. The last thing I need is to have a younger replica of her ideal invited on board.'

'Her ideal?'

'Do you know who her first love was?'

'Some mythical paragon, by the sound of it.'

'No, I could have coped with that. Arthur Whelford.'

'Arthur…as in George's brother? Arthur Whelford, the vicar? You cannot be serious. He was old enough to be her father.'

'Precisely. Her own father was a wastrel—a gambler and a rake who drowned in a puddle during a drunken stupor and left his family deep in debt. Whelford was the kind of man who helped her plan her kitchen garden because he knew he was dying and she would have to assume responsibility for her siblings' future.'

'Chase, I know love can addle one's brain, believe me, but you have officially taken leave of your senses. If there is anyone who can succeed in setting one's affairs on the right path, it is you.'

'That isn't what she wants. She wants what was denied her and everything Whelford symbolised—a home, stability, safety... And even you must admit those are not my strong suits.'

Lucas threw up his hands.

'Did she tell you she wanted any of these things? For someone who is yearning only for home and hearth she does a fantastic show of being as excited about adventure as Sam ever was.'

Chase tried to ease the tension out of his shoulders. He didn't want to have this conversation, but he couldn't stop.

'Yes, this is an adventure for her, but eventually she will yearn for home. She needs someone like Mallory.'

'Mallory. My God, are you actually contemplating arranging *that* for her? I take back what I said—this is not taking leave of your senses. This is crushing them underfoot, roasting them on a fire and feeding them to the jackals.'

Chase turned away from the incredulity in his brother's voice and focused on the statues flanking the arches—dark granite figures of the lion goddess Sekhmet looking kindly but rather sternly down at the human folly being played out beneath her.

'It's killing me.' Even he could hear the pain, the confusion. He tried to recover his equilibrium. 'But I want what is best for her. The worst thing is that someone like Mallory is probably better for her than I will ever be.'

'Hmmm. According to the little you told me, this woman singlehandedly kept her family afloat for years despite Fergus Walsh's best attempts to destroy them, then entered into two charades to further her ends, one of them involving standing up to Aunt Ermy and the other travel to a foreign and potentially dangerous locale with a man she knows possesses a dubious reputation. In addition to which she managed to overcome Sam's resistance and to endear herself to my all-too-suspicious Livvy. Do you really believe someone like her would prefer prim and proper Mallory?'

'Her father...'

'Is dead and apparently good riddance. Even if she thinks she wants an antidote to her untrustworthy sire, so what? One of your most valued skills for Oswald was always that you could see beyond what people thought they wanted to what they ought to want. You certainly did in my case. And in Sam's. Why don't you try some of your medicine on yourself?'

Chase considered saying something about overbearing older siblings, but Lucas was already striding off so he returned to glaring at Ellie and Mallory instead. She was smiling, but as Chase forced his mind to separate from his heart he could see what Lucas did.

Ellie in love and loved should be one long 'oh, look' moment, but there was no hint of wonder on her face. She looked very much as she had during those dinners at the Manor—polite, amused, attentive...distant. Eleanor, not Ellie. She might think she would be safer as Eleanor, but she wasn't. Safety could be as much a prison as uncertainty.

Mallory would probably never even realise Ellie existed.

Ellie was his.

He moved towards them as the musicians began the first flourishes of the next dance.

'My dance,' he announced and Mallory blinked, but bowed with a smile.

'We can continue this discussion in Qetara, Miss Walsh. Meanwhile, I look forward to our dance later.'

Chase locked his jaw against the atavistic urge to make it as clear as pain that Ellie was out of bounds.

'What discussion? Why is Mallory arranging assignations with you?'

'Mr Mallory merely promised to show me his copy of *Description de L'Egypte* which he left in Qetara. That is hardly an assignation, Mr Sinclair.'

'A fine excuse,' he scoffed.

'It isn't! He said there is a drawing there of what you called the White Desert. I expressed an interest in seeing it and he is merely being obliging. I think he is trying to atone for his dismissal of the Desert Boy books.'

'You cannot possibly be that naïve. In less than a day the man has done everything short of writing a poem to your left eyebrow while you were smiling at him as if he has just discovered a new pyramid and laid it at your feet.'

'I was not!'

She looked a little stunned at his accusation and he didn't know whether to be relieved or furious at the surprise on her face.

'It looked like that from here. And if you think... Where are you going?' he demanded as she turned away.

'To find someone who won't ruin my first-ever ball. And if you don't wish to dance with me, you have only to say so.'

* * *

Ellie regretted walking away within three steps, but pride kept her moving. She passed through the arches where the warm breeze ran close to the ground, tugging at the hems of her skirt like a playful wave.

She had been so looking forward to Chase asking her to dance—a chance to gather another memory of his closeness for the treasure chest that was to last her a lifetime. Instead, within two days of arriving in Egypt they were fighting. The bittersweet friendship that grew in Huxley's study felt far away, a dream already fading in the light of day. Tomorrow they would depart for Qetara and once he found Huxley's package he might leave them altogether and disappear on another of those quests he performed for his uncle.

The arched corridor led to a smaller court-yard garden and she went to sit on a stone bench tucked under a vine-covered bower. The music from the orchestra dimmed as her dance drew to an end and the reverberating drums from beyond the walls took its place, layered with a plaintive faraway ululation. Tears burned in her eyes and she closed them, listening to the clash of drums and violins as the orchestra began to play a waltz.

'I do wish to.'

She opened her eyes slowly.

'Dance with you,' Chase elucidated. The only light was a pair of oil lanterns at the entrance to the corridor and it outlined his breadth, but gave her no clue to his expression. He bent and took her hand. 'Come. I will try not to ruin this any more than I already have.'

'You don't have to dance with me out of duty, Chase.'

'I never do. Which is why I very rarely dance. Come.'

She moved towards the corridor, but he stopped her by placing his hand on her waist.

'Here. I claim my dance here.'

She didn't bother arguing. The music was faint, but the rhythm of the waltz slid gently along the marble floor, mixing with the rumble of the music beyond the palace walls and with the sweet scent of the tiny white flowers on the vines that covered the bower above them. She looked up from the sinuous folds of his cravat to meet his hooded gaze and didn't even try to resist the familiar rush of heat that struck through her.

It was always like this.

It was not merely that he and his brother were by far the most impressive men at the ball. She'd noticed she was not the only one to think so—she had seen the glances he received from many of the women—some furtive, some lingering.

For once he was dressed with strict propriety in dark evening wear and a shirt and cravat of immaculate white. He looked magnificent and as far out of her reach as the moon and stars.

She realised with a further fall of her spirit that he hadn't even remarked on her dress. She had so hoped to at least elicit a compliment; well aware this was as good as she was ever likely to look. But he'd barely noticed her new plumage. She was such a fool. Her hopes to impress Chase with her meagre charms were as ludicrous as an ant trying to kick a bear.

He hadn't appeared aware of much, in fact. All evening he seemed caught in his own world and she wondered again at the hostility he'd shown earlier that day. It simply was not characteristic of Chase and finally her own hurt fell away under a surge of worry.

'I know something is wrong, Chase. Are you still worried about Sam?'

His lips parted on an indrawn breath that was as peculiar as the rest and she tightened her hold on his hand. But he shook his head.

'No. Not as much now we are here. But you should be angry at me for being an imbecile, not providing me with excuses for being so, Ellie.'

'If it was merely you being an imbecile I wouldn't. But something *is* wrong, isn't it? Are you worried what you will find in Qetara?'

His smile was brief, but finally she saw the return of the affection she'd so depended on at Huxley, but he shook his head.

'I don't want to think about that now. Or about anything else the moment. Just dance.'

'But this is a waltz. I never learned how to waltz,' she said with a spurt of panic, pushing back a little, but his arms tightened.

'One day I shall teach you. But you don't need to know how to waltz to move to the music. Like this. Just close your eyes and try not to think. I know that's a challenge for you, if not a complete impossibility, but try.'

He pulled her closer and she closed her eyes as commanded. Like a curtain falling, she became aware of a whole different world in the darkness. Above all of his body—even where his arm wasn't around her and his hand holding hers he was so close his warmth was an entity in itself. It was like floating in a warm bath; she wanted to sink into him, luxuriate in being encompassed by him. She sighed at the wonder of it, at the brush of satin against her skin, at the breeze sliding under her skirts and over her heated cheeks and neck.

When he spoke his breath was warm against her temple.

'Do you hear those drums? They are called *darbukas* and that sound above them, that's an *oud*, like a lyre. Someone is getting married.'

His voice sank into a reverberation of its own and their dance became little more than a gentle swaying as they listened.

'But the singer sounds so mournful,' she whispered.

'She is singing for the end of one life and the beginning of another. There is a sadness to that, too.'

'I wish I could see such a wedding.'

'One day you will. I will take you.'

She didn't respond to the lie. This moment was all that mattered because this was borrowed time. Soon he would continue in his life, free of all fetters, and she in hers.

Without thinking she leaned her cheek on his shoulder and his arm brought her still closer until her body pressed the length of his, his other hand cupping her head against him, his fingers moving with the same seductive rhythm on her hair. He felt so solid, all around her, enveloping her in the strength of his body. The fabric of his coat was soft under her cheek, but she wanted to feel him closer. She did not care that this was not done.

The vibration of drums reached through the floor and the beat of his pulse was against her cheek, fast and sharp. Even the skirts of her dress felt alive, sending shivers of sensation through her as they brushed against her legs. Every pent-up frustration and memory of his touch, his kiss, tumbled over the ramparts of her defences and entered the dance, tangling inside her like the twisting souls in medieval paintings. The world was vibrating with tension and life and nothing mattered but the moment, the inexplicable combination of fire and comfort she felt nowhere else.

She was a world away from Ellie, from Eleanor, from everything that fettered her. She was alive.

She'd been waiting for this dance all her life. For this man, for this place, this moment.

She was at home and in heaven all at once.

She raised her head, rising on tiptoe, her mouth a breath away from his throat, absorbing the scent of musk and soap and that essence that was just him. She hoped she would remember that scent until she died.

He stopped, frozen, but didn't push her away and so she touched her lips to the taut sinew of his neck, only her breath shifting her against him, filling her lungs, filling every inch of her. The music swirled on around them—drums and violins, lyres and a lone flute, but as distant as a receding storm.

She moved slowly, finding the heat of his pulse and then, because it was the most natural thing in the world, she tasted it.

It wasn't at all strange that he swept her up with something between a cry and growl and they were suddenly deep in the shadow of the vines, her back against the pedestal of some pagan god, her thighs pressing hard against his waist, one hand splayed on her behind and the other deep into her hair, his fingers taut against her scalp as his mouth found hers.

Oh, God, I'm coming undone. I will never come back from this.

She sank into him, trying to pull him closer, her hands sliding under his coat to fist and tug at his shirt, her fingertips finally finding flesh.

It was so right she couldn't stop the whimpers pouring through her in the rhythm of her blood. She could feel their echo inside him, the way he gasped her name against her mouth as her hands worked their way higher.

This was how it was meant to be, flesh on flesh, his mouth drinking, tasting its way from her lips to her neck and downwards, brushing over the swell of her breasts, the faint roughness of his jaw a beautiful contrast to the firm pressure of his lips. His breath was ragged, slipping under the silk of her bodice and the constricting tautness of her stays, his fingers already easing away the shoulder of her gown when the sways of music were joined by series of mournful yowls beyond the high walls.

Chase shuddered and froze, holding her still half-raised against the cold marble statue, his breath as shallow and uneven as hers.

'What is that?' she whispered.

'Nothing. Just jackals. They roam the grave-yards. God, I must be mad. We can't do this. Not here. Anyone could come by.'

He lowered her gently, pressing her head to his chest before moving away, his hands shaking as he dragged them through his already dishevelled hair.

'I will return you to the others before I do something even more unforgivable. Tomorrow we will talk.'

Talk.

She didn't want to talk. Talk meant dragging back the common sense that for a brief, ecstatic moment, she'd managed to forget all about. Talk meant he would tell her this perfect bliss was wrong, a mistake. What had he called it? Unforgivable.

How could something so perfect, that made her heart soar like the doves that rose in waves when they drove through the streets of Cairo, be unforgivable?

She didn't want to talk. She wanted to howl like the jackals.

'Why must people always talk?' she moaned and, absurdly, he laughed.

'Blast you, Ellie. Why can you never say what one expects?'

He took a step back towards her, but a not-so-subtle cough from the archway stopped him in his tracks.

'May I go tell Olivia and Sam I have found the missing members of our party?' Lucas enquired politely with a very direct look at his brother. 'I hate to disturb your tête-à-tête, but Mallory has been enquiring for you, Miss Walsh. Apparently, you have promised him a dance and he is a far more resolute fellow than he appears. I'll send

Livvy to you in the ladies' withdrawing area,' he added quietly as he led her through the arches. 'You might wish for a moment to…compose yourself before you face the world.'

Ellie flushed in embarrassment as she allowed herself to be led away, resisting the urge to look back. She touched the trailing strands of hair lying on her shoulders, but Lord Sinclair's smile was sympathetic rather than condemning.

'I am impressed you have made my brother act so far out of character. That is always a good sign. He is too used to arranging the world to his will.'

'Out of character?' She could not keep the incredulity from her voice.

'Completely out of character, my dear Miss Walsh. Ah, Livvy, just in time to stop me from saying something I oughtn't. Enjoy your dance with Mallory and then I think we had all best retire for the night. We must be up at dawn to begin our journey to Qetara.'

Chapter Twenty

'Still cursing my soul because I offered Mallory a place on the *dahabiya*?' Lucas asked as he leaned on the *dahabiya*'s railing by Chase's side.

Chase didn't turn from his contemplation of the dark-teal water slipping past and the women filling pitchers of water from the banks of the river while children played between the reeds.

He'd always found these trip soothing, just watching the shifting landscape as they wound up the Nile, but it wasn't exerting its magic now. It certainly wasn't distracting him from what was happening by the table on the other side of the long deck where Ellie and Olivia sat reading and Sam sketched while Mallory hovered above them.

Or from the memory of the kiss as Jasperot's ball.

Nothing succeeded in distracting him from that for long. It was worst at night—in the dark, listening to the lapping of the water against the wooden boat and knowing she was asleep in her own narrow cabin just a few yards away, so present he could almost imagine if he reached out he would find the soft curve of her waist and she would make that soft sound in her throat as he pulled her towards him and finally do something about this damned fever that wasn't like any fever he knew. It just climbed and climbed like that idiot Sisyphus pushing a boulder uphill.

Even in the civilised light of day with everyone buzzing around them like fruit flies it took an increasingly conscious effort not to snarl at everyone and everything that approached her. It was ridiculous and pathetic, but it had him by the throat like a mystical possession.

He wished he'd made an utter fool of himself at the ball and compromised her and then they would be betrothed and this would all be behind him already. She would be his and that was that. Then he wouldn't have to listen to all the voices inside him that told him he wasn't right for her, that her life should follow a very different path from any he could offer her. That he had to tread carefully and consider whether this was truly what he wanted, to set himself up for failure and her for disappointment...

He wished they could go back to Huxley's study so he could just suffer alone with her. He'd been confused then, too, but more comfortable than he would have imagined possible. Just being with her. If he could go back, stop time until he was absolutely certain...

You will never be absolutely certain, said a snide voice inside him and sank its talons into his boots. He glanced down at Inky, who had abandoned Olivia and come to test her claws on him. Her round eyes stared up at him mournfully, as if she hadn't just spent the whole morning being petted and fed by everyone.

'Apparently it's your turn to pay tribute to this spoilt spawn of Bastet.' Lucas grinned as Lucas detached claw from leather. 'Did you have to bring Inky with you from the Hall?'

'She didn't give us much choice. She jumped into the carriage and on to Sam's lap as if it was obvious she was part of the journey and Sam didn't have the heart to put her out.'

'And you didn't have the courage to put her out.'

'I haven't seen you standing firm when Inky's determined to get between you and Olivia.'

'Point taken. At least Livvy was happy to see her. Besides, Inky might put in a good word with the local gods for you. By your morose mood since we boarded, you need a stroke of divine intervention.'

'It hardly matters,' Chase answered, turning back to the water slipping by beneath them. 'These past three days have only confirmed my point.'

'I must be more than usually dense, because I am missing that point.'

'That he is perfect for her.'

'Mallory? I admit I don't know her well, but if that young woman prefers Mallory to you, she is not only far less intelligent than she appears, but also an excellent actress. I don't see anything between them that would hint at the mutual combustion you two engaged in at Jasperot's.'

'That's not the point. I know I can make her lust for me. I even know she likes me. But I don't know if that is enough to compensate for what I cannot offer her.'

'You will have to be clearer. I'm having a hard time thinking of something you lack.'

Chase laughed again.

'Don't be an ass.'

'I take that back. You lack a strong dose of good sense. If she had wanted Mallory, she could have had him in her pocket by now. Now, would you stop thinking about what you think is right for her and concentrate on what is right for you?'

'But...'

Lucas slapped the railing.

'If I was this annoying when I first fell in love with Olivia, it's a wonder she agreed to wed me. Do you know what your problem is, Chase? You think too much. Stop thinking!'

'I'll think about it.'

Lucas met his rueful smile with one of his own.

'This is not good for the family reputation, you know. Two Sinclairs felled in a single year. I meant what I said. She is not a child, she is a mature woman and you are on occasion a sensible man. Do what mature, sensible people do and talk to her.'

'Like you talked to Olivia.'

Lucas grinned.

'You have the benefit of learning from my mistakes. But let me tell you, if she prefers Mallory over you, she's a fool.'

'Or a very wise woman. I'm hardly husband material. I don't even have a home.'

'One doesn't have a home. One creates it. I may have inherited houses before I married Olivia, but we're only creating a home now. This hot and sticky desert is as much a home to me at the moment as Sinclair Hall ever was. Of all of us I never thought you would be the coward. When you thought something was right, you acted.'

'It has nothing to do with cowardice and I *am* acting.'

'No, you are arranging matters for others. Not for yourself. Ellie might not be a young miss, but you have a lot more experience than her. In all the years I've never seen you lust after a woman you can't in conscience bed. The Chase I know would have put a continent between himself and such a challenge and laughed it off until it went its merry way and you went your merry way in another woman's arms. The last thing I would wager you would do was secure her on the same ship for a long voyage. Unless you were finally considering taking the plunge and wanted to make absolutely certain this isn't a passing whim.'

'I told you why I brought her. I needed help with Sam and she needed help saving her family. It was a sensible solution.'

'I will ignore the insult to my intelligence by trying to sell me the same nonsense you sold her and Sam. For heaven's sake, Chase. If you believe you are right for her—'

'I don't,' Chase interrupted and Lucas fell silent.

'Then perhaps she's not right for you,' Lucas finally said gruffly.

'You don't understand. Her life is one long struggle to reach stable ground. The only stability I could offer is monetary. I don't want to find myself tied to someone who is fated to realise I cannot provide what they really need. We've been there before, you and I, and I'm damned if I'm going there again for someone who isn't already tied to me. I'm not being selfless here, Lucas. I'm being as selfish as any hell-bound Sinclair was before me. I don't want the responsibility. I don't want to witness the inevitable death of whatever friendship and respect she has for me. I just don't want any of this.'

They were far enough away to ensure the others did not hear their low conversation above the desert winds, but perhaps something in the force of his voice carried because Ellie glanced up from her book and met his eyes.

It was like standing on the apex of a dune— standing still was impossible as the sand slowly skittered away underfoot, so he was reduced to shifting constantly to keep his centre of balance until he no longer knew what it was. He didn't know if what he told Lucas was the truth or pure cowardice. All he knew with absolute certainty was that he was desperate to go to her. Suddenly Ellie smiled the same smile he knew from Huxley's study and the world fell away, leaving only one, ringing truth.

He might not be right for her, but she was right for him.

If only he could get rid of Whelford's reincarnation.

'Do me a favour, Lucas, and find something to occupy Mallory before I do. Just look at him hanging over Ellie.'

'He's hanging over Sam at the moment,' Lucas pointed out. 'In fact, she looks like she is about to stab him with her pen any moment now. I'm so glad to see she's recovering her foul temper.'

'Sam is only an excuse. The idiot is smitten.'

'Which idiot?'

Chase shot his brother a look of dislike.

'Glaring at me won't help, Chase. Come, I will go rescue him from our womenfolk.'

They moved forward just as Ellie set down her book and went to stand by the railing, beckoning to Mallory.

'Do you know what that ruin on the bank is, Mr Mallory?'

Mallory hurried to join her and Sam rolled her eyes at Olivia and hunched over her sketch once more.

'See?' Chase growled at Lucas.

'I do. You don't. She was saving Sam. Now go do the same for her.'

'That is Bait Sobek,' Mallory was explaining to Ellie. 'A minor temple and not of great interest apart from the fact that its name refers to the crocodile god which is peculiar, because most sites with imagery of Sobek are upriver where crocodiles were more prevalent.'

'Maybe a few of the species find this stretch of the river welcoming, Mallory,' Chase said as he came to stand by Ellie's side on the railing. 'You could always test that theory by diving off the *dahabiya*.'

Mallory frowned, inspecting the tangle of reeds and rushes where long-necked herons waded in search of fish and frogs.

'I hardly think that is a sensible approach to testing the possibility, Chase.'

'Not sensible, but certainly entertaining.'

'Chase...' Ellie admonished, her voice wobbling a little.

'What? Hugh would approve of my Baconian method.'

'Hugh is fourteen.'

'But a very precocious fourteen...'

'Mallory, could you come with me?' Lucas called from the stairway leading to the lower deck. 'I want your advice when I discuss the next leg of our trip with Hamid.'

'Of course. With pleasure.' Mallory smiled at Ellie and Chase and went after Lucas.

'I thought you liked Mallory,' Ellie said when the two men disappeared down the wooden stairs.

'I do.'

'Then why have you been needling him these past couple of days? Are you jealous? That Huxley entrusted him with the box rather than wait for you?'

He gripped the railing hard. For that brief moment before she qualified her question he thought he'd been as obvious to her as he was to Lucas.

'I'm not jealous.' *Not of that, anyway.* 'I've merely forgotten what a tiresome bore he can be.'

'I realise he can be a little pedantic, but there was no need to make it clear you would prefer he jump overboard.'

'I was merely suggesting he test his theory.'

'By swimming in crocodile-infested waters.'

'Why the devil are you defending him? He's

a grown man, not one of your charges. And neither am I for you to scold. I'm not Henry or one of your siblings.'

'I'm well aware of that, Mr Sinclair.'

The flickering amusement in her eyes drained immediately and for once he didn't feel the need to snatch it back.

'Are you? You seem to treat us all the same, as if we survive on this planet by grace and it's only your superior good sense that can point us in the right direction...'

They stood for a moment in silence. Her face was flushed and her breathing fast and he wanted to take back his words, or at least explain...

'Ellie, I'm sorry.'

'I always tell my *charges* not to apologise for speaking the truth. Good day, Mr Sinclair.' Each word dropped like a boulder on his ragged soul and he didn't try to stop her when she returned to the others.

She was right. He wasn't truly sorry. For hurting her, yes, but not for his words. He was tired of her worrying about him. He wanted her to...

Oh, hell, he just wanted her. On whatever terms. He had no idea which way was up any longer. All he knew with absolute certainty was that he was desperate to just be with her, the two of them alone. He knew it with a vicious fever that worsened with each day and it just became more and more complicated.

During the long weeks from England to Egypt he'd still had a hope that one day he would awake and discover he was cured of this malady. That some miracle of time and reality would numb this pulsing core of him that was constantly crying out to close the distance between them, physical and otherwise.

Because he hated it. Sometimes he even hated her.

He wasn't surprised he felt these surges of queasiness. He was making himself ill just thinking about what a weak, lustful fool she'd reduced him to. He'd never in his life been so at sea with a woman, literally and figuratively, and he hated it. Hated that she could walk by him with no more than an impersonal nod and sit by Sam and Olivia and Mallory, responding to his comments as if they had never spent hours together alone in the study, as if he had never touched her more intimately than any man had...

Damn, damn, *damn* her.

Chapter Twenty-One

Bab el-Nur was beautiful.

Sam had pointed it out to her from the river—a great sprawling white structure set against a rising cliff and surrounded by gardens within tall earthenware walls. But it was even more impressive once inside the eight-foot walls. They hid from view a palace which satisfied the fantastical imaginings sparked by the Desert Boy books— the walls were decorated in patterned tiles and the windows with wooden shutters so delicately carved the light streaming in studded the stone floors with jewelled stars.

They were met by a host of servants who embraced the Sinclairs like long-lost children before handing them into the care of the Carmichaels, a grey-haired couple who beamed with pleasure as they patiently awaited their turn. Ellie and Olivia stood a little to one side, smiling at each other a little nervously at this whirlwind of very un-English affection.

Mr Carmichael was a bear of a man, not quite as tall as Chase and Lucas, with a head of unruly black-and-grey hair and an even more unruly beard, while Mrs Carmichael was tiny, her hair steel grey and her eyes a surprising sapphire that glistened with happy tears. After introducing Lady Sinclair and Ellie she turned to Sam and pulled her into another embrace, lingering unashamedly before drying her eyes with an enormous handkerchief she extracted from her husband's pocket.

'Finally. It has been too dreadfully long, my dears. Now you all go refresh yourselves and later we shall have tea in the garden. Off with you.'

Ellie's room overlooked the garden and beyond it rose ochre-coloured hills slashed at the top into a dramatic cliff fall overlooking the murky green ribbon of the Nile.

A wave of pure misery swept through her and she turned her back on that perfect tableau and went to sit on the bed. She had no right to expect anything from Chase, but she hated the way he was turning against her. He might have been grateful for her presence on the *Seahawk*, but he was clearly regretting his impulse to bring her to Egypt now that she'd made a fool of herself at the ball. She was losing even his friendship—the warm, approving acceptance that made her feel more herself than she ever had. Like the

fairy tales, she'd been granted a dream only to
see it twist around her into a mirror of her pain.
She'd known there would be a price for accepting Chase's proposal. She'd not thought it would
be exacted so soon and so harshly.

She straightened at a knock on her door.

'Aanisah Walsh? Miss Walsh?' Hamid called
through the door.

'Yes, Hamid?'

'It is Effendim Chase, *aanisah*. He says to join
him in the garden, please.'

Ellie followed Hamid through the whitewashed
corridors, her heart flopping about like a landed
fish. Was this the 'talk' he had threatened her
with at the ball? Was it perhaps why he had been
so distant and tense on the *dahabiya*? Had he been
gathering his resolve to face what he felt was his
responsibility?

And if this was the moment of truth—what
would she say?

She had a rather terrifying sensation that trying to stop herself from throwing herself at him
again would be as impossible as stopping her
breath.

What would she say? She would have to say
something.

No, Chase, I cannot marry you.

'Oh...*inalabuk*,' she mumbled, copying Chase's
curse, and Hamid stopped on the stairs, blinking
back at her.

'Excuse me, Aanisah Walsh?'

Ellie flushed.

'I lost my book,' she offered and Hamid's dark-brown eyes sparkled.

'You wish for me to look for it, miss?'

'I am certain it will turn up, Hamid, *shukran*.'

'Very well, miss. You must not worry. What is lost is often found when one least expects it.'

Not my heart, she thought as they continued. It is lost and I knew precisely where it is.

Inalabuk, she repeated—internally this time. She liked this curse. It started with a languorous role and then slammed into the wall like a cudgel. Wham. She must have Chase teach her a few useful juicy Arabic curses so she could at least take those back home with her when her time was up and hurl them at walls and at the heavens.

Home.

She didn't want to go home. She wanted to stay with Chase.

How on earth would she find the strength to say no?

Of course she wouldn't say no.

Would she be so very wrong for him? He might not wish to settle, or be in love with her as she was with him, but then how many people truly found the kind of love she felt for him? Perhaps with his losses and fears he must learn to trust before he could care? She could at least give him her love and perhaps children... Whatever he professed to the contrary she knew he would love his children wholly and without reservation. And he would be a most excellent father. So if by chance this was to be a proposal, even a reluctant one, she would...

Her heart was slamming around her chest so brutally she had to press her hand to her mid-riff to calm its acrobatics as Hamid led her to a shaded courtyard with a tiled fountain and large urns tumbling with flowering bushes.

Despite this beautiful setting, her sorely abused heart gave a protesting creak and slowed from its gallop to a disconsolate trot as Poppy Carmichael beckoned her to come join him and Chase. Not even the sight of an elaborate wooden box on the marble-topped table countered her disappointment.

There would be no 'talk', apparently.

'Miss Walsh, come sit by me. Chase was explaining about Huxley's letter and the confusion. Dear me, what a brouhaha. If I'd known... But how could I? I was surprised enough when Mallory arrived with the box and news Huxley was ailing, only to receive the lawyers' letter a few days later. Mrs Carmichael is very cut up, very cut up indeed. There were no blood ties, but you are all family to us. He sent both of us a letter, Chase. Explained everything to me and told me to keep the box by me until you arrived and could decide what was right. She was your mother, after all.'

Ellie watched Chase's face as he listened. His

mouth was drawn tight, the grooves at either side sharply marked. She leaned a little towards him, but did not reach out as she wished. When he didn't speak she turned to Mr Carmichael.

'I'm afraid I don't understand, Mr Carmichael. What is in the box?'

Mr Carmichael sighed and raised the lid to extract a thickly folded letter.

'There are two letters—one for you, Chase, and another to be included in the box when it is put in the shrine.' He held it out to Chase, but he shook his head and turned to Ellie.

'You read them, Ellie. Please.'

It was the 'please' that did it. Ignoring the surprise on Mr Carmichael's face, Ellie unfolded the two sheets of paper and read aloud.

Chase, my dear boy,
If you receive this letter first no doubt you are in Egypt, hopefully at Qetara. I had hoped to see you yet in England, but when Mallory reported you were off once more I worried you might already be on your way to Egypt.

I hope we might yet meet one last time before this illness wins the battle, but I feel myself fading fast. Strangely, I think my quest to discover the author of the Desert Boy books staved off the end, but now my quest

*is over I find I have little strength to resist
the siren pull of peace.*

*I'm weary, my boy. I've had a good life.
And what I could not have I have still cher-
ished. So if that compassionate heart of
yours is worried for me bid it quiet.*

*I am only sorry I probably shall not have
the chance to confer with you about whether
to tell Sam about Edge. I dare say Poppy
knows he is the author, though he never
even hinted to me that he was, nor did your
mother. Perhaps you already guessed as
well, but if not, you should know, for Sam's
sake. But I leave it to you and Lucas to decide what to do with that knowledge.*

*So—you may read my letter to Tessa. You
are all old enough now to know my feelings.
In fact, it would be a relief to me for all of
you to know. Your mother was the most precious thing in my life, even if I could never
be more than a friend to her. I know you
were often frustrated with her, and frightened for her, but rest assured she loved the
three of you above all and knew you loved
her, which is as important.*

*This box carries all that matters to me in
the end. The memories of my true family. I
am only sorry I am fading too fast to spend
time again with all of you. But in truth I pre-*

*fer you all remember me as I was in these
tales I gathered.*
Goodbye, my boy

Ellie's throat was thick with the pain she could
see in Chase's half-averted face, but at a sign from
Mr Carmichael she unfolded the second sheet. It
was long and tightly written, as if Huxley had
hunched over his task like a fist around a thorn.

My darling Tessa,
*I never had the right to say these words, but
now I am fading, and you are gone, so I give
myself leave to write what I never spoke.*
   *I knew my fate the day I arrived at the
Palazzo Montillio and saw you for the
first time in many, many years. I came to
Venice motivated by responsibility and
compassion—Oswald showed me the letter Chase sent him and, from the unspoken plea hidden behind the determination
and the careful schoolboy's writing, we
knew someone must intervene and force
your return to England if necessary, so
we could see to the children's welfare if
nothing else.*
   *But when I walked into that salon and you
turned from the arched windows overlooking the canal everything changed. I cannot
explain, but that day I decided you would*

all come with me to Egypt and I would find some way to heal you. And between me and the children we took that first step.

I know I failed in that ambition—I never healed you as I wished. Even in your pain and confusion and loss it was always Howard. But I found a corner in your heart, did I not? We found no peace, you and I, but a little solace.

Each of your smiles is a gift I carry with me and relive as I read through my notebooks. The one before me tells of one day when you were in your favourite corner of the garden, when we sat reading the first Desert Boy books and exclaiming over Sam's marvellous illustrations. It was a perfect day, was it not? You had Sam back with you, a respite from her wastrel husband. She was pacing to and fro as she read passages from the Desert Boy manuscript the publisher sent, remember?

I can recall the moment I saw realisation dawn in your eyes, but when I tasked you as to the author's identity you said it was only conjecture and possibly harmful if the truth were known and would say no more.

It pained me that once again you kept me outside, but now, knowing it is most probably Edge, I realise why you refused to tell. Sam was so excited about being asked to do

*the illustrations for the Desert Boy books—
for the first time in so long she was once
again our 'bright, particular star'. I realise
that had she known Edge was the author
she would have seen in it an act of pity or
charity, and would never have accepted it—
never from him.*

*I don't understand why they parted on
such poor terms, but if you knew more than
I that was another thing you kept from me.*

*You would call it foolish vanity, but the
need to uncover what you knew has assumed
a runic power over me this past year—my
last quest, I am afraid. In the end it was
a matter of being methodical—each book
held its own clues, but it was the tomb of
the bulls near Saqqara and the oases of the
White Desert that settled the question. Of
those remaining on my list of possible au-
thors, only Mallory and Edge were present
in both and I would be most shocked if my
most efficient Mallory's imagination could
extend to the fantastical.*

*Did you ever tell Lucas or Chase? I feel
it is important they know and will tell Chase
when he comes as Lucas, most amazingly,
has married and is off with his new bride,
but I shall leave it to them to decide whether
it is right for Sam to know.*

I was always grateful for the gift of your

*time and your wondrous trio. How proud
you would be of them today, Tessa, for all
their struggles. I am.*

*As I read through my accounts I am
swamped with love and longing for those
days. I am gathering the best of them—
those where your presence is strongest—
and will put them in my offering and have
Poppy place them in the Temple of Sekhmet
at the bottom of the garden, precisely where
I came that evening and found your soul
had left.*

*One day I, too, will board the Ship of the
Dead and perhaps by some magic like that
in Edge's wondrous tales I shall find you
and your beloved Howard happy and together, and even that pain will be pleasure,
Tessa dear, if only I could sit with you again
at the bottom of that garden.*
Your loving servant, always,
Huxley

The birds picked up their chatter again and
after a moment Chase took the letter from her
hands and folded it, replacing it by the vase nestling in its flannel bed. The framed drawing was
on the table, staring at the sky glinting through
the vines.

It was a simple drawing, but as vivid as its subjects—Sam had captured the smile Huxley men-

tioned and Ellie realised Chase was correct—his mother had not been pretty, her face too strong for beauty, but the smile was full of love. Huxley looked very like his brother, but with a hint of stubbornness that Arthur Whelford lacked.

'Will you tell Sam? About Lord Edgerton being the author?' Ellie asked.

'No. She has few enough anchors in her life and I don't wish her to think Edge gave her the commission because she was in a bad way at the time. Understood, Poppy?'

'Of course, Chase. Not only for Sam's sake. Edge, too, does not need either more upheaval or notoriety in his life. I suggest placing the letter and the vase in the temple, but I think you should keep the notebooks. Tessa would have wanted you to have those memories. We should find a separate box for them, though. I will see if Janet has something appropriate.'

He took the box, laid his hand briefly on Chase's shoulder, and wandered off with a sigh. Ellie knew she should leave as well, but didn't. In the silence that fell she heard the steady chirp of small brown sparrows flirting in the palms and the low steady cooing of a dove.

'Well, that is the end of that,' Chase said. 'Come. She is buried at the bottom of the garden. You may as well see.'

Ellie wanted to take his hand, but she walked beside him through the greenery, the path climbing a little as they approached the rise of the cliff. It was a simple structure with eight adorned pillars like those she had seen in a temple half-covered with sand on the river bank. Inside there was only a marble bench, but the entrance was flanked by two statues, one of the lioness-faced woman and the other a seated woman with a disc above her head.

'Sekhmet and Hathor,' he said at her unspoken question, his voice as bland as his expression. 'Huxley chose them because my mother always said it made such good sense to have female goddesses that dealt in the practicalities of life and didn't allow men to make all the decisions, which was ironic because even if she had once been like that, she certainly wasn't after my father's death. The only significant decision she made was to be buried in Qetara. My father was buried in Boston and she said she did not wish to be buried at Sinclair Hall, so Huxley did as she wished.'

He walked into the shaded space, looking at the simple bench at the end. Only a small plaque on the wall with nothing more than her name and the years of her birth and death indicated this was a grave.

'I never realised Huxley...'

She waited for him to continue, but he didn't and she came to stand beside him.

'There was no reason for you to realise, Chase.

It was between the two of them. You are not the only one adept at hiding emotions.'

He turned away, but she saw the slight flush mark his high cheekbones and wished she had kept silent. He was probably all too aware of her weakness for him; there was no point in forcing that realisation upon him at every turn.

When he took her arm and began leading her away, she went with him. She didn't even notice he wasn't leading her back into the house, but up another gravelled path that crunched beneath their feet as they followed its twisting between tall hedges of dotted with tiny white flowers. It led downwards to a small bower with cushioned benches shaded by trees with large dark-green leaves and tightly closed buds.

'Lemon trees,' he said curtly. 'You will like it when they flower in a month or so.'

Her mind wouldn't encompass the thought that she might be there in a month, with him.

'Hopefully we won't be interrupted here. It is time you and I talked.'

She closed her eyes briefly at the yearned for and dreaded words. She would never be strong enough to reject his proposal. She wanted this, *him*, too much.

'You look as though you are being asked to walk the plank, Ellie. I know I am far from your ideal, but you seemed happy enough to receive my kisses at Jasperot's, one would think you would

be a little more reconciled to receiving the inevitable proposal.'

His mouth twisted at her silence.

'I've crossed the lines with you so often I've all
but erased them. You do realise this is discussion
is merely formality? Did you honestly believe that
after everything that happened between us there
was any other option?'

'There are always other options if one is willing to accept the consequences, Chase. I still don't
believe marriage without affection is wise. Imagine if our parents had to face all their challenges
without even that bedrock—it would have been
a thousand times worse.'

Perhaps she wasn't strong enough to say no,
but now the moment of truth had come she didn't
know if she was strong enough to say yes. She
would almost rather be his mistress and his friend
and live on borrowed time and affection than become the mistake that could sour his life.

Finally, he flexed his hands, turning to tug at
one of the tiny closed buds on the trees. Immediately the tart and sweet scent of citrus filled the
air, but then he tossed the mangled bud to the
ground and turned back to her.

'I don't think you should use either of our parents' tales to back any argument concerning wed-
lock, except those of the cautionary kind. You
don't trust a union not based on love? Well, I
wouldn't recommend a union which is only based

on that debilitating state. I watched my mother use that as her excuse for transforming from a force to be reckoned with to a well-intentioned rag doll. I would wish for many things from someone I planned to share my life with other than love.'

'Chase, I…'

'I'm not done. Those options you spoke of are a fine fantasy, Ellie. It was always going to end here. The moment you told me you weren't betrothed to Henry I knew that. I know I am far from your ideal, but I hoped this trip would help reconcile you to my limitations. And if you are hoping Mallory will offer…'

'What? Of course I'm not…'

'Good, because *this* is the right course of action, Ellie. I've done little else but want you from the moment you tried to push me down the Folly stairs, and you want me just as much, admit it. Blast it, your dissembling talents aren't good enough to hide that. If I hadn't come to my senses at Jasperot's ball, you wouldn't have stopped me. Don't deny it.'

'I course I don't deny it, Chase. I know I have no will when you touch me, but…'

'To hell with "buts"…'

His words descended into a growl and he pulled her against him, his hands moving down her back, moulding her against him, his fingers pressing deep into her waist. She leaned back in his arms. His face was a hard mask, but his eyes were dark with fire and even in her inexperience she couldn't mistake the pressure of his arousal against her.

'This is right, Ellie. This.'

He kissed her, flinging her back into that magical moment at the ball, his mouth against hers, coaxing and teasing and drawing her soul from her. His hands were sending crashing currents through her, making her want to do a thousand things until she didn't know what to do except press herself against him as closely as she could, her hands clinging and seeking, trying to encompass and possess just as he was doing to her.

His pulse was evident everywhere they touched—fast and hard like hers—and her mind, half-lost and fading, clung to the beat of his blood, to the simple message—*He wants me. Me—plain, on-the-shelf, managing me. Wants me enough to change his whole life. What else matters?*

And, God, she wanted him.

She hadn't known it was possible to want someone so swiftly and desperately that any thought of consequences, even of emotions, mattered as much as a grain of sand to the star-filled sky. Nothing mattered but his mouth grazing hers, teasing her lips into opening for him, his tongue touching lightly, skimming the parting seam with a heat that lit a blaze throughout her body, telling her things she hadn't known until this very instant. That she wanted this heat everywhere, she wanted him to touch and taste her skin, she wanted to rub herself against him, ached with this demand he show her what she was capable of.

'Chase… Show me…'

'That's right, love. Trust me. Just feel…'

She wrapped her hands around his shoulders and surrendered to the sensations, and he kissed her as deeply as she needed, his hand releasing her behind to skim upwards over her bodice, coaxing it aside to cup her breast and the warmth, the firm pressure of feeling herself held in the palm of his hand, his fingers splayed against the weight of her, slowly abrading her dancing nerves.

I love this. Oh, God, I love you, Chase. Please love me back.

'Chase. Love me…'

'Oh, God, Ellie…' His arms closed around her, hard, a shudder like the fever making his body buck against hers. Then his hands moved lower, one cupping her behind as the other gathered the fabric of her petticoat until the tips of his fingers grazed the skin of her thigh.

Nothing had ever felt like that, the way his fingers were brushing along the rise of her thigh, moving upwards and inwards, drawing a vortex of heat tighter and tighter between her legs, making her aware of the pressure of his arousal against her hip as he held her hard against him, his knee sliding between her legs, parting her. It should have scared her, but it didn't, it felt more natural than her own hands on her skin, necessary, inevitable.

Then his fingers, warm, firm, brushed through the soft down at her apex of her thighs, dragging a cascade of stars along with them. Her legs tightened against her will, clamping about the hardness of his thigh pressed between hers, but she didn't pull away. She was afraid, but she had to know what came next so she stayed there as his fingers stroked closer and closer, finally tracing the moist skin of her cleft, grazing what every inch of her recognised as another core of her being.

It was like opening a treasure chest, knowing something precious was inside, but only now realising how utterly unique and beautiful and unbearable and she never wanted it to end, but it had to. Something had to end it. It was like being shoved up a cliff, higher, higher, knowing at some point there would be nowhere to go but over the edge and that the fall could be horrible and the most wonderful thing ever.

When the fall came it wasn't a fall at all, but a soaring. She was cut loose from her moorings, her thoughts, her very identity and went up into the sky like a spark from a fire—swirling into darkness but utterly alive. The last thing she felt and heard was herself laughing his name.

She surfaced layer by layer out of the lovely, dream-like state, her senses slowly separating from the warm honeyed puddle of sensation they'd become. Not even her mind could ruin her well-being, at least not yet. She knew that would come, that she would have to give up the cocoon of his arms. She didn't want to. It felt so perfectly right to be just where she was, seated on his lap on the bench, hidden from the world by the vines, the warm flush of his breath against her hair, the soft comfort of his thumb brushing idle patterns on the back of her hand. It was so intimate and so natural even though she'd never experienced anything remotely similar. She sighed, nestling closer, and his hand tightened on hers.

'Don't squirm. There are limits to my self-control and you are testing them all.' The words were half-whispered against the hair falling over her cheek and she drew back. He looked as dishevelled as she felt—his dark hair mussed, probably from her fingers pulling at it, his cheekbones marked sharply with the heat of their encounter, his cravat crushed. But even as she watched she saw his guard being raised again as he approached the battle lines once more. This time bringing with him the cannon she had just supplied him with.

'I doubt there is an Anglican priest in the area, so we will have to go to the embassy in Cairo to wed…'

'No, Chase, we still haven't resolved…'

'Resolved? Devil take it, Ellie. Are you aware

that but for a Herculean effort at restraint on my part we would even now be in danger of begetting a bastard? Out here in the garden where everyone might have stumbled upon us? You do realise that, don't you?'

It felt like a slap and her face stung with it—with embarrassment and pain at the anger in his voice, but mostly with fierce remembrance of pleasure.

He cursed as he watched her face.

'You see? This is precisely the problem! I brought you here to talk, not... I never thought keeping my hands to myself would be a daily struggle. Every day on that boat I had to remind them they have no business reaching for you as if it was their right and every night I lie awake thinking of you just a few yards away, in your bed, warm and soft...' He stood, tugging at his hair and sending it into even greater disorder. 'And the worst of it is that I can't guarantee this won't happen again because around you I am like a fool who after drinking three glasses of brandy still thinks he is being perfectly sensible when he decides to accept a wager to walk backwards to Brighton. Oh, hell, that didn't sound right. You know what I mean.'

She did. What had just happened was evidence of that.

'Oh, God, I don't know what is right to do, either. I don't want to hurt you, Chase.' The words were wrenched out of her and Chase turned away with a short laugh. For a moment it was only the birds and the faint tinkle of the fountain. Then they both raised their heads at the sound of someone approaching.

'Chase?' Mrs Carmichael's voice carried over the hedge and Chase sucked in a breath and hurried to intercept her.

'Oh, there you are, dear boy. Sheikh Khalidi heard you had all arrived and has sent his carriage. You know how he is and it would be best if you all went and paid your respects first thing. Poppy and Lucas and Sam and Lady Sinclair are already gathering. He will have to forgive me because I refuse to miss my afternoon rest, or I shall be quite prostrate. Do hurry along, my dears.'

'You should go with them,' Ellie said once Janet disappeared again.

'Curse Khalidi. We are not done here yet. You cannot run away from this, Ellie.'

'I don't intend to. But we cannot talk while everyone is waiting. At least I cannot. Please go with them and later...' Later. By then perhaps some miracle would occur and show her the right choice.

He shoved at the pillar, like Samson trying to tumble the Philistine temple in his frustration and pain.

'Come with me,' he said at last, holding out his hand, but she shook her head.

'I think I shall stay here with Mrs Carmichael, if you do not mind. I need time to think. Hopefully I can meet Mr Khalidi on another occasion.'

He looked so quietly furious she felt scorched inside and out. But he left without another word and she remained standing there long after she heard the carriage pulling away on the road beyond the wall.

Chapter Twenty-Two

'I need some time to think.'

Devil take her. What was there to think about? He'd seduced her and she'd loved it. Hell, she'd seduced him, again, and *he'd* loved it.

There was nothing to think about except where and when to do that again.

Then why the devil did he feel as though it was all wrong? That he never should have left her to think. Ellie thinking was a recipe for trouble.

Chase paused at the foot of the broad marble stairs leading up to Khalidi's palace. He felt as though he'd swallowed a wasp's nest whole, his body still humming angrily at the control he'd exerted not to take advantage of Ellie, demanding he go back and do what he should have done from the very beginning. But he knew that wasn't right.

He didn't want Ellie to marry him because she had to. He wanted her to want him, to need to be with him. Which meant he would have to keep his hands to himself from now on and woo her until he worked through all her reservations and he convinced her he was right for her.

If only he could convince himself.

She would not marry him for his money or his name or even for the pleasure he could and did bring her. There had to be more for her to give him a chance. And he did not know if it existed inside him.

And if it didn't?

He wanted to go back right now and beg her to give him that chance. Either that or hide somewhere in the desert until this confusion was burned out of him and left him bare like a camel's skeleton bleached by sun and sand.

'Coming, Chase?' Lucas asked with a frown from the top of the steps.

'Tell Khalidi we will join you in a moment,' Sam intervened, hooking her arm through Chase's. 'I want to show Chase something in the garden.'

Lucas considered them, then gave a brief nod and continued inside with Olivia.

'Sam…'

'Do not "Sam" me. You should not be here. I don't know what happened between you and Ellie just now, but you should not have run away.'

'I did not run away. I proposed. She said no. If anyone is running away from responsibility it is she.'

'I didn't say anything about running away from responsibility, darling Chase. You never ran away from that, only from what you wanted, but were afraid to demand. Did you tell her how you truly feel?'

'For heaven's sake, Sam, leave it be!'

'Just like you left me be? Or did I imagine you prodding me and harassing me to make this trip? Even then I meant to tell you I would not, but what did you do but come and tell me about Ellie and I knew I had no choice because I realised that for the first time you needed something from me, even if you were still blind to how much. I knew before I even met her you were in love with her and that is why I forced myself to suffer that voyage from hell and didn't put a pistol to the captain's head and force him to turn the *Seahawk* around that very first night. And, yes, I'm very glad I came here, for myself, but that doesn't change the facts, Chase. You need her and I would wager my very last farthing you never told her how much. Why on earth should she consider your proposal when you are concealing the truth from her?

'Sam…'

'You were always the one to face the truth first, Chase. I remember the day you told me Mother wasn't strong enough to change, that she would be a rudderless vessel for ever, tossed about by other people's currents. I hated it because it meant abandoning the hope she could be strong for me when I needed her more than ever, but I knew you were right. At least you and Lucas were always there for me and now you have found someone who can also be as strong for you as much as you are for her. Go back, tell her the truth. Tell her you need her. *That* is what she must decide upon.'

Chase raked his hands through his hair. She was right. He'd taken the coward's way, hoping he could still reach his destination. He'd asked her to spend her life with him and lied, even if only by omission.

He knew he had to fix it, but he was terrified. If she rejected a real proposal based on his love, he would have nothing left. He would be like Huxley, living in the shade of what he could not have, but without Huxley's acceptance of his fate. He could not be like Huxley and be pleased the woman had found happiness with another. It would be unbearable. He *needed* her.

'Now, Chase.' Sam squeezed his arm and turned back to the palace entrance. He watched her go and went to find Abu-Abas.

'Please convey my apologies to Sheikh Khalidi, Abu-Abas. It is imperative I return to Bab el-Nur immediately. Oh, and I need a horse.'

Abu-Abas tugged at his white beard and sighed.

'You Sinclairs have not been back in Qetara one day and already there is trouble, *al-Jinn*?'

'This time it is only trouble for me, Abu-Abas.'

'She went where? With *who*?'

'*Whom*, Chase dear, with *whom*. And do not shout, I can hear you quite well.' Mrs Carmichael patted his arm soothingly. 'Miss Walsh went up to the Howling Cliffs with Mr Mallory. She said she wished to see the view. You needn't look so thunderous. She is quite safe with him, you know. After all, it is only Mallory.'

Chase refrained from saying what he thought about 'only Mallory'.

The cliff path from the garden was not a difficult one, it switched back and forth along an old goat path and the first level of the cliffs was little higher than the Tor back at Huxley. But even at the pace he set it felt far too long for Chase.

Once he reached the first plateau he scanned the view—the sun was sinking towards the far desert to the west, turning the Nile into a twisting snake of olive green shot with gold, winding its way through a fur of reeds and palms, and the eastern hills into a palette of orange and purple. But Chase neither saw nor cared. His mind shrank the universe into a single object—the woman seated on a boulder at the edge of the cliff.

'Where is Mallory?'

Ellie surged off the boulder and his heart

lurched in fear, calculating her distance from the edge and his distance from her, but she merely stood, the afternoon desert breeze making her skirts bloom about her, the lowering sun spinning honey and gold into her hair and eyes. She looked lovely and free, and as vivid as the desert around them. She'd not arranged her hair since the garden and it was gathered only by a ribbon which was losing the battle against the wind. The thought that Mallory might have contributed to her state of disarray...

'Where is Mallory?' he demanded again and she smiled.

'Behind you.'

Chase whirled. He hadn't even noticed Mallory standing rather warily by the path coming down from the upper plateau.

'You were looking for me, Chase? Miss Walsh asked I show her the cliff path. I did suggest waiting until the others returned, but...'

'But I insisted,' Ellie explained. 'I wished to see the cliffs before the sun set. I needed some place quiet to think. Thank you for accompanying me, Mr Mallory.'

'My pleasure, Miss Walsh. Perhaps... I should return to the house now?'

'Perhaps you should.' Chase nodded, trying very, very hard to remain calm. His heartbeat was still racing from catapulting himself up the path, from his jealousy and from the sight of her.

She looked very much like a desert sprite herself, his own fantasy conjured from the emptiness of sand and stone to a being of warmth and light.

'Chase…'

'No, please, before you say anything, I need you to listen to me. Please. I want to tell you the truth.'

Her warmth receded into fear, but she straightened her back, clasped her hands before her and nodded. The look of a woman expecting bad news and used to it.

He took hold of her hands. 'I made a hash of things today, Ellie. Not just today. In fact, judging by my dealings with you, I couldn't be trusted with even the hardiest of the seventeen pugs. I kept telling you what was the right thing to do because I was… I *am* scared it is wrong for you. You deserve someone like Arthur Whelford— stable, reliable, with a home to offer you. I don't think I can qualify as offering any of those three. I could cheat and say I can offer you a home, but that's not quite the truth because though I could purchase a house I've never had the kind of home you have at Whitworth. You deserve someone to give you that rather than once again have to assume responsibility for creating it. I will probably fail, too. I try to imagine myself in a house like Whitworth and I split down the middle—I want it, but I want to run for the hills because I don't know if I have it in me.'

Her hands flickered in his and he tightened his hold.

'No, please, let me finish. This is the difficult part. I wanted to marry you from the moment you told me you weren't betrothed. It is true I would have been happy to give you the money for Whitworth even if I hadn't felt anything but friendship for you, but in that case I would never have manoeuvred you into becoming Sam's companion. That was purely selfish—I needed you near me. I hated the thought of leaving for Egypt and not seeing you for months. I told myself the voyage would give us time to become acquainted and I promised myself I would behave in a manner that would rival Whelford's. But I knew the moment I saw you with Mallory I was lying to myself. I will never be like him or Whelford. I don't know if I can create a home for you—I have no real experience in the matter. I have no real experience being stable, either—I've never stayed in one place more than a few months at a time and, to be honest, I never thought I would. I hope I am reliable, but perhaps not in the way you would wish.'

His heart was thudding, all his instincts telling him to veer away before he went off a cliff again, but he trudged forward.

'I know I am not what you need, Ellie, though I wish to heaven I was. I also know you are what I want, what I need, what I crave, what I cannot contemplate living without. I have never been so at ease and so ill at ease with anyone in my life. You make a fool of me every time I look at you, but I can't look away. I do not know if I can create the home you want, but I will try to my last breath if you give me a chance. Because you are the only home I want. All I ask is that you take time to consider my offer during this trip and grant me some leeway as I try my best to become better. And if at the end of it you tell me you would rather ascend in a hot air balloon with Inky and seventeen pugs than ally your life with mine, I will try to accept that. Or not. I shall never force your hand, but I cannot promise to stop trying to convince you to care...'

As if a wave rose under her, Ellie suddenly flung herself at him and he found himself clutching her warmth against him.

'Oh, God, Chase, I love you so much.'

Chase steadied himself before they both ended up over the cliff. His heart was slamming so hard he was afraid it would do lasting damage. He could barely hear her tumble of words over the rush of blood in his ears.

'I never knew you could be so blind. I was absolutely certain you knew I was in love with you and that was another reason you felt obliged to offer. Sam knows and Olivia knows and I am rather certain your brother knows. Why on earth do you think I came to Egypt? It wasn't for the pugs, I promise you...'

'You came…for Whitworth. For adventure.'

'I came because it meant three more months with you. It was as simple as that.'

'Simple!' He laughed, tightening his hold on her. 'And I object to being called foolish. By the same token how could you not realise I was in love with you? I can hardly keep my hands off you.'

'Well, I did think it was strange you wished to bed someone as plain as I, but for all I knew it was merely a case of my being in the vicinity and there being no other presentable females. It made little sense to me otherwise.'

His arms tightened around her, unsure whether to laugh or be thoroughly offended.

'Good God, woman, if this is your opinion of me…'

'It isn't; it is my opinion of *me*. At the ball I began to hope it was more than just friendship and lust. But then you barely spoke to me on the *dahabiya*.'

'How could I when Mallory was hovering over you like a shadow? All I could think was that around him all my faults would become as plain as day and you would realise just how far I was from someone like Whelford.'

'What on earth is your obsession with poor Mr Whelford? Yes, I cared for him, but not in the way you think and I certainly am not in the least interested in Mr Mallory. And Whitworth was never,

ever my dream—it was my home and it became my obligation. You say you don't have a home to give me, but you give me something much more precious. I don't think I ever fully allowed myself to be myself until I met you and suddenly there was room for me—you always make room for me. I never realised how lonely I was until I wasn't any longer, and that has only ever happened to me with you. *This* is my dream—being myself, with you, exploring and learning what I can be, seeing you with people you love, seeing you happy. This past month—I've been in heaven even if I knew it could not last. The only home I want is with you, wherever that is. And I want to believe you love me so very, very, very much.'

Hope was a strange beast. He hadn't much experience with it and it shocked him how powerfully it swept everything aside and staked its claim on him. He closed his eyes for a second, allowing it to finally reach him and settle. Then he raised her hand, resting his mouth on it, breathing in her warmth and sweetness.

'That is two of us, then,' he said against her skin. 'I love you, Ellie. I have from the first week. You knocked me off a cliff and I'm still falling which might explain how abysmally I have handled myself. I will try to do better from now on, but I cannot guarantee I won't make an utter fool of myself again. Just please don't let that cloud the issue—I love you. I've been yours from the moment you knocked me off my feet in the Folly.'

Her hands stiffened in his hold, her body gathering, and he could almost feel the surge of resistance. For a moment he thought of heading it off, but then he just waited. She had a right to her fears as much as he.

'I want so much to believe you, Chase, but what if in a few months you realise this is all because you met me at the wrong time—when you were hurting because of Huxley and your parents and because of you being *al-Jinn* and fixing things, and perhaps a…a carnal attraction that clouded your judgement. But you might meet someone lovely and wealthy and sweet and… everything I'm not and you will regret this. It would break my heart.'

'I see. This is where we each don our hair shirts and I go on about not being like Arthur Whelford and you spout some nonsense about giggling debutantes.'

'I'm serious, Chase. I'm too old and plain and managing and…'

Chase pulled back a little, cradling her face between his hands.

'We are both are guilty of a great deal of nonsense. Saying you are old is a four-year insult to me. As for being plain, I have never in my life derived so much pleasure from looking at anyone or anything as I enjoy looking at you. I can't help myself. Just seeing you smile lights me up from inside. I'm not fully alive every day until I meet your amazing honey eyes. And as for managing…well, that is quite true. You are.'

'Well, then, so are you.' Ellie leaned her forehead against his chest and he could feel the tension slowly ebb from her body. He smiled. There would more such waves, but he would hold her through them until they learned to trust each other.

'You are far worse than I,' he coaxed, smoothing his hand over her hair and settling her more comfortably against him. God, he loved holding her. He loved that she nestled against him so trustingly. However much her mind distrusted him, her body was proving a very useful ally.

'Impossible. You are merely less obvious about it.'

'You have a point. Any other objections to your admitting I love you?'

'Plenty, but I don't want to think of them at the moment. I would much rather you kiss me again.'

'Finally you said something that makes sense.'

Ellie smiled up at him. She'd come up to the Howling Cliffs to search for answers and for the strength to make hard decisions, but one look out over the bleak and beautiful landscape confirmed she'd already made her decision—Chase was her home.

Meeting the warm glow in the grey eyes, she wondered how she hadn't seen the love that was so obvious to her now. He needed her as much as she needed him.

'Well?' she prompted.

He touched her cheek, his fingers leaving ribbons of silvered warmth as they slipped over her skin, her neck, dislodging the ribbon holding her hair as they eased through her hair. Her body clenched about the flares and sparks shooting through her at his touch, at the promise of so much more.

'*Very* well,' he murmured. 'Better than I've ever been in my life. There is no going back on an oath spoken on the Howling Cliffs, Ellie, and a kiss here is sacrosanct.'

The glow in his eyes turning dusky and dark as his head bent to hers, the words shaping themselves in soft brushes against her skin as his mouth explored where his fingers ventured. Finally his lips settled on hers, rested there for a moment, the whole of the world radiating outwards from the warmth of his skin on hers. The bare world around them, the orange warmth of the setting sun was a blanket holding them together, holding in such a wave of love and pain her eyes burned with it, with gratitude and fear and love.

'Chase…'

That single, half-breathed word cracked the peace and his control. His arms pulled her against him with almost desperate strength, his mouth fusing with hers, and her lips parted on a gasp, at the shock of heat and near pain at the contact.

'Ellie. God, Ellie, I want you. I want to be inside you *now*.'

His breath seared her lips, blood scorching through her like the crudest spirits, and the tingle burst into flame, hot, pulsing flame. She wanted to do something, take hold of him, but the kiss was encompassing her, taking her will away, melting her under him.

She could not help it or stop it. Her body arched against his, her arms wrapping about his neck as she rose to press her mouth to his, kissing him as if she was sinking away into quicksand and this would be the very last time they touched.

By the time he let her go the sun was just the remains of an orange-red puddle melting into the distant desert. He took her on to his lap as he sat on the boulder and they watched it drain away into dusk.

'I think I'd best get you to Cairo as soon as possible.'

'Oh, no, Chase, must we leave here?'

'Most definitely. There is no place for us to wed in Egypt but at the Embassy. I want to ensure you're safely tied to me before you meet someone far more worthy than me.'

'And before you meet someone beautiful and

far less managing than me. But I hate to ruin the trip for Sam and Olivia.'

'It will only be for a week and I can't deny Lucas the pleasure of gloating over my downfall as I gloated over his. But I think I will arrange for our own *dahabiya* once we are safely wed; I want you to myself on the return trip to Qetara. I will have Hamid put plenty of those soft cushions on the upper deck so we can watch the stars while I convince you categorically you and I are meant for one another.'

'I already know that. And you were wrong, by the way.'

'Impossible. About what?'

'A good kiss is far, far better than a good book.'

Chase's laugh was as soft as the breeze wrapping around them, pressing the musky warmth of the desert air between them and sneaking like smoke under skirts and up sleeves, as if the spirits were absorbing them into the desert itself. Then Chase gathered her against him, leaving no room for anything, anyone, but him.

'I'm glad, because I am in desperate need of the next volume before we return to Bab el-Nur.'

Epilogue

Bab el-Nur—one month later...

Bab el-Nur was settling into the quiet of the night when Chase entered his room. He stopped in the doorway and smiled at the woman curled up against the pillows wearing a very flimsy cotton nightdress. Ellie smiled back.

'I have something to show you.'

'Good.'

Chase had shed his clothes by the time he reached the bed and slid in beside her. Ellie pulled the sheet over them, but he twitched it back.

'No, you said you have something to show me and I don't want to miss a thing. This is our last night in Bab el-Nur for quite a while and I mean to make the most of it. I'm in need of more nectar of the gods from Madame Ambrosia to fortify me for the trip... Ouch. Why am I sharing my bed and wife with Gabriel?'

She laughed and tugged the book out from under him. He reached out to tweak the book from her hand, but she grabbed for it.

'Wait. This is what I meant to show you. Remember that note of Huxley's we found mentioning page ninety-seven? How he says it struck clean to his heart? I forgot all about it until I read Sam's copy of the most recent Desert Boy book. See? I found it.'

'I don't care if you found the panacea for all the world's ills, Ellie love. At the moment all I care about is right…here…'

The book wavered in her hand, her lashes dipping as his hands and mouth weaved their magic. It still shocked her how little control she had over her body when it came to the marital bed. The release that pleasure brought was so terrifyingly absolute, so different from everything she knew. For the first days after their marriage it had reawakened all her old fears—the fear of what might follow such a loss of control, that her tentative and precious new world with Chase might be lost with it.

She hadn't even been able to explain, embarrassed and convinced Chase would be miserably disappointed by her stumbling, stammering inexperience. She'd waited for his inevitable realisation of what she still suspected—that she was a mistake. But she'd underestimated him, again. He took his time. Soothed and coaxed her patiently out of her fears and into the trust and release that she began to realise was far more who she was than the cautious Eleanor Walsh.

'You wouldn't be so scared if you didn't want to be wild, Ellie,' he said as he'd slowly stroked her back as she lay on their bed on the *dahabiya*. 'But we will take our time and enjoy the journey.'

'Don't be noble, damn you,' she murmured into the pillow. Even nervous, she loved those moments, his hands sloping softly up and down her back, just shaping her, stroking as if she were Inky. Inch by inch she would sink into the rhythm, as if she was being rocked by gentle waves.

'I love it when you curse. Try the latest one you heard in the camel market today.'

She'd laughed, her muscles relaxing, and tried the latest addition to her growing vocabulary of profanity as his hands soothed over her shoulders. And bit by bit she'd melted.

Now, a month later, she couldn't remember why she'd been so scared. All she knew was the rising tide of that wildness, a swirling storm like the great sandstorms roaring their way across the desert planes to the east—inescapable and building with a ferocity until they devoured the world before them.

That same storm was building now, fed by the slide of his legs against hers, the silky roughness of the hair on his chest as he brushed his body against hers, bringing her breasts to tingling peaks. Her hands slackened and the book fell beside her with a thump, reminding her.

'Wait…'

'No.'

'Page ninety-seven, paragraph three…'

He groaned, untangling his legs and resting his forehead on her shoulder before pushing up on his elbow.

'You have three minutes and then I am going ahead and doing what God put me on earth to do. As of tomorrow we will have to make do with the bed on the *dahabiya* and then on board a much less comfortable arrangement on a ship back to England and I want to make hay while the bed is wide and comfortable, Mrs Sinclair.'

She turned towards him, sliding her bare leg between his until it rested against the very definite sign of his intentions, and he curved his hand over her behind, bringing her close, his mouth brushing the sensitive shell of her ear as he spoke, his breath coiling about it, about her, melting her into mist, into nothing but sensation.

'Ever since you had me flat on my back that first day in the Folly tower I have suffered from the most debilitating fantasies about your legs firmly anchored between mine and your thigh doing this…'

'Chase…'

She let the book drop over the side of the bed. Page ninety-seven, paragraph three would wait.

* * *

It waited two long hours on the floor before Chase stepped on it by mistake on his way to open the wooden shutters to let in the evening breeze. Cursing, he picked up the book and handed it to her.

'The three-minute clause still holds because I am not through with you. Now, what grand plot, secret code or magical incantation did you discover, love of my life?'

She patted the bed, curling up against him and tilting the book to the light of the oil lamp.

'Listen. Page ninety-seven, paragraph three. *"Leila knew love was never intended for her kind and she had no such expectations. So when love came she hid it deep inside the caverns of her soul and turned her back on it though it blazed hotter than the August sun. But even the best hiding places must eventually be abandoned or they become graves. And so when she stood at Gabriel's side above the valley and felt his pain strike sharper and deeper than the swords that decimated her family and dreams, she finally said the words that would bring either damnation or release. 'It was only ever you, Gabriel, my one and only love.'"*

Ellie cleared her throat. 'I am no desert sprite, but those words are from my heart, too, Chase. Because it was only ever you, Chase, my one and only love.'

He stroked the tears from her cheeks and touched his mouth to the damp, his tongue tracing the crest of her cheekbone, the corner of her mouth where the skin turned smooth and over the soft sweep of her lips, his breath warm and soothing as it caressed each surface in turn. When he answered, the words warmed her lips, filling her with joy.

'And it was only ever you, Ellie, my one and only love.'

* * * * *

COMING SOON!

We really hope you enjoyed reading this book. If you're looking for more romance, be sure to head to the shops when new books are available on

Thursday 25th July

MILLS & BOON

Coming next month

MRS SOMMERSBY'S SECOND CHANCE
Laurie Benson

'How can I help?' he asked, tilting his head a bit as he looked at her with a furrowed brow.

'I'm stuck.'

'Pardon?'

'On the hedge.' She motioned to her back with her gloved hand. 'The lace on my dress is caught on a branch and I can't move. Would you be so kind as to release me?'

He glanced around the small wooded area she was in and even appeared to peer over a few of the lower hedges as he made his way closer to her. When he stood a few feet away, the faintest scent of his cologne drifted across her nose as it travelled on the soft breeze.

Clara was petite in stature and had to look up at him as he stood less than two feet from her. Facing him, without the busyness of the Pump Room, she was able to get a better look at him. His firm and sensual lips rose a fraction in the right corner, softening the angles of his square jaw. Although he was clean shaven, there was a hint of stubble on that jaw and on his cheeks. She appreciated impeccably groomed men so it was surprising that she had the urge to brush her fingers against his skin to see what that stubble felt like.

He leaned over her and her breath caught as his lips

drew closer to her eyelids. His finely made arms, defined through the linen of his blue coat, came around hers. He could have easily stood to the side of her to free the bit of fabric, but being surrounded by all his quiet masculine presence, she was glad he had decided not to.

'You truly have got yourself caught.'

He looked down at her and flecks of gold were visible in his blue eyes. 'I know I haven't spent much time in your presence, however, this is the quietest I think I have seen you,' he said with a slight smile.

'I don't want to distract you.'

'You already have.'

She lifted her chin and now their mouths were a few inches apart. The warm air of his breath brushed across her lips. The last time she had kissed a man was ten years ago. And even then, she couldn't ever recall her pulse beating like this at the thought of kissing her husband.

Continue reading
MRS SOMMERSBY'S SECOND CHANCE
Laurie Benson

Available next month
www.millsandboon.co.uk

LET'S TALK
Romance

For exclusive extracts, competitions
and special offers, find us online:

f   facebook.com/millsandboon

🐦 @MillsandBoon

📷 @MillsandBoonUK

Get in touch on 01413 063232

For all the latest titles coming soon, visit
millsandboon.co.uk/nextmonth